THE VOICES GREW LOUDER AS THE EXECUTIONER APPROACHED

Bolan drew back around the corner, out of sight. The hardmen of Liberty Arizona had returned to retrieve something they had left behind.

A tall gangly man reached behind a filing cabinet and pulled out a package wrapped in brown paper. Which was the exact moment Detective Devlin chose to plant his foot on the bottle cap Bolan had just stepped over.

The cap snapped like a gunshot under Devlin's bulk, then scraped the concrete almost as loudly as his booted foot dragged it across the floor.

The militiamen turned, looked toward the sound and spotted the Executioner.

A second later, Bolan stared down the barrels of four guns.

D1167999

DON PENDLETON'S

MACK BOLAN®

STONY MAN™

Enemy Within

A GOLD EAGLE BOOK FROM

WORLDWIDE®

TORONTO • NEW YORK • LONDON
AMSTERDAM • PARIS • SYDNEY • HAMBURG
STOCKHOLM • ATHENS • TOKYO • MILAN
MADRID • WARSAW • BUDAPEST • AUCKLAND

If you purchased this book without a cover you should be aware that this book is stolen property. It was reported as "unsold and destroyed" to the publisher, and neither the author nor the publisher has received any payment for this "stripped book."

First edition January 1999

ISBN 0-373-61922-7

Special thanks and acknowledgment to
Jerry VanCook for his contribution to this work.

ENEMY WITHIN

Copyright © 1999 by Worldwide Library.

All rights reserved. Except for use in any review, the reproduction or utilization of this work in whole or in part in any form by any electronic, mechanical or other means, now known or hereafter invented, including xerography, photocopying and recording, or in any information storage or retrieval system, is forbidden without the written permission of the publisher, Worldwide Library, 225 Duncan Mill Road, Don Mills, Ontario, Canada M3B 3K9.

All characters in this book have no existence outside the imagination of the author and have no relation whatsoever to anyone bearing the same name or names. They are not even distantly inspired by any individual known or unknown to the author, and all incidents are pure invention.

® and TM are trademarks of Harlequin Enterprises Limited. Trademarks indicated with ® are registered in the United States Patent and Trademark Office, the Canadian Trade Marks Office and in other countries.

Printed in U.S.A.

Enemy Within

PROLOGUE

Virginia Beach, Virginia

The pain never really left his legs, even when he was stoned out of his mind on the morphine. Sometimes it was sharp. Other times dull. But the pain was always there.

Except when he worked.

Desmond Click rolled his wheelchair to the computer terminal and thumbed the power button. He reached to the table at his side, lifting the CD player and wrapping the earphones around his head. Flipping the switch, he leaned back, resting his arms at his sides. The rap group Spice *1* chanted into his ears as the computer components warmed up.

At the moment, the pain in what was left of his lower limbs was little more than a numb ache, like his muscles were trying to cramp up on him. Not much different than that hot August day years ago when he'd gotten dehydrated playing baseball at Cub Scout camp.

A wave of depression swept over Click as he recalled the camp. How long ago had it been? Twenty years? At least. Long before he lost the use of his legs. During the days when he could walk and run and jump as well as any of the other boys and better than most. Before the fire that had bound him to the wheelchair and burned his face so badly that even the strongest men turned their eyes when they saw him.

"'Kill 'em all,'" Spice *1* screamed in his ears.

A series of clicks, buzzes and flashing lights told him that the hard drive and modem were almost ready. Then the screen flashed a brilliant series of reds, ambers and rust. The colors, combined with Spice *1*'s rising fervor, reminded him of a small fire that steadily grew until it had become a roaring inferno. He felt a stirring in his lower abdomen.

A few moments later, Click had typed himself into a chat room and begun searching for the man who called himself Zulu. As he sent out his probe, Click remembered the first time he'd met the black man—a black boy then. It had been at the same Cub Scout camp and Bernell Dixon had been the only one of the other boys who didn't pick on Desmond Click.

Click knew why. Both of them had been social outcasts. Dixon was the only black at the camp, and Click knew even then, even before his deviation had completely manifested itself, others had recognized him as "different."

A smile crept across the face of the man in the

wheelchair. It was fun communicating with Dixon again after all these years, and he found it amusing that the same little boy who had called himself Zulu when they'd played Capture the Flag and other games had chosen that appellation to use on the Internet. He had thought of Dixon immediately when he'd come across the name on the Internet, and a few leading questions in anonymous cyberspace had confirmed his suspicions that this Zulu was the same boy he had known so many years before.

What made it even more fun was that the leader of the Free African Nation, Bernell ''Zulu'' Dixon, had no idea who the man calling himself Maestro actually was.

Zulu came on line and Maestro recommended they enter a private room. They did.

Are things in place? Maestro asked.

Affirmative, Zulu replied.

Any problems? Any last minute changes?

No. All shipments arrived on time. Components were assembled on schedule. Delivery has been made. Awaiting a Go.

Click giggled in his wheelchair as the excitement in his abdomen spread upward into his chest, then dropped into his groin in anticipation of what was to come. The pain in his legs was all but nonexistent now as the blood rushed to other areas, arousing his body and stimulating his brain. He lifted his hands in front of him, folding them together as if in prayer, closed his eyes and reveled in the moment.

The chase was almost as good as the climax.

Opening his eyes, Click cracked his knuckles, leaned forward, and typed *Then Go!*

Affirmative, came back the response on his screen. *Will notify with results.*

Click's hands trembled with excitement as he whirled his wheelchair at an angle from the computer screen. Lifting the remote control from the console, he pressed the Power button and watched the television in the corner of the room light up. Betty Jean Livingston, newsanchor for KJVC TV, appeared. Click glanced back to the computer screen. No change.

He watched the pretty newsanchor sum up the local events of the day. The DEA and the local sheriff's office had served two dozen search warrants and arrested close to forty people. Two bank robberies. Four murders—three apparently gang-related.

Click shook his head. All that violence. What was the world coming to? The satirical thought made him laugh out loud.

He felt the stirring in his groin. He should think of other things. If not, he might reach the point of no return before he could watch his work on TV. He let his thoughts drift back to the days, not so long ago really, when he had been willing to set up firebombs for anyone. He had worked for both right- and left-wing terrorist groups without remorse, much like an unattached playboy nailing every woman who came his way. Then, by chance, he had made cyberspace contact with Zulu. He had realized during their communiqués that though he was white, the discrimination blacks had experienced was the same as he had known.

Since then he had worked specifically for Bernell "Zulu" Dixon's Free African Nation. And like a playboy who had finally found the one woman to whom he could devote himself exclusively, Desmond Click now helped only FAN.

A buzz from his modem alerted Click that a message was coming in. Cold shivers raced down his spine as he turned to face the screen. His breathing quickened. He saw the first letter appear on the screen—a capital *B*.

Turning to face the screen again, Click's hands rose to the sides of his face. His fingers gently massaged his cheeks. A low moan escaped his lips as the *B* was followed by an *O*, then another *O*, then an *M* and finally *!*

His entire body quivered in delirium. It had happened. They had done it. *He* had done it again.

As his exhilaration leveled off, Click felt a warm glow engulf his body. He turned back to the television in time to see a flicker of a frown lower Betty Jean Livingston's eyebrows. She stopped speaking, cocking her head slightly to one side as if listening to something.

Click knew what had caused the change in expression and the pause. He had seen it many times before. The first report of the explosion had just come in over the Interrupted Feedback Device in her right ear.

The lapse in the woman's professionalism was only momentary. She looked back up at the camera and said, "This just in—reports of another explosion, this time at the Federal Courthouse in Miami. Police and firefighters are en route to the scene. KJVC will keep you informed as more information comes in." Turning to a man seated next to her, she said, "So, Bill, how's the weather look for this weekend?"

Click tapped the Power button and killed the television. Turning back to the keyboard, he typed *Well done, my good and faithful servant,* sent the message to Zulu, then switched off the computer.

Still basking in the afterglow, Click wheeled across the hardwood floor to his bed. He reached up, grasping the sling suspended from the ceiling and pulling himself onto the mattress. The covers tucked under his chin, he snuggled into the pillow and closed his eyes.

It had been good, he thought. Not as good as the days when he could actually set the fires himself and then watch them, and not as good as what he had planned in the next few days. But good nevertheless. Something like making love to a beautiful woman you'd just met.

Click felt his groin stirring again as he relived the moment in his mind. Yes, it had been good. But if tonight had been like making love to a beautiful woman, what he had planned to come would be like an orgy with a year's worth of *Playboy* centerfolds.

A knock on his bedroom door jerked Click from his fantasies. He bunched the covers over his groin to hide his excitement. The interruption irritated him. With a sigh he said, "Come in, Mother."

The old woman creaked the door open and padded into the room in her housecoat and slippers. She crossed the room and tucked the bedspread tighter around her son's neck. Leaning forward, she kissed him on the forehead. "Good night, Dezzie," she said. "Do you need anything?"

"No, Mother," he said. "I don't need anything." The sooner he ended the old bag's nightly ritual the sooner he'd be able to return to the world of his thoughts.

"I love you, Dezzie. Sleep well."

Click smiled up at his mother like a little boy. She liked that smile, he knew. It would make her happy and she'd go away quicker if they didn't get into an argument. A few cross words, or if she even sensed his irritation, and she would hang around trying to smooth things out.

"Good night, Mother," he whispered. "I love you, too."

Mrs. Click smiled a compassionate smile at her

son, kissed him on the forehead once more and left the room.

Although he had turned the CD player off long ago, Click went to sleep with Spice *1* screaming ''Kill 'em all'' in his ears.

CHAPTER ONE

Stony Man Farm, Virginia

The mood in the War Room was somber at 0400 hours. But then the mood in the War Room was always somber, for somber issues were the only kind deliberated there. It was here that men prepared to go to war.

Hal Brognola, high-ranking official in the U.S. Department of Justice and director of Sensitive Operations at the Farm, took his place at the end of the table. To his right sat Barbara Price, Stony Man's mission controller. To his left, Aaron "The Bear" Kurtzman had rolled his wheelchair up to the table from his usual post in the Computer Room.

Pulling a half-chewed cigar from the breast pocket of his rumpled gray suit, Brognola stuck it between his teeth. Just past Price, he saw the men of Able Team. On the other side of the table were the commandos of Phoenix Force.

At the far end of the long conference table sat a

big man with hawkish features and piercing blue eyes who was dressed in black. The man's name was Mack Bolan. He was also known as the Executioner, and by a half-dozen other aliases, and he was the very soul of Stony Man Farm.

Brognola nodded as he opened the manilla file in front of him on the table. He sifted through the papers inside. The teams looked fit and ready to ride, even if David McCarter and his teammates still had sleep in their eyes. Phoenix Force had just returned from rescuing an American oil executive held hostage in South America, and couldn't have grabbed more than three hours of shut-eye before being awakened for this emergency meeting. Still, they were drinking coffee, and Brognola knew they would be as good as new in a few more minutes.

The man from the Justice Department pulled the cigar from his mouth and cleared his throat. "There's no point in beating around the bush," he said. "You guys know as well as the rest of the U.S. that there were more political bombings in the past six months than in the rest of our country's complete history. Some of the strikes were carried out by ragged-assed radical groups who got lucky and pulled things off. But follow-up investigations have led us to believe that others are highly sophisticated operations that have been expertly planned. So without further ado, I'll turn this meeting over to Aaron." He paused. "He'll tell you exactly where things stand at the moment."

Aaron Kurtzman opened his mouth to speak but before the words could come out the combination lock on the steel security door to the outside buzzed. The door opened, and an attractive middle-aged woman in a red pants suit walked in. She was followed by a distinguished-looking black man wearing a cardigan sweater and club tie. Behind the black man came a young Oriental dressed in ragged blue jeans and a faded denim jacket decorated with silver studs.

The three newcomers took up standing positions behind Kurtzman.

"As all of you already know," Kurtzman began, "my cybernetics team—" he hooked a thumb over his shoulder at the three people standing behind him "—runs periodic spot-checks of the Internet. The reason is simple—while computers have given humankind a valuable medium of anonymous communication, that medium, like any other, holds tremendous potential for abuse. Right now I could take you upstairs and tap into advertisements for snuff films, kiddie porn, surplus Russian chemical and nuclear weapons, and about four thousand other items that not only present a danger to the mass populace but—" and here Kurtzman's voice took on a mildly sarcastic tone "—dare I say it in this age of political correctness? Items that are just flat immoral."

He shook his head in disgust. "There's little chance of tracing these things to the source. But I digress.'' He reached for the water glass on the table in front of him, took a drink and set it back down. ''I'll cut to the chase. For several months we've been tracking a guy who calls himself Maestro on the Net. I won't bore you with all the details, but we've got every reason to believe he's the brains behind the explosions at the World Trade Center, Oklahoma City and several other lesser-known strikes.''

Halfway down the table, Carl Lyons shook his head. ''Bear,'' the leader of Able Team said, ''I just can't buy it. The World Trade Center was Muslim extremists. Oklahoma City, supposedly, was whacko far-righters. You trying to tell us those two groups are in bed together?''

Kurtzman suppressed a smile. Warriors didn't come any finer than Carl Lyons. But the ex-LAPD detective was basically a kick-ass-and-take-names type of guy. Computers simply weren't his thing.

''No, Ironman,'' Kurtzman said, using the nickname Lyons's attitude had earned him over the years, ''we've got no reason to believe that. I'm just saying we suspect that this Maestro did the homework for both groups.''

David McCarter, the former British Special Air Service officer who now led Phoenix Force, cleared his throat. ''But what would Maestro's motive be?'' he asked. ''Why would he be helping such diverse—even contradictory—groups?''

Kurtzman shrugged. ''That's the sixty-four-thousand-dollar question. I don't know the *why*, David. Just the *is*."

He took another sip of water, then went on. "Okay. The latest Intel leads us to believe that Maestro's setting up a bomb for some group in San Antonio. We don't know who, where or what. But the Alamo Tavern—there's one listed in the San Antonio phone book—has come up in several pieces of intercepted information."

Kurtzman moved into another area. "Unrelated to all this," he said, "we've also picked up on a threat on the President's life."

"Damn shame," Lyons said.

A dirty look from Brognola kept the Able Team leader from speaking further.

Again, Kurtzman had to hold back a smile of amusement. It was no secret that Carl Lyons had little use for the current commander-in-chief. The Able Team leader was as conservative as the President was liberal, and while Kurtzman knew Lyons wouldn't hesitate to lay down his life for the man in the Oval Office—simply because he *was* the man in the Oval Office—Brognola had decided to send Phoenix Force to the White House to avoid personality problems. Lyons, Kurtzman knew, was symbolic of a tremendous number of good, patriotic Americans who had begun to openly question the federal government. They believed Uncle Sam had grown too big, too strong and far too oppressive. In short, they wanted the United States to go back to being the "Land of the Free" instead of moving continually closer to socialism as the rest of the world gave it up.

"The President is worried," Brognola said. "He suspects there's a Secret Service leak. And he's requested that we send personnel to work with his protection team." The big fed pulled the cigar from his mouth and returned it to his pocket. "That's you guys, David. That's where Phoenix Force is headed."

Kurtzman watched puzzled looks spread over the faces of David McCarter, Calvin James, Rafael Encizo, Gary Manning and T. J. Hawkins. Phoenix Force usually worked outside the U.S., with Able Team handling domestic affairs. If a comparison to the "regular" federal government had to be made, Phoenix Force operated somewhat like a CIA strike team with Able Team more of an FBI counterpart.

The frowns on the commandos' faces turned to shrugs and nods as they accepted their assignments.

The big man at the end of the table had remained silent so far. But now he spoke.

"I assume you've got something for me to do, Hal?" the Executioner asked.

"Oh, yeah, Striker," the big Fed said, "do we ever. Those two white extremist guys in Chicago. You read about them in the papers, I'm sure."

Bolan nodded.

"They got caught trying to plant a bomb in the

IRS offices last week. You're set to interview them and then go from there. Anything you want to—''

Brognola was interrupted as the security lock buzzed again. The gray steel door swung open and two hard-looking men, both dressed in blacksuits, entered the room carrying cardboard boxes. They were followed by another man in blue jeans and cowboy boots.

''Brought you guys some new toys,'' John ''Cowboy'' Kissinger, Stony Man Farm's chief armorer, said as the two blacksuits set down their boxes on the conference table. ''And from what I've gathered from Hal so far about your missions...'' His voice trailed off for a moment. Then a stern look replaced the smile on his face. ''You're going to need them all and more.''

Illinois

DAWN CAME AND WENT. A light rain began to fall over the Windy City.

Jack Grimaldi, Stony Man Farm's ace pilot, set the wheels of the Learjet 60 on the tarmac as Bolan unbuckled his seat belt, rose and walked back into the passenger area. He listened to the PW305 turbofan engines grow quiet as the plane reached the end of the runway.

Bolan crossed the floor to the lockers bolted against the side of the jet. Once there had been eleven seats in the passenger area, but now there were six. The rest of the space had been converted into equipment storage and the series of diverse-sized lockers that circled the cushioned chairs. Opening the second locker from the front, the Executioner pulled out a black briefcase, then exited the plane.

The rental car was waiting in the parking lot, and five minutes after landing, Bolan was piloting the Buick Road Master through Chicago's wet streets. Twenty minutes after that, he was parking in front of one of the city's ancient gray precinct houses.

The sergeant behind the glass at the front desk was a walking, talking police cliché. Gray-haired and a good forty pounds overweight, his uniform shirt bulged over his Sam Browne belt, completely hiding the buckle. "What do you want?" he asked in a surly voice.

"Belasko, Justice Department," Bolan said, pulling his credential case from the inside pocket of his suit coat and holding it against the glass. "I'm here to see Detective Dwight Graham."

The sergeant picked up the phone. "Yeah, Detective," the portly man said. "Some Fed here to see you." He hung up and looked at the Executioner, hooking a thumb over his shoulder. "Go on back."

A buzzer sounded as Bolan walked toward the door the sergeant had indicated. He pushed through the electronic lock and found himself in a narrow hallway in dire need of new paint. A door toward the end opened as the one behind him swung closed, and the half-remembered face of Dwight Graham appeared.

Bolan walked forward as Graham came down the hall and extended his hand. A big grin covered his face as he spoke in a hushed voice. "You remember me, Belasko?"

Bolan smiled, doing his best. In addition to engaging in counterterrorist strikes throughout the world, he, Phoenix Force, Able Team and the other personnel at Stony Man Farm occasionally conducted advanced training classes for select police and military personnel. Flown into the Farm blindfolded, the men left the same way, never fully knowing who had trained them but aware that they had received instruction far above that found through conventional channels. Dwight Graham had been one such trainee a few years before.

"I remember your face, Dwight," Bolan said. "Refresh me a little more."

Graham's smile didn't fade. "You and a black guy—Cal, I think it was—taught the close quarters combat section. You used me to demonstrate on several times, and I had bruises for two months afterward."

Bolan chuckled. "Learn anything?"

"Yeah," Graham said. "Mainly that the ten years I'd already trained in the traditional martial arts didn't amount to shit when it came down to the nut-cutting. And that if I ever have to face Cal with a blade, I should just cut my own throat to save time.''

Bolan laughed. Calvin James, a former Navy SEAL, was Phoenix Force's edged weapons expert. There was no one better than him with a blade.

Graham turned, indicating with his head that the Executioner should follow. ''I've studied karate, judo, aikido—little bit of everything,'' the Chicago cop said as they walked down the hall. ''But I've never seen any form of fighting as simple, direct and effective as what you guys taught.''

''The system is basically the same one that American servicemen went through during the World War II era,'' Bolan said. ''When a lot of men had to be taught to defend themselves, and they had to be taught fast. Before things got over-fancy.'' He glanced at the shorter man walking at his side. ''Traditional martial arts are okay if you can learn to make that bridge between the artificial atmosphere of the dojo and the streets.''

They reached the end of the hallway and Graham opened another door, stepping back to usher the Executioner through. ''Yeah, but what I liked about your system at the Farm was that there wasn't any bridge to cross. It was reality training from the word go.'' He stepped through the doorway behind Bolan and started down another hall toward a steel door at the end. ''And I think I've still got a few bruises to prove it after all these years.''

Bolan smiled. He was remembering Graham better now, and remembering he liked the man's enthusiasm.

Several lockers stood against the wall next to the door, keys extending from the locks. Graham reached up and twisted one, opening the door. "Got to leave our weapons out here," he said. "The holding cells are on the other side. To save time, I talked a couple of Cook County deputies who are buddies of mine into bringing our boys over from the jail." He pulled a Glock 21 pistol from under his sport coat and shoved it into the opening.

Bolan drew the sound-suppressed Beretta 93-R from under his left arm and the .44 Magnum Desert Eagle from his side. Jerking the Gerber Applegate Folding Fighter knife from a horizontal speed sheath, he added the blade to the other weapons inside the locker.

"I remember that about you, too," Graham said, closing the locker door and pocketing the key. "You never went underarmed."

Bolan chuckled again. Graham's enthusiasm was contagious. "No future in that," he said.

"Literally," the Chicago PD detective added.

Graham led the way past a trustee who was busy with a mop and bucket on the concrete floor. They passed a black-and-yellow sign that read CAUTION! Wet Floor, and moved to another glass-enclosed office. "Got a Justice man who needs to talk to Spivey and Burkett," Graham told the jailer on the other side of the glass. "If you want to go get them, we'll meet you in the conference room."

The jailer, a tall kid with acne scars, sighed as he stood. As soon as he was gone, Graham shook his head. "Kid gets irritated when he has to work," he said disgustedly. "Thinks his job is to smoke cigarettes and read *Penthouse* all day long."

Graham led the way again, taking Bolan down one of the cell runs past prisoners smoking and playing cards at the steel tables bolted to the floors. A few catcalls made their way through the bars to welcome the Executioner. He ignored them.

The conference room looked as if it had once been a cell itself. A one-way mirror was the only opening other than the solid steel door. It was unlocked, and Graham swung it open, again stepping back to let the Executioner go first.

Bolan stepped inside the small room, finding another of the CAUTION! Wet Floor signs on the damp concrete. The walls were lined with carpet, soundproofing the room to allow prisoners to confer with their attorneys in confidence. Bolan took a seat at the table in the center of the room, facing the door. Graham dropped into a chair next to him.

They had just seated themselves when the door opened again. The tall jailer stepped back and two men dressed in Cook County Jail coveralls strutted cockily into the room. Graham indicated the two other seats at the table, then waved the jailer away.

The heavy steel door closing sounded like a hammer striking an anvil.

"Well, hello again, boys," Graham said pleasantly.

"Hello, asshole," the taller of the two men said. Bolan looked him over. Heavily muscled, he had rolled up the sleeves of his coveralls to make sure everyone knew it. Badly inked jailhouse tattoos covered the skin of his exposed arms. Long greasy hair hung to his shoulders, and he had one bushy eyebrow that ran from one side of his face and crossed his nose to the other, looking very much like an obese caterpillar.

"This pleasant character is Dwayne Spivey," Graham told Bolan. "His little buddy here is Jason Burkett." The detective's tone became sarcastic. "Both Dwayne and Jason must be treated with the respect appropriate to their station in life. You see, they're both members of the Master Race."

"You got that right," Spivey said. "Fuckin' National Aryan Army." He shot out his arm in a Nazi salute.

"Yeah, got that right," Burkett repeated. He, too, saluted.

"Oh, I fully intend to treat them the way they deserve to be treated," Bolan said, smiling. He eyed Burkett. Short and fat, unlike Spivey he sported no tattoos. But he might as well have had the word *follower* printed across his forehead. He kept looking to Spivey every few seconds to see how he should act.

"This is Special Agent Mike Belasko, boys," Graham said. "He'd like to ask you a few questions."

"We want our attorneys," Spivey stated.

"Yeah," Burkett piped in. "We want our attorneys."

Bolan stared hard at Spivey. The man averted his eyes after a few seconds. "Gentlemen," the Executioner said, "maybe you've noticed I haven't informed you of your rights." He paused, then said, "And I don't intend to."

Both men looked up in surprise.

"The reason for that is simple," Bolan went on. "I don't intend to use what you're about to tell me against you. I won't testify at your trial. In fact, after I leave here today you'll never see me again."

Spivey fished a cigarette out of the pocket of his coveralls. Burkett looked at him and did the same.

"Well, that's good you don't plan to use what we say against us, pig," the tattooed man said as he struck a match and held it to the end of his smoke. "'Cause we ain't sayin' shit."

"That's right, pig," Burkett chimed in. "We ain't sayin' shit."

"All I want is the name of the man who's the brains behind your bombings," the Executioner said. "You tell me that, and I'm out of here."

"Right," Spivey said, taking a deep lung full of

smoke and letting it trail out his nose. "And I'm the fucking Easter bunny."

"Yeah," Burkett said as the smoke rose to the ceiling from his own nostrils. "I'm Santa Claus."

Bolan fought the urge to slap the smirks off the men's faces. He knew well that might bring down repercussions on Graham. At the very least, it could put Graham in a position where he had to decide whether to later perjure himself.

"What do we get in return?" Spivey asked.

"Yeah, pig, what do we get?" Burkett repeated.

Graham turned to Bolan. "You hear an echo in here?"

"You get to know you helped me put an end to the deaths caused by your bombings," Bolan said simply.

"Well, we don't want that reward," Spivey said. "It's far more fun to blow up you Feds."

"Yeah."

Next to the Executioner, Graham cleared his throat. Glancing at the detective, Bolan saw the man frowning toward the black-and-yellow caution sign on the wet floor. Slowly Graham's habitual smile returned to his face.

"Anybody want some coffee?" Graham asked pleasantly.

"Good idea," Bolan said. "Black."

"That figures, black-ass lovin' Fed," Spivey said.

It took Burkett a second to get it, but when he

did, the fat man burst into a girlish giggle. "Yeah, you would like it black!" he said.

"I'll be sure to put enough milk in both of yours to turn them white," Graham said, standing. "Or at least khaki. I'll try to get it the color of the führer after a week on the beach." He walked to the door, then turned, pointing to the caution sign. "Be real careful while I'm gone, guys," he said. "This floor's still slippery." He winked at Bolan and was gone.

The steel door had barely ground shut again before the Executioner's right fist shot across the table. Bolan's knuckles made contact with Spivey's jaw, and a loud crunching sound exploded as the bone cracked. Spivey screamed.

Without hesitation, the Executioner swiveled in his seat, following up the right cross with a left hook that snapped Burkett's head backward on his neck. Burkett, of course, screamed just like Spivey. Both men tumbled out of their chairs and hit the concrete floor.

Bolan stood and circled the table as the two white supremacists began to moan. He reached down, lifting Spivey by the lapel of his coveralls, and slammed him against the wall. "Who's behind everything?" he demanded, his nose an inch from the other man's. "Who's your strategist?"

"You son of a bitch!" Spivey said painfully out of the side of his mouth. "You broke my jaw!"

"He broke my nose!" came from Burkett, still on the floor.

Bolan held Spivey against the wall with his left hand as his right drew back. A short hard uppercut to the sternum sent the air shooting out of the prisoner's lungs. Spivey choked, coughed and started to slide down the wall.

The Executioner turned to his friend. Lifting Burkett, he saw blood pouring from both of the man's nostrils. Bolan threw him against the wall and drove another fist into the rolls of fat covering the man's solar plexus. Burkett grunted. Bolan dropped him in time to avoid the spray of vomit that shot from his pudgy lips.

Returning to Spivey, the Executioner jerked him to his feet and slammed him back into his chair. By the time he got back to Burkett, the man had finished retching. Bolan repositioned him next to his friend, then returned to his own seat.

Bolan looked over the two men as he gave them time to catch their breath. They were hurt, but not so bad that they wouldn't heal. And it couldn't have happened to a nicer pair of guys.

The National Aryan Army was a hate-driven group of racist Nazis. They not only hated the federal government, they wanted everyone who wasn't exactly like them off the shores of the U.S. And if they couldn't get the Blacks, Hispanics, Jews and other races out of the country, they wanted them dead.

When the moaning, whimpering and blood-sputtering had tapered off to where it looked like they could talk, Bolan said, "Okay, guys. I'm going to ask you my question again. You can answer, or we can dance the next dance together—it's all up to you." He paused. "Who's the one who sets things up for the Aryan bombings?"

Spivey started to lip off—Bolan could see it in the eyes above the quickly swelling jaw. Then the man thought better of it and mumbled painfully, "Don't know. That's the truth. There used to be a rumor about some big brain guy who did it with a computer. But I don't know anything more."

The Executioner turned to Burkett. "Nothing more," the man with the broken nose said, sounding like a little kid with a stopped-up nose.

"Since you like to be just like your friend," Bolan told Burkett, "maybe I ought to break your jaw to go along with your nose." He turned back to Spivey. "Of course then I'll have to go to work on *your* nose so your little sidekick's feelings won't get hurt."

Spivey shook his head. "I'm tellin' you the truth, man," he mumbled. "I don't know anything else about the guy. Except I don't think he's worked for us for quite a while."

Burkett started to speak, but the Executioner held up a hand. "I know," Bolan said. "He hasn't worked for you for quite a while."

There was a racket at the door, then a pause.

Bolan knew it was Graham announcing his presence, then waiting so the Executioner could be in a position he wouldn't have to testify to later. A few moments later the door swung open, and the Chicago PD detective came in carrying a cardboard tray with foam coffee cups wedged into the cutouts.

Graham set the tray on the table, handed Bolan a steaming cup of black coffee, then slid the two with milk across the table. He shook his head. "I warned you guys about the slippery floor," he said, pointing to the sign. "Can't you read? Some Master Race."

"What else can you tell me?" Bolan asked.

With Graham back, Spivey mistakenly thought he'd be protected. "Nothin', pig," he spit. "Not a damn thing."

Graham glanced at the Executioner and grinned. "Damn," he said. "I forgot the sugar." A second later he was gone.

Fear clouded the men's faces.

"I suggest you give me something to go on," Bolan said, "or we're going to have to play games again."

Spivey looked up at the ceiling, racking his brain for anything that might keep him from another beating. Then, looking back down, he said, "New Breed."

"What's New Breed?"

"Group down in Kankakee, man. A militia." He

glanced around as if the walls might sprout ears. "Just don't tell them you got it from me."

"Or me," Burkett chimed.

"Tell me about them," Bolan said.

"Rumor has it they've got something going down."

"What?"

"I don't know."

Bolan turned to Burkett. "I'm sure you don't know either, right?"

The puppet shook his head violently back and forth. "I don't know," he said through his blood-clogged nostrils.

Graham came back in with several packs of sugar and tossed them on the table.

Bolan leaned forward. "Where do I find these New Breed characters?" he asked Spivey.

The white supremacist gave him directions to a wooded area outside of the city.

The Executioner stood. "The deal still goes. Nothing you told me will be used against you. But there's one other thing." He watched the two men for a moment. He could almost see the words "lawsuit," "civil rights," and "police brutality," written in their eyes. He waited a moment, then pointed to the caution sign again. "You both fell down, you understand? Like I said, you'll never see me again—unless I find out someone's trying to bring heat down on this guy." He indicated Graham with his head. "If that happens, you'll see me and you'll pray to God you hadn't.'' He paused again. ''Understand?''

Both men nodded.

Bolan walked out of the conference room and headed down the hall.

proved God will bear it," the bandit had muttered.

Bolan had nodded.

Bolan walked out of the conference room and
headed downstairs.

CHAPTER TWO

Texas

It was late morning by the time Able Team drove
under an overpass, then turned off St. Mary's onto
Mission Road. Charlie Mott, Stony Man Farm's
number-two pilot, had landed them in San Antonio
only minutes earlier, and now they entered the old
Roosevelt Park area of the city and passed the
world-famous Lone Star Brewery on the right, then
the Yturri-Edmunds Historic Site on the left. Mission Road dropped beneath the traffic of Interstate
10, and shortly they arrived at the Alamo Tavern.

Lyons pulled the rented Suburban into the parking lot, threw the transmission into Park and killed
the engine.

The Able Team leader looked up from behind the
wheel. From where they sat, he, Herman ''Gadgets'' Schwarz and Rosario ''Politician'' Blancanales could see the front and one side of the large
building. The side wall was fabricated of corrugated
steel. The front, Lyons suspected, had once been

the same—it was probably originally a warehouse or industrial business of some type. But now a layering of stucco covered the steel to mimic the walls of the real Alamo at Alamo and Houston streets in central San Antonio.

"Wonder how they came up with the name for this place?" Blancanales cracked.

"Got no idea," Schwarz replied, shaking his head. "How about you, Ironman? You know?"

Lyons ignored the question. Except on rare occasions, he let Schwarz and Blancanales handle the humor division of Able Team, not understanding why they wasted their time and energy on things he rarely found funny, and knowing he felt no desire to enter into their banter even if he had. He opened the door, twisted out of the Suburban and said, "Okay. Let's see what's inside."

"Gee, Ironman," Blancanales said, "do we have to? This is going to be rough duty sitting around this place drinking beer all day."

Lyons started across the gravel toward the front door as the other two men got out. "I've got a feeling there'll be a little more to it before we're done," he called over his shoulder.

"There always is," Schwarz said as he and Blancanales hurried to catch up to their leader.

Lyons glanced at his teammates as they fell in to flank him.

Both wore faded jeans, cowboy boots, and snap-button Western-cut shirts tucked into their waistbands. Wide hand-tooled belts, cinched together with large silver and gold buckles, circled their waists.

Even to the discerning eye, the three men appeared unarmed. But hidden beneath the shirts, readily accessible as soon as the snaps down the front were ripped apart, each man wore at least one pistol and assorted other weapons in an elastic Bianchi bellyband holster.

"What do we do once we're inside?" Blancanales asked.

"Look and listen," Lyons said. "The Alamo has some connection to an upcoming bombing—that's all we know. So go easy. We'll see a way to work ourselves in sooner or later. Just don't get us all burned by being too eager."

"We going with the ex-Special-Forces-currently-out-of-work story?" Blancanales asked, as he opened the door and stepped back for the other two men.

Lyons nodded. It was as good as any, and better than most of the phony background stories Able Team used when going undercover. He suspected it would be perfect for the atmosphere they'd find inside the Alamo.

The men of Able Team stopped just inside the door. Years earlier, as a rookie LAPD patrolman, Carl "Ironman" Lyons had learned to stop just inside the door when entering a bar. It took a few seconds for the eyes to adjust to the dimmer light usually found inside such establishments, and it provided an opportunity to take a look around at what was going on before jumping into the middle of something.

Or as Lyons's old training officer used to say, "You get hit with fewer chairs that way."

As his pupils dilated now, the Able Team leader saw that they were inside a small vestibule. It was similar to the outside of the building in that the walls were covered with stucco. Three large and not particularly well-sculpted stone figures stood against the wall. If it hadn't been for Davy Crockett's coonskin cap and the huge clip point blade in Jim Bowie's stone hand, Lyons doubted he would have recognized the men. He assumed the third man, wearing a more formal military uniform, had to be William Travis.

Like the quality and workmanship that had gone into the stucco walls both inside and out, the poorly done statues cheapened the Alamo rather than added character. Gadgets put it more succinctly as he took it all in. "This place is tasteless as hell," he said.

Lyons led the way into the tavern proper. The three men crossed a large deserted dance floor, then made their way through the tables to the bar at the far end of the room. The sign on the wall inside the front door had said the fire marshall restricted the Alamo to a capacity of 425 patrons. The place was easily big enough to hold that many people. But there couldn't have been more than a dozen present at the moment.

Lyons stopped at the table closest to the bar and took a seat facing the door. Schwarz and Blancanales dropped into two of the three other chairs. An attractive young blonde wearing a short buckskin skirt, matching halter top and coonskin cap dropped several coins into a jukebox against the wall, then sashayed her way across the dance floor to Able Team's table as Garth Brooks began to sing. She stopped next to Lyons and smiled. "Hi! My name's Amy," she said in the perky Southern accent found nowhere but Texas. "I'll be your waitress, and I bet you old boys could use a beer."

"Right and wrong," Blancanales said, returning her smile.

Amy looked puzzled.

"Right about the beer," he explained. "Wrong about the *old* in old boys." The Able Team psychological warfare expert reached up, grabbing a handful of the hair over his ears. "We're not that old," he said. "This stuff's just prematurely gray."

Amy flushed red. "I didn't mean—"

Blancanales's good-natured laughter brought the smile back to her face. "Like I said, you're right about the beer," he said. "Make mine a Lone Star. And it's getting close to lunchtime. You have a menu?"

"Sure do, sugar," Amy said. "I'll bring them

with the beer." She turned to Lyons and Schwarz. "What can I bring you to drink?"

"Lone Star's fine," Lyons said.

Schwarz nodded.

Amy wiggled off in her short buckskin skirt.

Amy came back a moment later with three long-neck bottles, glasses, cardboard coasters and menus. After a brief perusal of the list, all three men ordered cheeseburgers and french fries to go with the beer.

"My cholesterol gets dangerously low if I don't eat like this," Blancanales told Amy.

The young blonde was enjoying the attention shown her by the attractive older man. She leaned over the table, giving him an eyeful of cleavage. "Well, we can't have that now, can we sugar?" she said, then twirled away to take her order pad behind the bar to the cook.

Stopping to take a read on the situation at the front door wasn't the only lesson Lyons had learned years ago as a rookie cop; scrutinizing the people inside the establishment individually was just as important. Twisting casually in his chair, the Able Team leader's gaze moved to the bar. Behind the long wooden counter, a stocky man with a handle-bar mustache polished shot glasses. Seated on the row of stools in front of the rail were the usual assortment of unemployed human casualties with broken veins across their noses.

Lyons shook his head. They could be found in

any bar, in any town, in the nation—early in the morning—drinking to get over the hangover of the night before and into the new one they would have the next day.

Scattered around the tables were a variety of types. Several construction workers, off for lunch, were still wearing their hard hats. A man seated by himself kept glancing nervously around the room. In the corner farthest from Able Team sat a middle-aged man and a red-haired woman of equal years. They held hands across the table, looking into each other's eyes as they spoke in hushed voices, pausing occasionally to kiss or sip their drinks. Lyons saw the sparkle of wedding rings on both of their left hands. The rings didn't match. One was white gold, the other yellow, and he quickly recognized the situation for the extramarital liaison it had to be.

The burgers and fries arrived and Lyons ordered another round of beer. They were halfway through lunch when the phone on the bar rang.

A man Lyons hadn't seen before appeared from a door at the side of the dance floor and walked to the ringing instrument. About five foot eight, he looked close to that in width. He wore a brown Western-cut suit that had been too small for him many calories ago, lizard-skin cowboy boots and a small-brimmed "rancher" hat. A short unlit cigar extended from between his teeth, and he carried what looked like an account book.

The man in the rancher hat grabbed the receiver from the cradle. "Alamo," he grunted.

There was a short pause during which the man's eyes flicked to the couple in the corner. Then he said, "No, Grant. I told you before, she ain't here. She doesn't ever come in here. Now quit botherin' me, will you?" He hung up and began to talk to the bartender.

Able Team finished eating and sat back as Amy carted off the plates, bringing them each another beer without being asked. Lyons studied the fat man in the hat. He had dropped the account book on one of the tables against the wall and was huddled over his figures. He had to be the Alamo's owner or manager, or both.

And Carl Lyons's police instincts were getting a very bad reading on the man.

The Able Team leader was still watching the fat man when the front door suddenly burst open. A man of around forty-five, at least six foot four and weighing in at a good two-fifty, stomped inside the bar, carrying a long-barreled shotgun at port arms. Dressed in a khaki shirt, matching pants and work boots, he paused as Lyons had done to give his eyes time to adjust to the darkness.

Lyons glanced at the corner table.

The couple seated there were frozen like statues.

"Aw shit," grunted the fat man at the table against the wall.

The newcomer got his sight, and it fell on the man and woman in the corner.

"You whore!" the man with the shotgun screamed as he started toward them.

Lyons saw Schwarz and Blancanales both move their hands toward the snaps running down the fronts of their shirts. The Able Team leader did the same. The-second-to-last thing he wanted to do was blow the cover they were trying to establish. But the very last thing he'd do was watch a double murder go down without stopping it.

In his peripheral vision, Lyons saw the fat manager pull what looked like an undersized TV remote control device from the side pocket of his coat. He pressed a button.

A moment later, two burly men appeared from the door behind the bar that Lyons assumed led to the kitchen. A third, equally large man entered from the foyer.

The man with the shotgun stopped ten feet from the table and raised the weapon to his shoulder. "You lyin', cheatin' bitch!" he screamed. "I'm goin' to kill you and your boyfriend both!"

"Now hang on a minute there, Grant," the manager said, standing. "There ain't no reason to jump to any conclusions."

The man called Grant swung the weapon away from the couple at the table and onto the manager. "Just stay where you are, there, Cube!" he said. "You're a lyin', low-life, lizard-crawlin' bastard, too. You told me my wife wasn't here, you son of a bitch! When I've done settled with them, I may just have me some buckshot left over for your greasy gut!''

The two men who had entered the room from the kitchen—bouncers, Lyons assumed—had been making their way slowly across the dance floor toward Grant. The big man with the shotgun had been too absorbed with what he was doing to notice them earlier. But now he saw them.

Swinging the long barrel of the goose gun their way, he said, ''Stop right there now, Harley! I got nothin' against you and Tommy Lee, and I don't want to have to kill you. But I damn sure will if I have to. I damn sure will.''

The third bouncer—the largest of the three who had appeared in the foyer—had been behind Grant the whole time. Lyons had watched him take special pains to move slowly and silently, and now he was less than twenty feet behind the shotgunner. As Lyons slowly began to unsnap his shirt, the woman at the table spoke. The Able Team leader glanced back at the table.

''Put your squirrel gun down, Grant,'' she said. ''You know it's over between you and me. You raised your hand to me one too many times. I ain't never comin' back to you. Never.''

The woman had turned to face her husband, and now Lyons could see the other side of her face. The eye that had been hidden from him earlier was black and swollen.

Grant swung the shotgun back to the table. "You better say some prayers, and you better say 'em fast," he screamed. Tears of rage ran down his face. He swung the weapon slightly to cover the man. "You better do the same, Claude. 'Cause you're goin' to be right after her!"

Lyons let his hand fall into his shirt and come to rest on the butt of the Colt 1911 Government Model. To his sides, he saw Schwarz and Blancanales were ready as well. He was about to draw when the bouncer behind Grant made his move.

The man was fast for his size, and he covered the last ten feet in a blur. As he moved, a flat black leather slapper appeared in his hand. Bringing it up high over his head as he got within arm's reach of Grant, he brought it down on the back of the big man's skull.

For a moment, Grant stood still, blinking his eyes. Then the eyes closed, and he dropped the shotgun before toppling forward on top of it.

Lyons, Schwarz and Blancanales quickly resnapped their shirts. A fast glance at the manager told the Able Team leader that the man had been too preoccupied with the dangerous situation to pay any attention to them.

The other two bouncers rushed forward. The one who had been addressed as Harley knelt next to Grant and jammed a finger into his neck. "Ol' boy's okay, Cube,'' he man said after a moment. ''Just out cold.''

''Well, get him the hell out into the cold, Harley,'' the manager said. ''Drive him home and stick his ass in bed until he sobers up. And leave the damn shotgun here.'' He pulled the soggy cigar from his teeth and turned to face the other Alamo patrons. ''No extra charge for the floor show, folks,'' he called out. ''Entertainment's always free at the Alamo.''

The few chuckles the lame joke got were more nervous than amused.

Lyons and his teammates watched as the three bouncers carried Grant out the front door. ''That biggest guy handles himself well,'' Schwarz commented, nodding toward the man who still held the leather slapper in his hand.

''Yeah,'' Lyons said. ''But what if he came up against something he couldn't handle?''

''Like what?'' Gadgets said. ''You mean us?''

''In a roundabout way.'' Lyons glanced at Blancanales. A big grin spread across the man's face. He figured out what Lyons had in mind.

Lyons stood and crossed the dance floor to the row of pay phones in the foyer. Careful that there were no inquisitive ears within hearing distance, he dropped a quarter into the slot.

When he returned to the table, the Able Team leader glanced at the check Amy had left.

''Who'd you call?'' Gadgets wanted to know.

Lyons fished into the pocket of his jeans, found two twenties and dropped them on the table next to the bill. "I'll explain on the way to the motel," he said, turning toward the front door.

"What motel?" Schwarz asked.

"The one we're getting ready to check into," Lyons replied.

CHAPTER THREE

Washington, D.C.

David McCarter sat in the middle seat of the limousine behind the Treasury agent who was driving. Gary Manning was against the opposite window, with Rafael Encizo, Calvin James and T. J. Hawkins in the rear of the vehicle. Hal Brognola, the stump of unlit cigar clenched between his teeth, rode shotgun in the front.

McCarter, Phoenix Force's leader since the retirement of Yakov Katzenelenbogen, watched the driver pull up to the security checkpoint. A uniformed Secret Service man stepped out of the guard shack and walked forward carrying a clipboard. The driver showed his credentials.

"The President is expecting us," Brognola said, leaning across the seat into the Secret Service man's view.

"Oh, Mr. Brognola," the man said, stiffening. "Sorry, I didn't see you there." He jotted something on the clipboard, stepped back and waved them through.

The limo waited as the electronic barricade rose overhead, then rolled through onto Pennsylvania Avenue. McCarter had been on this street many times in the past. It had been always busy with tourists and bureaucrats, and seeing it so deserted now gave him an eerie feeling. As there had been several incidents with guns, the street was closed to general traffic.

The former British SAS officer straightened the solid burgundy tie around his throat as the limo stopped again at the front gate. He was a British subject rather than an American citizen, and he still felt allegiance to the Crown. But he had lived and worked out of the United States for so long now that it was indeed his second home. And he took it somewhat personally when crazy men shot at the White House and forced the closing of Pennsylvania Avenue.

Such incidents seemed a precursor for worse things to come.

The limo pulled through the gate, circled the White House and rolled into a parking place at the rear marked Secret Service Only. McCarter, Brognola and the rest of Phoenix Force exited the vehicle and walked toward a steel door. The Phoenix Force leader glanced at Brognola as the high-ranking Department of Justice official came to a halt and pressed a buzzer.

Brognola had decided it best that he escort Phoenix Force personally to this initial meeting with the President in order to break the ice with the Secret Service. What Phoenix Force was about to do—join the presidential family's protection team—was practically unheard of. For many years that had been the duty of the Secret Service, and they guarded the responsibility jealously.

McCarter wasn't expecting a warm welcome from the Secret Service. Waves were about to be created. And while the Secret Service worked out of the Treasury Department rather than Justice, Brognola was high enough up the ladder to deliver serious political clout if it became necessary.

The steel door opened electronically, and four more uniformed guards appeared inside a semilit corridor. The fact that the men had their hands resting on the grips of their pistols didn't escape McCarter's eyes. Neither did the fact that the retaining straps on their holsters were unsnapped.

McCarter shook his head. He had never seen security around the White House so tight, nor the guards so tense. It wasn't a good sign. But like the closing of the surrounding streets, it said plenty about the current atmosphere of the nation.

A metal detector was positioned just inside the doorway. Brognola held up his Justice Department credentials as he walked through. The alarm buzzed.

"I'm sorry, sir," a guard in his midtwenties said. "We'll have to have your weapons."

Brognola shoved his credentials closer to the man's face. "Read this," he said.

"I know, Mr. Brognola. But we've got orders. No one but the uniformed staff and protection team is allowed to carry a weapon inside the building."

Brognola bit down on the cigar until McCarter thought it might snap in two. "Carrying weapons is our business, son," the Justice man said. "And these men are about to become the President's protection team." Without another word he walked past the guards toward an elevator at the end of the corridor.

The rest of the team followed, each sending the metal detector screaming as he passed through. McCarter noticed the young guard pulling a walkie-talkie from his belt as he brought up the rear.

No one spoke as the elevator rose. When the doors rolled back, they found themselves staring at six more uniformed men. This time, the guard in charge was older. "Hi, Hal," he said in a Southern drawl.

"Hello, Henry."

The man Brognola had called Henry had thick gray hair that might, or might not, have been a toupee. He smiled with his lips, but his eyes showed stress. "I understand you refused to give up your weapons downstairs."

"You understand correctly, Henry."

The gray-haired man's sigh was almost inaudible. "Hal, we've got orders direct from the President himself on this. It's going to be my ass if you don't cooperate."

Brognola pulled the cigar from his mouth and used it to indicate the office down the hall. "We've got orders from the President ourselves," he said. "And those orders are to show up here and join his protection team. How do you want us to protect him and his family without weapons, Henry? Judo, maybe?"

Henry sighed again, louder this time. "Damn, I've always loved politics," he said. "Okay, Hal." He took a step back. "But do me a favor, will you?"

"What?"

"Fade the heat for me if the Man gets his tail caught on the fence, huh?"

Brognola nodded and led the way down the hall again.

Two men in suits—one navy blue, the other gray—stood outside the door to the Oval Office. Both were well over six feet tall, muscular, and had neatly trimmed mustaches. Brognola flashed his ID again, and the man in blue squinted at it. "So you're the top-secret team of bodyguards sent here to teach us our job, are you?" he said, smirking.

Brognola had to look up to meet the man's eyes. But that fact didn't slow the Justice man down. "You might put it that way."

It was the tall man in the blue suit who lost the staring contest.

"So," Brognola said, "you want to let us in?"

The two men in suits stepped reluctantly away from the door. They didn't open it.

Brognola ignored the subtle insult and opened the door himself, holding it back while the men of Phoenix Force walked through. He took the lead again once they were in the outer office, stepping up to the secretary's desk and saying, "Hello, Eileen."

"Good afternoon, Mr. Brognola," the attractive brunette behind the desk said. "The President is expecting you."

Tapping a button on the intercom, she spoke into a speaker-phone. "Mr. President, Mr. Brognola and his men are here."

The voice that came back over the speaker-phone had a mid-South accent. "Thanks, Eileen," the President said. "Send them in."

McCarter followed the other men into the Oval Office. Three more Secret Service agents sat in overstuffed easy chairs against the wall. They rose to their feet as Brognola and Phoenix Force entered the room.

The President stood behind his desk. "Hello, Hal," he said, extending his hand.

Brognola shook it briefly. "Mr. President."

The man behind the desk turned toward his protection team. "George, Howard..." he said. "I'd like you and William to wait outside. I need to discuss a few things with these gentlemen."

A Secret Service man in dark gray pinstripes frowned and took a step forward. "Sir," he said, "I'm not so sure—"

"That will be all, George," the President said. "Thank you."

George looked like he wanted to say something else, but he didn't. Reluctantly he led the other two agents through the door into the outer office.

"Have a seat Hal, gentlemen," the President said, indicating the chairs and couches around the office with a wave of his hand as he sat. When they had all found a seat, he went on. "I wanted to speak to you privately before we introduce you to the current protection team." He cleared his throat. "As you might imagine, my decision to bring in bodyguards from outside the Service has created a certain amount of dissention within the ranks."

Brognola nodded. "That's to be expected," he said. "No one wants somebody else doing their job. Or telling them how to do it."

"Precisely. But sometimes unpleasant decisions are unavoidable. Especially when you sit here," he said, tapping the desk.

Brognola leaned forward in his chair. "Perhaps you could tell us exactly why you decided you wanted Phoenix Force to protect you," he suggested.

The President shrugged. "A variety of reasons.

First, as I'm sure you already know, there have been several attempts on my life over the past few weeks.''

McCarter felt his eyebrows lower slightly. Unless the Phoenix Force leader was mistaken, he was referring to two incidents in which men were found carrying weapons inside the outer security perimeter during the President's speeches in different states of the U.S. In neither case had there been an actual assassination attempt, and follow-up investigations gave no indication that any was planned.

"I assume you're speaking of the incidents in Buffalo and Detroit?" Brognola asked.

The President nodded. "Of course."

McCarter glanced at Brognola but saw no change in the Stony Man director's deadpan face. Buffalo and Detroit were the incidents all right. Was there a real threat or had the President succumbed to the paranoia the pressures of office sometimes induced? McCarter watched the big Fed out of the corner of his eye, knowing Brognola would be asking himself the same question, and wondering what that answer would be.

"What are the other reasons you brought us here, Mr. President?" Brognola asked. The fact that he had changed the subject without pursuing the matter told McCarter everything he needed to know.

"I want someone I can trust not only watching me, but the Secret Service, too," the man behind the desk said. "One of them—maybe more than one—has to be in on this."

Now Brognola did frown. "Are you saying you believe there's a leak?" he asked.

"Leak, treachery, treason, call it whatever you will. Of course there's a leak."

"And what leads you to believe this, Mr. President?"

"Isn't it obvious? Unless someone on my protection team is dirty, how did those two men get their guns through perimeter security?"

McCarter knew that there were about a thousand ways that could be done, and was tempted to tell the Man so.

Brognola looked like he might do it himself but instead said, "I'll instruct Phoenix Force to keep an eye on the protection team as well," he said.

The phone on the desk buzzed. The President poked a button with his index finger and spoke into a speaker-phone. "Yes, Eileen?"

"Sorry to interrupt you, Mr. President. Mr. Taft on line four."

McCarter recognized the name and wasn't surprised at the call. Theodore Taft was the current Secret Service director.

The President punched another button and said, "Good afternoon, Ted. What's on your mind?"

"Good afternoon, Mr. President," came a brisk voice on the other end of the line. "I'm calling because I'm greatly concerned."

"What concerns you, Ted?"

Taft cleared his throat. "I understand you have called in men for your protection team from some outside agency. I also understand they refused to give up their weapons at two security stations within the White House."

"Well, Ted," the President said, "we can't really expect them to protect me without guns, can we?"

There was a long pause on the other end of the line. Then Taft said, "Sir, we haven't run a background investigation on these men. I don't even know who they are. I don't understand why you felt the need to—"

"You don't need to understand it, Ted," the President said, his voice growing a bit harsher. "You only need to accept it." His tone lightened again. "Hal Brognola's here. I'll let him talk to you."

Brognola leaned toward the speaker-phone. "Good afternoon, Ted."

"Hal, what have *you* got to do with all this?"

"These are my men," Brognola said, "and they're the best. You have nothing to worry about."

"What kind of bureaucratic coup are you trying to pull, Brognola?" Taft asked, his voice rising slightly. "Trying to get protection duties transferred to Justice?"

Brognola straightened the lapel of his coat. "No,

Ted. I'm just taking orders from the President of the United States. Just like you.''

Another long pause followed. Finally Taft said, ''Mr. President, if this is your will, so be it. But I want to go on record as strongly objecting to the use of these unknown men in such a sensitive position. And I can take no responsibility for your safety if anything goes wrong.''

''Your objection is duly noted, Director Taft,'' the President said. ''Anything else on your mind?''

''No, sir.''

''Good.'' The President punched the button to kill the line. Turning his attention back to the men seated around the room, he tapped the intercom button again. ''Eileen, are the First Lady and the children here yet?''

''Waiting right here, sir.''

''Send them in.''

A moment later Eileen opened the door. A boy of around ten, blue-eyed with sandy hair and wearing the uniform of an expensive private school in the Washington area, entered the office. He was followed by a young woman with frizzy blond hair who looked to be about sixteen or seventeen. The girl wore a faded denim skirt even shorter than Eileen's, blue hose and denim Western boots. A tight white blouse—the top two buttons left carelessly open—covered her upper body. She was attractive, but the clothes and the heavily applied makeup she wore weren't what one expected of the President's daughter.

The last person through the door was that of the well-known First Lady. She passed her children and strode to the President's desk. She wore a dull gun-metal gray suit and flats. Her hair was chopped off bluntly at the neck, and she appeared to be some-what irritated. "How long is this going to take?" she demanded of the President. "I have meetings, appointments..."

"It won't take long, dear," the President said.

Introductions were brief, with the First Lady's eyes revealing her anger as they fell in turn on Brognola, McCarter and the men of Phoenix Force. The boy was Wallace, the girl, Kelly.

"Well, then," Brognola said when the introduc-tions had been completed, "I suppose the next step is to break up into teams. David, I'll turn things over to you."

McCarter cleared his throat. "Mr. President, I, along with Mr. Manning, intend to remain with you at all times, working in conjunction with those al-ready on your protection team. I'll assign Misters Encizo, James and Hawkins—one man to join each of the teams covering the First Lady and your chil-dren." He turned to James. "Mr. James, please ac-company this young man to school. Mr. Encizo, you'll be with Kelly. That leaves Mr. Hawkins to—"

As he spoke, the President's daughter had moved

in front of T. J. Hawkins. Now, looking up into the face of Phoenix Force's youngest member, she gave him a smile that bordered on lewd. "I want *him*, Daddy," she interrupted, purring like a kitten. Then, stepping in at his side, she took Hawkins's arm and pirouetted to face her father.

Hawkins turned red.

McCarter found himself suddenly wishing that Phoenix Force had a female member. This young woman was going to be trouble with a capital *T;* she already had eyes for Hawkins. The Briton thought a moment. He could assign one of the other men to her, but he doubted that would solve the problem.

"Do you have any objections to this gentleman escorting Kelly?" the President asked McCarter.

"No, sir," McCarter said. "That will be fine."

"Good," the man behind the desk said. "Because Daddy's little girl seems to always get what she wants. Regardless of anyone's objections." He beamed across the room at his daughter.

Kelly squeezed Hawkins's arm and smiled back.

McCarter was fighting the urge to regurgitate when the first rifle shot sounded outside the White House.

For a moment, no one spoke or moved. Then three more rounds were fired in rapid succession. McCarter dived over the desk and landed on the President. Holding him down, he looked back to see that the other members of Phoenix Force had taken the rest of the First Family to the floor.

"Rafe!" the Phoenix Force leader yelled as he rose to his feet. "You, Gary and T.J. stay here and take charge of the protection teams! Calvin, come with me!"

"Without another word, McCarter and James raced for the door to the Oval Office.

Stony Man Farm

AARON KURTZMAN reached to the console next to his computer, lifted the coffee cup and took a sip. The bitter brown liquid was lukewarm, and he made a face he could see in the blank monitor screen in front of him. Setting the cup back down, he swiveled his wheelchair toward the ramp that led down to the other work areas in Stony Man Farm's Computer Room.

Huntington Wethers walked slowly up the ramp, followed by the other members of the Farm's cybernetics team, Carmen Delahunt and Akira Tokaido.

As they gathered around him, Kurtzman asked, "Are you still working on the serial killings, Carmen?" The female member of the cybernetics team, an old-line former FBI agent who'd been lured from Quantico by Brognola, had taken it upon herself to solve a particularly vicious series of rape-murders that had taken place in Massachusetts and Maine, then spilled over the Canadian border into Quebec and New Brunswick. The victims had been dissected and mailed in pieces to family members.

Carmen Delahunt was taking the attacks personally. The victims were all middle-aged women much like herself.

"That's affirmative, Aaron," Delahunt said. "And I'm not giving up until that son of a bitch is behind bars." She paused. "Or more preferably, in the ground."

Kurtzman nodded. "What would it take to get you to put it on the back burner for a little while?"

Delahunt smiled again. "I'm sure a simple 'please' would do the trick."

"Good. I want you to start running down the names and dossiers on all known strategy experts with terrorist connections. Start with those in the U.S., then go to Canada and Mexico. If we don't come up with anything in those places, try Interpol."

"Got it. Anything else?"

Kurtzman shook his head. "Not for the moment."

Without another word Delahunt turned on the balls of her feet and hurried back down the ramp to the bank of computers in front of her chair.

Kurtzman turned his attention to Akira Tokaido. The young man was dressed in his usual garb: torn and faded jeans tucked into a pair of well-worn black combat boots, and a sleeveless denim jacket covered with silver studs. His head bobbed back and forth as he kept time to the music blasting in his ears from the ever-present Sony Discman CD player.

The computer genius fought the urge to shake his head. He didn't know how the kid could work with that noise he called "alternative" music in his head all the time. But Kurtzman didn't care as long as Tokaido did his work. And the young Japanese did it. Well.

"Unplug that mainline into your cranium a minute, will you, Akira?" Kurtzman said.

"What did you say?" Tokaido asked.

"Take that thing out of your ear so you can hear me."

"What?"

Kurtzman raised his voice. He had already said, "Take that thing out—" again when he saw the smile spread across Tokaido's face. The Stony Man computer wizard chuckled as he realized he'd been had.

Tokaido jerked the cord from his ear and turned off the CD player.

Kurtzman couldn't help but shake his head. "You still on the mass murder in Oklahoma City?" he asked. Several years ago, five women had been discovered bound, gagged, stabbed and strangled in what police knew had been a crack house. Authorities still had no leads.

"Yes," Tokaido said, "but I am getting nowhere fast."

"Then you won't mind pulling off and tapping into the library files across the country."

"Libraries?" Tokaido repeated. "I'm so glad you plan to read. A mind is a terrible thing to waste."

Kurtzman ignored the joke. "I want you to make up a list of references on military strategy and find who's been checking them out. I want to know who's been reading Sun Tzu, Musashi, Genghis Khan, George Patton, all of the classics. But don't forget the more modern stuff, too. There's a relatively new work by Frederick J. Lovret entitled *The Way and the Power*. Make things like that get on the list."

"Sure thing," Tokaido said. "Your wish is my command. Anything else?"

"Yeah. When you've finished the libraries, start on the bookstores."

"Bookstores? I didn't know they kept such records."

"They don't, most of them. But many of the major bookstore chains have a preferred-customer or frequent-reader program these days," Kurtzman said. "You buy a membership, then get a discount on each purchase made the rest of the year. They *do* keep track of what the members buy, and if our boy Maestro has a card, we may be able to cross-check him with what Carmen comes up with."

Enlightenment filled Tokaido's eyes, and he turned and headed down the ramp.

Kurtzman watched the young man take his seat, then turned to Huntington Wethers. By appearance, the tall, distinguished black man was Akira Tokaido's exact opposite. Conservatively dressed in dark brown slacks, a beige cardigan sweater, white shirt and paisley tie, Wethers carried an air of dignity wherever he went. He had been a professor of cybernetics at Berkeley when his talents had been discovered and he had been invited to work at the Farm.

"How goes the DNA thing, Hunt?" Kurtzman asked. Wethers was working on a theory that it might be possible to lift DNA directly from clothing even when no tissue or body fluids were found.

The man smiled. "Steady, but slow, progress. It may all be in vain, Aaron. But I haven't given up hope." He held up two crossed fingers.

"Can you give it up long enough to help me out for a little while?"

"Of course. What can I do?"

"I want you to step up the periodic spot-checks we do on the Internet," Kurtzman said. "Go at it full time. Let's try to pick up this Maestro character again and find out all we can about him."

"Will do," Wethers said.

Kurtzman watched him walk down the ramp, then turned to his own computer. He had handed out the assignments and had all the confidence in the world that his people would carry them out to the best of their abilities. And their abilities were better than those of any other human beings in the world. With one possible exception.

Maestro.

Kurtzman tapped several keys and began to program his own machine. He had had a feeling in his gut all along that whoever this Maestro was, he was in a league of computer expertise that they'd not yet encountered at Stony Man Farm. Well, so be it. Maestro might be good. He might even be great.

But Aaron Kurtzman seriously doubted that the man, whoever he was, could outsmart all four of them.

For a moment, the Stony Man Farm computer genius thought of Carmen Delahunt and how she was taking the serial killings personally. He guessed he was beginning to take Maestro personally.

He let the computer beep its ready signal, then his fingers began to fly across the keyboard like a maestro himself. He loved computers. He had a special relationship with them, and a serious respect for all the good they could do for humankind.

But he didn't like them being used for evil. Yeah, he thought, that got things down to a personal level, all right. He clicked the Sign On button and entered the World Wide Web.

So he'd just have to find this guy who called himself Maestro. One way or another, he'd get this bastard who liked to plan fire bombs.

Virginia Beach, Virginia

THE HARSH RHYMES of West Side Connection's "Bow Down" filled Desmond Click's head. But the music did little to lighten his mood as he stared from the balcony outside his bedroom window at the waves rolling in over the Atlantic coast. Wheeling his chair to the rail, he looked down the shoreline at the tall buildings along the edge of the sea. The sight brought a thin smile to his face as his eyes fell on the tallest of the structures. But the lapse in melancholy was short-lived.

A light breeze blew across the balcony, and Click tucked the blanket tighter into the sides of the wheelchair, then pulled the shawl close around his throat. He knew it wasn't particularly cold outside today. But *he* was cold. Since the accident his circulation had been poor and it seemed he was always freezing; even inside his mother's apartment he could turn up the heat to ninety degrees and still find himself shivering.

As the breeze continued to tickle his face, Click glanced down toward the shriveled tissue he knew lay beneath the blanket—the hideous mess that had once been his legs. Calling them legs now was stretching the term. If they looked like legs of any kind, it would be the legs of a Thanksgiving turkey just removed from the broiler. The sight was enough to make him weep.

The breeze blew harder, and Desmond Click

shuddered. Turning in his wheelchair, he grasped the handle of the sliding glass door, slid it open and wheeled back into his bedroom. He shut the door again, then turned toward the glass just as the sun drifted out from behind a cloud. Click faced the sun but the new angle of light entering the room had turned the glass into a mirror.

Click stared at his reflection. His face and hands were covered with the deep pink scars left by the fire, and were as grotesque as his legs. He turned away and closed his eyes.

He shivered again. He missed the warmth he used to feel in the sunshine. He missed the warmth he got in his body when he ran, or lifted weights or played the other sports. But most of all, he missed the warmth of fire. Not the warmth it brought to his body but the warmth it brought to his soul. And yes, he thought as he opened his eyes again, the warmth it brought to his groin.

Click sat back against his chair. The sun was hidden by a particularly thick cloud now. A dreary darkness had fallen over the shoreline. He had never noticed how depressing the sea could be when he had had use of his legs. He had never known depression in those days. Oh, he'd had a few bad days along with the good—no different than anyone else. But in those days, he could always go out and light a fire.

Fire had always cheered him up, and what he'd thought to be depression he now knew to be nothing more than a mild case of the blues. Certainly not this dark, hollow, hopelessness that drifted over his body and soul for days, weeks or even months at a time.

Click wheeled away from the window and over to the nightstand by his bed. He lifted the pack of unfiltered Camel cigarettes, shook one loose and tapped it on the table before sticking it between the scarred tissue where his lips had once been. He rolled the wheel of the lighter with his thumb and the flame shot up. For a moment, Click stared at the small blaze in fascination, then lit the end of his cigarette.

A knock sounded on the door. Click didn't answer. He inhaled as hard as he could, watching the orange glow at the end of his cigarette shoot halfway down the shaft. He held the smoke in his lungs as the knock came again, finally letting it drift out his nose and mouth when his mother's voice said, "Dezzie? Dezzie? I've brought your lunch, dear."

The door started to open and Click whirled his chair violently toward it. "Dammit, Mother!" he screamed at the top of his lungs. "I've told you never to come in here before I give you permission!"

The door quickly closed again. There was a long silence, then, "Dezzie?"

"Yes, Mother."

"May I come in, sweetheart? I've brought your lunch."

"Yes, Mother. Come in."

The door opened wider this time and Mrs. Click, still in her housecoat and slippers, walked across the threshold. She carried a tray with a cheese sandwich, potato chips, an apple cut into sections and a Snickers candy bar. The elderly woman looked nervous as she stopped in the middle of the room. "Shall I bring it to you, darling?" she asked.

"No," Click said. "Set it down on the desk." He looked at what the tray held in disgust. It was the same lunch she had packed him for school every day when he was a child. It was the same lunch she had fixed for him every day since he was forced to move back in with her after the accident.

Mary Click set the tray on the desk next to her son's computer modem and brushed a loose strand of gray hair from her face. "Will you come eat, Dezzie? I'll stay with you if you like."

"I'm not hungry."

"But you've got to eat something, sweetheart. You've got to keep your strength up."

Click wondered for what. How much strength did it take to push keyboard keys or wheel his chair from the bed to the computer to the window and back again?

"I'll eat later," Click said, turning back toward the window.

"Dezzie," Mrs. Click said, taking a tentative step toward her son's back, "let's do something today. Let's go for a walk along the beach. Or we could go to the mall."

"I don't want to go anywhere."

"But you need to get out, darling. You can't just stay in this room all the time."

"I've done a pretty good job of it for the last three years," Click said. The anger he felt toward his mother was always waiting to rise in his chest. Most days, he controlled it. But recently, that control had been slipping. And today, with the depression he felt...

Click looked back at her. She was always dawdling, wanting to get something for him; do something for him. She thought she was helping, but all it did was remind him of the helpless monster he'd become. Most of the time, he simply didn't like her for it. Sometimes, like now, he hated.

"But it's not good for you son. You need to get out. You need to see people."

"That would involve them seeing me," Click said through clenched teeth. He turned back to the window.

"Oh, Dezzie, it's not so bad. Not as bad as you think. People have seen much worse. They don't stare or—"

Click whirled so hard in his wheelchair this time that it tipped over onto its side. He went flying onto the floor, spewing every curse word he had ever known.

"Dezzie!" his mother shrieked, stepping forward.

"Get back, dammit!" Click screeched, flailing his hands. "Get away from me, you old bitch! I don't need your help, and I don't fucking well want it!" Rolling onto his side, he reached out, righting the chair again. He set the brake, grabbed the arms and started to drag himself into the seat.

The sun came out again over the ocean and forced him to watch his pathetic movements in the window.

"Dezzie, let me help you...please?"

"No!" Click shouted. "Stay the fuck away from me!"

Finally back in the chair, Click wheeled toward the table, his chest heaving for oxygen. He grasped the tray of food, lifted it over his head and hurled it at his mother. Mary Click flinched as the tray and plates sailed past her, missing their target by inches.

"Now get the fuck out!" Click screamed.

A deep sadness covered the woman's face as she stood motionless for a moment. "All right, Dezzie," she said softly through her tears. She turned and left the room, closing the door behind her.

Click spun his wheelchair back to the window. The sun was still shining and he could see himself. He rolled close to the glass, staring at his reflection, forcing his eyes to look at the ghastly tissue that had once been a face. He ripped the shawl from his shoulders and threw it on the floor, then jerked his

T-shirt over his head. Again, what he saw was a monstrously deformed parody of what had once been flesh and skin.

He held his arms in front of his face. His eyes widened in horror. His mouth opened to scream, but no sound came from his empty soul.

Click's lifeless arms fell back into his lap. He had nothing left to live for, he thought, and his eyes moved to the desk drawer where his father's old Colt Single Action Army revolver lay beckoning.

Then his eyes flicked up to the computer.

He did have something to live for. At least for a little while longer. He had his computer, and that computer was hope.

Click slowly turned his wheelchair toward the desk and began to roll across the room. He had work to do—a fire-bomb strike to set up—he should get to it now. With any luck, that work would let others experience the pain he had known.

Let them know what it was like to be a monster like Desmond Click.

CHAPTER FOUR

Illinois

The Learjet 60 dropped through the sky as Grimaldi guided it over Kankakee. Bolan watched the city streets and buildings grow fewer along the highway below, eventually becoming farm and pastureland. A few minutes later, he spotted the thick wooded area that Spivey and his friend had described. "There, Jack," he said, pointing through the windshield. "Take her east a little."

Jack Grimaldi nodded, banking the plane toward the trees and dropping the altitude farther.

Bolan raised the rubber armored Zeiss 10 X 40/GA binoculars to his eyes and adjusted the focusing. He stared through the lenses as they flew over the woods, scanning the branches and leaves for any sign of the New Breed militia Spivey had said would be there. He saw nothing.

The jet cleared the woodland and Grimaldi banked the wings over another pasture, heading back in the direction from which they'd come. Bolan squinted into the opticals, the sun hitting his line of vision at an angle that made viewing difficult. Again, he saw no signs of activity within the trees.

"You sure this is the right place?" Grimaldi asked. "There's a bunch of wooded areas farther down." The Stony Man pilot nodded toward the horizon.

The Executioner shook his head. "This has to be it," he said. He straightened in his seat and dropped the binoculars into his lap, rubbing his eyes with his free hand. "See those two streams running parallel to each other over there?" He didn't wait for an answer. "Spivey mentioned them specifically."

Grimaldi shrugged.

"Let's try coming in from the west, Jack," Bolan suggested. "I want the sun at my back this time."

"Then the sun at your back is what you get, Sarge." Grimaldi cut the flyover short, dipping the wings into a wide arc that ended with them approaching the target from the new direction.

Bolan glanced at the man to his left as they neared the trees again. Jack Grimaldi had been the top flyboy at Stony Man since the Farm's origin. A former fighter pilot, he had taken a wrong step after leaving the service and wound up flying planes for the Mob. But Grimaldi was a good man at heart, and he had gratefully corrected that mistake after meeting the man known as the Executioner. Since that time, Bolan and Grimaldi had flown more missions together than either of them could remember.

The early-afternoon sun was still almost directly overhead, and the jet's new angle of approach provided the Executioner with almost direct lighting. He relaxed his eyes, moving the binoculars slowly back and forth across the treetops as Grimaldi cut the engines and glided over. Just as he was about to give up, a flicker of sun reflected off something hidden in the trees. Before he could identify the reflection, the plane had cleared the woods once more.

"Swing her around and drop lower," Bolan said. "I think I'm on to something."

Grimaldi did as instructed but said, "You sure you want to go down? We're pushing things as we are. If the bad boys are down there, they're likely to see us."

The Executioner nodded. "I know, but I don't see any way around it."

They dropped lower through the sky as they turned, finally banking to the west again. The jet all but skimmed the treetops now, and Bolan left the binoculars in his lap.

Halfway through the forest, the Executioner saw another reflection, then more light bouncing off glass and metal. He frowned through the windshield.

Pickups, a few Jeeps and other four-wheel drive vehicles were parked along a winding dirt road that led from the county blacktop just to the east. "You see them?" Bolan asked.

"Yep," Grimaldi answered. "I just hope they don't see us."

Bolan and Grimaldi had been together too long for further orders from the Executioner to be necessary. The pilot dipped a wing and took the jet back up, cutting a 180-degree turn through the sky before approaching the trees one final time. As he did, Bolan moved to the rear of the craft, shrugging into the parachute straps before slinging the Heckler & Koch MP-5 over his right shoulder.

A few seconds later, he was falling from the jet toward the pastureland three hundred yards from the trees.

The Executioner jerked the rip cord, sending the sky-blue day camou canopy over his head. The chute unfurled, catching the wind and dragging him momentarily back in the sky. Descending slower now, Bolan raised the binoculars to his eyes and searched the trees. From this distance, he could see nothing. But he hadn't really expected to.

Hitting the ground on both feet, the Executioner jogged three steps to catch his balance, then tugged the canopy by the lines. Quickly he folded the chute and found a large rock to weigh it down. The next step was a final weapons-equipment check. He scanned the wooded area in the distance as he began to pat himself down.

In addition to the HK MP-5 submachine gun that would serve as his primary weapon, the Executioner's sound-suppressed Beretta 93-R rode in shoulder leather over the woodland camou skinsuit that covered his body. His trademark .44 Magnum Desert Eagle hung from the matching camouflage ballistic nylon belt and holster on his strong side. Extra 30-round 9 mm magazines for the subgun were stored in his combat vest, with auxiliary loads for the two pistols in belt carriers on the other side of his shoulder holster under his right arm.

As he continued to search the trees in front of him, Bolan's hand fell to the grooved grip of the Applegate-Fairbairn fighting knife suspended upside down on his vest. Made by Colonel Rex Applegate's custom cutler, William W. Harsey, it was the final evolution in double-edged combat blades that had begun with flint weapons in the Stone Age, then progressed through the daggers of Medieval times and the classic World War Two Fairbairn-Sykes commando knife. Secured in a Kydex sheath, it differed from most military blades in that it was a weapon first, a utility blade second. It could be used to open cans, cut firewood for a bivouac or construct a shelter, if necessary.

But its main function was as a man-killer.

Satisfied that his equipment was in place, the Executioner double-timed it toward the trees. The terrain sloped up and down in a series of shallow peaks and valleys, and he stayed low to the ground, taking full advantage of the cover they provided. Fifty yards from the forest, he dived forward to his belly, bringing the binoculars back to his eyes for

a final search of the branches and leaves. He saw
the almost hidden opening off the blacktop. But
again, no signs of the New Breed militia.

Bolan rose again, sprinting the final distance to
the woods and disappearing inside the tree line. He
stayed hidden inside the foliage, ten feet from the
road, following its path. Tire tracks deeply embedded in the dirt after a recent rain led him deeper
into the forest. He moved quickly yet quietly, walking the fine line between speed and stealth.

Seventy yards from where he'd entered the trees,
he came across the first parked vehicle. The ten-
year-old Ford Bronco had seen its share of abuse.
Spots of gray primer peeked through the black paint
covering the dented body. Through the tinted windows, Bolan could see the outline of boxes.

Ammunition boxes.

He moved on through the woods, passing vehicles parked along the side of the road in front of
the Bronco. They pointed toward a clearing where
at least a dozen more pickups and Jeeps stood.
Pausing at the edge of the trees, the Executioner
frowned at the sight. He had seen roughly twenty
cars and trucks. That meant at least twenty New
Breed militia roamed somewhere deeper in the forest.

He started to move into the clearing when a sudden burst of automatic fire far in the distance met
his ears. Dropping lower behind the trunk of a thick
tree, the Executioner waited. A second later, the

gunfire died down and the faint sound of laughter sounded through the trees.

Then footsteps approached from the other side of the clearing. A man in his early twenties, sporting a thick brown beard, dirty pinstriped overalls and an AR-15 emerged from the foliage across from Bolan. He walked unsteadily through the parked vehicles to a blue-and-white Chevy pickup, and opened the door. Bolan watched him pull an almost empty half-pint bottle of whiskey from the bib pocket under his chin, finish it off and throw it into the trees with a loud crash. Reaching into the truck, the bearded man pulled out a box of .223-caliber ammo and dropped it into the pocket where the bottle had been.

Bolan let the New Breedman stumble back in the direction he'd come, then zigzagged through the parked vehicles in pursuit. He found the narrow footpath the man took but stayed inside the trees again, using them for cover.

Threading his way around trees and boulders, the Executioner again followed the trail to his side. More sporadic gunfire, louder now, sounded ahead. The laughter and voices grew more audible as he neared the source.

Fifty yards from where the New Breedmen's vehicles were parked, Bolan came to another, larger, clearing. Still a good ten feet inside the trees, he crouched and moved closer. The foliage grew thicker as he neared the opening, until the Executioner felt as if he were swimming through a sea of waist-high green and brown leaves. It was a mixed blessing; the natural concealment made silent movement tougher.

Reaching the new clearing, Bolan peered through the leaves to see men of all ages, dressed in a combination of ragged denim, flannel, overalls and camouflage clothing. They moved up and down the firing line of a three-hundred-yard rifle range. At one end of the line stood a beer keg. Next to it, on top of card tables, were buckets of ice, bottles of spirits, paper cups and mixers.

All of the men were armed to the teeth, with AR-15s and Chinese AK-47s being the rifles of preference. Government Model .45s, Smith & Wesson .357s, Browning Hi-Powers and various other side arms hung from their sides. Occasionally one of the men would take a break from drinking to fire a few rounds downfield.

Paper silhouette targets stood at the one-hundred, two-hundred and three-hundred-yard line. But they were all but ignored as the men took shots at the steel targets that stood closer. Bolan turned his attention to the marks.

And what he saw made him sick.

At ten yards stood three steel cutouts, which had been painted in vivid color. The one on the right appeared to be an Hasidic Jew, complete with black flat-brimmed hat and braids, holding an account book to his chest. On the left was a man with Hispanic features. He held a knife in one hand, a revolver in the other. The target in the middle was an elderly black man who sat cross-legged on the ground eating a slice of watermelon.

The nausea in Bolan's stomach turned to anger as one of the New Breedmen transferred his beer to his left hand, jerked a .45 from his holster and aimed it downrange. "You like watermelon?" he called out drunkenly. "Well, eat *this!*" He fired three rounds at the target.

The first two missed. The second struck the black man in the arm.

A New Breedman dressed in Nam leaf camou burst out in laughter. "With shootin' like that, Yulin," he said, "that old man'll have your wife before you know it."

"And the government'll give him your job," another man added.

The man called Yulin turned red in the face as more laughter followed. He cursed and skulked back toward the beer keg.

The Executioner's eyebrows narrowed. Militias had been getting a lot of bad press the past few years, and it was men like this that fueled that fire. Over the years, the Executioner had come across three distinct groups that the media was now lumping together as "militia." First, there were bigots like this who felt like big men when they played army. Most had never faced return fire and would wither in terror if they ever did. Second were the

far-right-wing crazies—men like those who had
bombed the Murrow Building in Oklahoma City. It
was these groups, which were actually few and far
between, that the press was attempting to convince
the public were in every city, on every street.

Third came the true patriots who might not like
the current administration but had no intention of
harming innocent people in any vain attempt to tear
it down. Often led by former U.S. military officers,
they felt obligated by the Constitution to be trained
and ready to assist the regular forces in the event
of foreign invasion or domestic discord. Their
hearts and souls were in the right place, and the
Executioner regretted that their admirable efforts
had been tainted by an overzealous media that cared
about nothing but headlines.

Bolan watched the New Breedmen continue to
drink, laugh and shoot. He listened to ongoing ra-
cial slurs and fought back the urge to rise from
cover and to confront them. Prejudice and bigotry
might be immoral, but as far as he knew, none of
these yokels represented any actual physical threat
to the races they slandered. And the Executioner
had never been in the habit of murdering people
just because their views were corrupt.

What he needed, Bolan knew, was to snatch one
of the men from the group and interrogate him, find
out if New Breed was involved with the computer
planner calling himself Maestro, and if not, who
was. He scanned the group for anyone who ap-

peared to be the leader, his eyes finally falling on a middle-aged man wearing starched OD green BDUs and sitting in a folding chair next to the beer keg.

The man was drinking a can of diet cola and appeared sober. Periodically other men would stop by for a few words, their body language communicating a respect Bolan hadn't seen them exhibit among themselves.

The Executioner nodded silently. This man was the leader. Now all he had to do was find a way to separate the man from the rest of the pack and—

The faint sound of a twig snapping behind him caused Bolan to whirl. As he did, Grimaldi's warning about flying too low over the trees flashed through Bolan's mind. It had been a calculated risk that he had to take. Without it, he'd have never located New Breed at all.

But the low-flying plane had been spotted, and the man to the Executioner's rear now raised an AR-15 and fired.

The bullet sailed high over Bolan's shoulder as the Executioner squeezed the trigger of the MP-5. A 3-round burst of 9 mm hollowpoints gutted the gunman groin to sternum. The man screamed in final agony as he fell to the ground.

Bolan turned back toward the clearing. Twenty rifles had swung his way. He dived behind the tree as full-auto gunfire struck the wood and stripped the bark from the trunk.

Texas

CARL LYONS LED the way through the double doors
of the Alamo Tavern, past the figures of Bowie,
Crockett and Travis, into the club proper. The same
table Able Team had occupied that morning was
available, and they resumed their seats.

Lyons glanced around the room to see many of
the same faces that had been there earlier. The construction workers had returned to work, as had the
nervous-looking man. The couple who had been the
catalyst for all the excitement had wisely vacated
the premises. But the stocky mustachioed bartender
was still behind the counter, and the drunks in front
of him were now joined by more men and women
who looked like they needed, rather than wanted, a
drink.

The fat manager Grant had called Cube, his cosh-
wielding man Harley, Tommy Lee and the other
bouncer were nowhere to be seen.

The Able Team leader scanned the rest of the
tables as Amy caught sight of them and flounced
their way. Not far from where they sat, four muscular young men wearing Trinity University letter
jackets held down a table littered with beer mugs
and pitchers. They talked quietly among themselves, primarily about football, occasionally laugh-
ing at a comment or joke. As Amy reached Able
Team's table, Lyons heard a broad-shouldered
young man tell his even larger friend with wire-

rimmed spectacles, "Damn, Berg. You get any dumber and the coaches'll have you playing offense."

The statement brought another round of laughter from the football players.

"Hi guys," Amy almost sang, her eyes lighting on Blancanales. "Just couldn't stay away from me, huh?"

Blancanales grinned back. "You got it, darlin'," he said in an exaggerated Texas twang.

"More beer?" Amy asked.

"More beer," he agreed.

Amy strutted off, the tail of her coonskin cap swaying almost as much as her hips. She returned with a pitcher and three glasses, and after several more exchanges of flirtatious banter with Blancanales, wiggled her hips toward the men in the letter jackets.

Schwarz shook his head at Blancanales, grinning. "You should be ashamed of yourself, you dirty old man."

"You sound jealous."

"No, no." Schwarz shook his head again. "I'm just attracted to grown-up women."

"Don't worry. It's not going anywhere. But it doesn't hurt to stay in practice. Who knows? Someday the million-to-one long shot might come through and we'll actually have some time for a little recreation."

The men of Able Team settled to sipping their

beer and listening to the quiet conversations at the tables around them. Carl Lyons scanned the room, looking for the manager and bouncers. They had disappeared somewhere into the back.

The quiet atmosphere inside the Alamo broke suddenly as the front door slammed open on its hinges. Four men burst into the room dressed in khaki pants, plaid shirts and work boots. They were covered in gray concrete dust.

"Find us a table and order us some damn beer," a tall slender man with a well-groomed mustache said as he veered toward the men's room. "I've gotta go drain the dragon."

"The expression is 'drain the lizard,' Leo," said a shorter man with a goatee.

"Not in *my* case, Phil," Leo said. "Not in my case." He disappeared into the rest room as the other three men took seats at a table catercornered from Able Team.

"That son of a bitch is gonna pay," a man with a red beard promised in a surly voice. "I'm gonna find his ass and kick it into next week."

"Right, Blake," answered the fourth man. His clean-shaven face made him look almost as young as the Trinity football players at the next table. "You go find the boss and do just that. My money's on him bein' the one who walks away."

Blake's red beard bobbed up and down as he answered. "It don't matter who can whip who, Doc," he said. "That bastard ain't got no right firin' us just for smokin' a little weed during our break." He paused as Leo returned from the men's room. "Hell, I been finishin' concrete for the man for almost three years. Never once missed a day."

"Quit your damn cryin'," Leo said. "I was with him for nearly ten." He dropped into the chair still vacant at the table. "Been thinkin' about startin' up on my own, anyway."

"You gonna need some help?" Blake asked. "I mean, I got payments comin' up and—"

His words were interrupted by Amy's arrival at the table. The anger the concrete finishers had been expressing at being fired suddenly turned to interest in the attractive young woman. "Well, sweet thing," Phil said, reaching out and encircling her slender waist with a hairy arm, "if you're gonna ask us what you can give us, I can answer that right now."

Amy shrugged out of his grasp with a practiced move. The smile on her face turned cold and professional. "What can I get you boys to *drink?*" she asked.

"Hell," Phil said, "purty as you are, I'd drink all of it I could."

Amy turned a light shade of red.

In the corner of his eye, Lyons saw the football players turn their attention toward the concrete workers' table.

"Bring us a pitcher," Leo said. "And shots. Bar whiskey for everybody."

Amy walked off in relief.

Blake reached in the shirt pocket of his concrete-stained shirt and pulled out a hand-rolled cigarette. He rolled the wheel of a cheap plastic lighter and a moment later the odor of marijuana filled the Alamo. Taking a hit, he passed it to Phil, who inhaled deeply before handing the joint to Doc. The youngest of the concrete men took his turn and was handing off to Leo when the side door off the dance floor opened. Harley, the grip of the leather cosh visible in his back pocket, crossed the open area to the concrete workers' table.

"You old boys gonna have to get off the property if you wanna do that," he said, forcing a smile. "Sorry, but we get off-duty cops in here sometimes."

The statement was probably a lie, but it had the desired effect, solving the problem by letting the concrete men think Harley was helping them. Leo dropped what remained of the joint into the ashtray.

"I'll get rid of the evidence for you," Harley said with a chuckle, lifting the ashtray and turning back toward the door. As he passed Able Team's table, Lyons heard him mutter, "Assholes."

Amy returned with the men's beer and shots and set them on the table, but not before Phil tried to snake a hand up her short skirt. Slapping it away, the young barmaid hurried off to check on the men in the letter jackets.

At the football players' table, a low murmur of anger began.

"Getting jealous?" Schwarz asked Blancanales, who chuckled.

The men of Able Team continued to sip their beer while the concrete workers guzzled theirs. Lyons glanced at the man called Leo and for a moment their eyes met. Then Leo looked away.

When the shots were gone and the pitcher empty, Leo raised it over his head and yelled for more. Amy reluctantly went to get it, staying on the other side of the table from Phil.

"What's wrong, sweet cheeks?" Phil slurred, holding up a hand and wiggling his index and middle fingers. "Come on over here. I can make you dance in delight."

The sound of a chair sliding back quickly from a table sounded across the room. The big man in the Trinity letter jacket rose to his full six-foot-six-inch height and marched toward the concrete finishers' table. Through the clear lenses of his wire-rimmed glasses, his eyes burned with anger.

He stopped at the table between Phil and Blake. "Tell her you're sorry," he demanded.

"Tony, don't..." Amy said. "Just let it ride."

"Like hell," Tony said. He took off his glasses, folded the ear pieces and tucked them into the pocket of his letter jacket. "You heard me," he said. "Tell Amy you're sorry."

The man called Phil held up a hand. "Hey, sorry kid," he said. "She your girl?"

"That's none of your business."

"Okay, okay," Phil said. His lips were smiling, but his eyes had taken on a cruel look.

He turned to Amy. "Madam," he said with mock respect, "please accept my most humble regrets..."

After a few seconds, Tony said, "That's better."

"...that I'm not on top of you right now humping you to a loud screaming orgasm," Phil finished.

With a loud growl, Tony drew back his fist.

It never found its mark.

Phil reached out, grabbed the young football player's groin with one hand and twisted. Tony roared in pain as Phil stood. Still holding Tony's crotch, the burly concrete finisher drove a hard hook into the young man's jaw with his other hand.

Tony's eyes closed and he went down as if he'd been blindsided by a blitzing linebacker.

By now the other football players were up and sprinting to Tony's aid. The broad-shouldered man who had teased Tony earlier launched himself into the air five yards from Phil, his arms outstretched in a flying tackle.

Phil stepped to the side and threw a knee into the young man's groin as he flew by.

In his peripheral vision, Lyons saw the side door off the dance floor fly open. Harley and the other two bouncers hurried through the opening, letting the door swing closed behind them. Harley had drawn his leather slapper from the back pocket of his jeans. The other two men carried sawed-off cue sticks.

Leo, Doc and Blake had risen to their feet as the remaining two football players neared their table. A tall athlete, not as massive as the others and looking more like a running back or a wide receiver, reached the table and drew back his fist. Leo trapped the attack with his left hand and drove a hard right into the young man's midsection. The kid bent in two, coughing. An overhand blow from Blake dropped him onto the floor.

The bouncers now joined the melee, with Tommy Lee swinging his cue stick at Doc's head. Doc dropped low, letting the club pass over his head, then bringing an elbow under Harley's chin. The bouncer's eyes rolled back into his head as he fell backward over the table.

Lyons glanced across the dance floor to see the side door inching open again. Cube stuck his head through the opening.

Leo moved in behind the third bouncer as the man drew back his cue stick to strike Blake. Catching the man's wrist just below the weapon, he wrenched it away and grasped it in both hands. As the bouncer turned to face him, Leo drove the end of the stick into his sternum like a lance.

Air whooshed from the bouncer's lungs as if someone had opened an oxygen tank.

The final football player suddenly realized he

was alone. Raising both hands in front of him, palms out, he took a step backward. "Hey, that's enough," he said. "I don't want any—"

Phil stepped in and drove a hard right to his jaw. Another Trinity letter jacket joined those already on the floor.

"Time for us to join the fun yet?" Schwarz whispered to Lyons.

"Not quite yet."

Harley was now the only bouncer left on his feet, and Leo, Phil, Blake and Doc began to circle him. Harley held his leather-covered cudgel in front of him, shuffling his feet and trying to get something behind his back. He had a look of resignation on his face as if he knew he had already lost. But he intended to go down fighting.

Blancanales glanced at Lyons, who nodded.

Able Team stood.

"Hey," Blancanales shouted across the room, "those odds look a little one-sided."

"Well," Leo said, his mustache curling up in a wicked smile, "why don't you jump in and even them up?" He waved the Able Team commando closer with the cue stick still in his hands.

Blancanales returned as Able Team closed the gap between them, the concrete finishers and Harley. Blancanales stepped toward Leo. The man with the neatly trimmed mustache brought the cue stick back behind him like a baseball bat and swung.

At the last second, Blancanales skipped back, letting the club pass by a half inch from his nose. Leo's momentum carried the cue stick around, and before he could recover, Blancanales moved in.

The Able Team commando shot a low kick into Leo's ankle that sent the concrete worker hopping up and down on the other leg. As he hopped, Blancanales followed up with a series of body punches that brought him down.

Lyons saw Schwarz block a hook from Phil and snap a front kick into the man's groin. The man bent over, bellowing like a bull. Schwarz hopped onto the other leg and snapped a second kick into the goatee on the man's chin.

With the odds suddenly against them, Blake and Doc quickly lost interest. In a parody of what the football player had done only seconds before, they both held up their hands and stepped back. "We've had enough," Blake said.

"You can't have had enough," Lyons countered. "You haven't had *any* yet."

The Able Team leader leaped the three feet between him and Blake. He feinted with his right, then drove a solid left into the man's jaw. The blow stunned the burly red-bearded man but didn't finish him. He swung a wild right, which Lyons parried. The Able Team leader turned sideways and drove an elbow into the man's gut.

As Blake fell to the floor, Lyons turned in time to see Schwarz pop Doc with a flurry of short right and left jabs to the chin, then slide in behind the man. Wrapping one forearm around Doc's throat, he braced his other on the back of the man's neck in a classic sleeper hold.

A few seconds later, Doc's eyes closed and he slithered to the floor.

For a moment, the Alamo Tavern stood silent. Then, from somewhere behind him, Lyons heard Amy say, "Wow!"

The door off the dance floor opened wider, and the fat manager squeezed through. The cigar stump in his teeth, he waddled across the tile to where Lyons, Schwarz, Blancanales and Harley stood. He surveyed the damage briefly, then turned to Lyons and extended a pudgy hand. "Travis 'Tex' Thompson's the name, old partner," he said around the cigar. "Some call me Triple *T,* and others T-cubed. But most just shorten it to Cube."

Lyons shook his hand.

Cube raised his rancher's hat over his head and used the sleeve of his jacket to wipe sweat off his balding head. "I appreciate what you've done," he said. "And all your beer is on the house the rest of the day. Fact is, you stick around long enough, and you've got the biggest steaks in the kitchen coming, too."

The Able Team leader nodded. "Thanks," he said. "But what we could really use is some work."

Cube frowned. "Don't have any openings at the moment," he said. Then he glanced from Harley to the other two bouncers, out cold on the floor.

"Then again, maybe I do." Taking a step in to the man still holding the leather slapper, Cube stuck his belly into Harley's belt buckle and looked up into the taller man's eyes. "Get your two pansy-assed playmates out of here," he said. "You're all fired."

Anger flared momentarily across Harley's face. Then Lyons, Schwarz and Blancanales stepped in behind Cube and the anger disappeared.

Cube turned back to Lyons as Harley began trying to revive the other two bouncers. "Now I got openings," he said. "And you're hired."

Lyons forced a smile. "Thanks."

"You can thank me by doing your job," Cube said. "And the first task is to get this trash out of my place." He looked down at the concrete workers, football players and bouncers still on the tile.

Most of the men were regaining consciousness. Lyons, Schwarz and Blancanales helped them to their feet and escorted them past the statues in the entryway and out into the sunshine.

When they returned, Leo and Tony were the only two still asleep on the tile. Lyons slung the concrete worker over his shoulder in a fireman's carry as Schwarz grabbed Tony's feet and Blancanales gripped the football player's wrists.

Able Team laid the two men down on the parking lot in front of the Alamo. As they did, the concrete worker with the neat mustache opened his eyes.

Lyons looked down into the face of Leo Turrin, Stony Man Farm's top undercover operative.

"How do you think it went?" Turrin whispered.

"Well," Lyons said.

"Good." Turrin nodded. "Just do me a favor, will you?"

Lyons waited.

"Tell Pol to watch the ankle kicks next time. And I feel like he cracked one of my ribs."

Before Lyons could respond, Tony rolled to his side next to Turrin. Brushing gravel from the parking lot off the sleeve of his Trinity letter jacket, he said, "I knew this training was going to be tough." His hand moved from the jacket to his jaw, which Phil had struck. "But right now, I think I can speak for us all when I say we'd rather get back into blacksuits and dodge bullets."

CHAPTER FIVE

Washington, D.C.

More gunshots rang out as McCarter and James sprinted past the surprised Secret Service agents in the hall outside the outer office. They had almost collided head on with George and Howard in front of Eileen's desk as the two men rushed past the secretary to check on the President.

William was already waiting at the elevator. He now wore a bright green armband over the sleeve of his charcoal gray suit. The two Phoenix Force warriors sprinted backwards through the metal detector as the uniformed men pulled more green armbands from their pockets. James, a step in front of McCarter, reached out as he passed to tear the circular elastic strap from the hand of one of the guards. He heard a "Hey!" as he ran on, then another voice shouted "What the hell?" telling James that McCarter had procured one of the identification emblems as well.

The elevator door swung open as James reached

it. Shoving William in ahead of him, he entered the car. McCarter had dropped James's lead to a half-step now. Another series of shots rang out as James turned in time to see the Phoenix Force leader whirl around and punch the first-floor button.

William's chest had slammed against the rear of the elevator. Now he turned, red-faced and scowling. "Who the hell do you guys think you are?" he demanded.

"We could tell you," James said, "but like the saying goes, then we'd have to kill you."

McCarter nodded, his face deadpan. "That's very true," he added. "And in this case, it's not even a joke."

The doors closed with excruciating sluggishness. James slipped the green armband over his wrist and up his biceps. The arm IDs were used by the protection teams and other Secret Service personnel for identification in times of emergency. The colors changed daily, and sometimes hourly, if a threat was perceived.

As they rode down, James patted the .45-caliber Glock 21 in the shoulder rig under his arm. His hand moved from there to the eight-inch blade of the Black Cloud *Prokopta* knife suspended upside down across his back. Satisfied that his weapons were in place, he waited.

The elevator seemed to take an eternity to descend, and James wondered if the threat outside— it sounded as if the shots had come from the front of the White House—had been subdued. They could hear nothing above the grind of the elevator.

James's question was answered as the elevator door opened to a new volley of rounds.

The gray-haired uniformed officer—Brognola had called him Henry, James recalled—stood just outside the door holding a walkie-talkie. A voice on the other end was speaking and James, McCarter and William paused to listen.

"...inside a barricade of four cars," came the voice over the walkie-talkie, "in the parking lot across the street."

There was a pause, then another voice came on the airway. "What kind of weapon has he got?"

"Looks like an AK," the first voice came back. "My guess is semiauto only. At least he hasn't fired any full-auto yet."

A third voice, deep, resonant and angry came on. "How the hell did he get whatever it is into the area?"

Another pause ensued, the lines silent except for several quiet crackles and pops. Then the original man said, "I don't know, sir."

The reverberant tones of the most recent speaker returned, chewing out his subordinates with language that would have burned the ears of the most hardened Federal Communications Control listener. "Anyone have a shot?" the voice finally asked.

"Not yet," came the response.

McCarter turned to James. "We've got to find

out if this guy is a singular nutcase or part of something bigger,'' he said. ''We don't want him dead.''

William stared at him, still red in the face. ''We'd like that, too,'' he said. ''But with all due respect, Mr. Have-to-kill-you-if-I-tell-you, the President's safety is the primary goal and if we have to kill this bastard to insure it, we will.''

McCarter chuckled. ''The President is quite safe upstairs,'' he said. ''And unless this bloke across the street has X-ray vision like Superman, he'll stay that way.'' He cleared his throat. ''Take us to a side entrance, William.''

''I'll do no such thing. You can't—''

James repressed a grin as he watched the Browning Hi-Power pistol leap into McCarter's hand. Without ceremony, the Phoenix Force leader shoved it under William's chin. ''No time for a row just yet,'' the Briton said. ''Take us to that side entrance, William. One where my man here can get out without the shooter seeing him.''

William's throat looked like a boa constrictor swallowing a horse. He nodded, then turned and led the way down a short hall, stopping at another steel door. Six more uniformed men, all wearing the green emergency armbands, stood guard. They stared in disbelief at McCarter's gun pressed into the back of William's neck.

''Jim?'' one of them said. ''What...?''

''Just let them out,'' William replied. ''They're on our side.''

"Our side. Then why—"

McCarter shoved the Browning harder into the back of his captive's neck. "Just do it!" William yelled.

McCarter turned to James. "You know what to do. You've got to get this guy alive before one of these dolts shoots him dead."

James nodded.

Another of the uniformed men opened the steel door, and James emerged into the sunshine, finding himself on the side of the White House. He could still hear sporadic fire from across the street. But it all came from the same weapon—an AK-47. Sprinting from the door across the lawn, the Phoenix Force commando stopped behind the shrubbery just inside the fence. Then, with a quick glance toward the front again to make sure he was hidden from the shooter, he climbed the bars and leaped over to the sidewalk.

The rifle fire kept up as James sprinted down the street away from the White House. He made a sharp turn to his left, cutting between two buildings and using another to shield himself from the shooter's position as he hurried back toward Pennsylvania Avenue. When he reached the front of the building, he pressed his back against the veneer and peered around the corner. Down the block, he could see the four vehicles the gunman had arranged as cover: two were Chevy Blazers, a third, a Honda Accord. Through the side window of the Buick Road Master nearest him, James could see the barrel of an AK-47 pointed straight up.

As he watched, the rifle barrel dropped until it was aimed across the street at the White House. Now James could see the top of a head. The barrel jumped twice as two more rounds exploded.

James used the shooter's preoccupation to make a mad dash across the avenue. He dived into the open entryway of another building as the shots died down. Craning his neck, he could see more of the gunman this time. He could even tell that the man wore a white dress shirt and had a flattop haircut.

The Phoenix Force commando paused. If *he* could see the shooter that well, so could the Secret Service snipers who should be set up by now. The fact that they hadn't shot him meant they had yet to receive the order. But patience would run short. And soon. If James didn't get to him fast, the man inside the vehicular barricade would be too dead to talk.

The Phoenix Force commando came out of the entryway keeping his back against the stone wall of the building. He moved quickly, sliding along the edifice toward a position to the rear of the shooter. The four-car barricade was approximately in the center of the parking area with other vehicles scattered throughout the lot.

James moved on, hoping the gunman wouldn't catch a glimpse of his movement in the windows of any of the vehicles. His hand fell to the Glock under his left arm, then moved away.

He could try to wing the man, but an unexpected move as he squeezed the trigger could turn the round into a kill shot. And the sound of new gunfire could easily trigger more rounds from what by now would be dozens of Secret Service weapons aimed between the cars.

The Glock wasn't the answer.

As he neared the edge of the parking lot, James dropped to his face on the ground. Crawling beneath the shooter's line of sight, he squirmed under and edged along the length of the nearest vehicle. He repeated the procedure several times, making his way across the asphalt toward the sound of the 7.62 mm rounds.

Six cars later, James looked between the tires of a GEO Storm to see the side of one of the Chevy Blazers. Beneath the body, he could see the squatting calves of a man wearing navy blue slacks and cheap brown brogans. Again, the Phoenix Force commando considered the Glock. From this new position, he knew he could fire at least one round, maybe more, into the gunner's legs. But that still might trigger a response from the Secret Service. And other things could still go wrong.

During his stalk across the parking lot, the only sounds James had heard were the sporadic explosions from the AK-47. But now, as he considered his next move, he heard the screech of a public-address system coming on.

"Attention!" shouted a voice from one of the guard stations across the street at the White House. "You, in the parking lot. Throw down your weapon and come out with your hands on your head!"

For a moment, silence fell over Pennsylvania Avenue. Then a voice rang out from inside the fortification of automobiles. "Like hell I will! And let you kill me? No thanks!" A 3-round volley of fire erupted from the AK-47.

The voice on the PA system returned. "Throw out your weapon and come out with your hands on your head," it repeated. "You will not be harmed."

This time, the rifle rounds were the only answer.

James knew his move had to come quickly. Whoever was running the show would soon give up and order the guards to fire. Drawing his knife by its curved handle, the Phoenix Force commando stared down at the dulled steel of the sweeping blade. With its radical clip point, the knife looked like a cross between a large Bowie knife and a pirate's cutlass. A near ideal fighter, it was nevertheless not the ideal tool for the task at hand.

But it was the best he had, and would have to do.

James had learned the high art of the blade as a tough kid on Chicago's South Side. Those skills had been fine-tuned during his years as a Navy SEAL. He was an expert with edged weapons, and knew they were far more versatile than firearms. They could inflict death, but they could also bring an opponent to what Filipino *kali* fighters called the "bargain point."

In western terms, James knew you could cut someone "a little"—just enough to make them stop what they were doing. Shooting someone "a little" was damn hard.

James looked out from under the GEO. Approximately twenty to twenty-five feet of open lot separated him from the shooter's barricade—not too great a distance for a surprise attack with a blade under ideal conditions. But these were hardly ideal conditions. First he had to crawl out from under the GEO without being heard. Then he had to hope the man wedged between the cars didn't catch his reflection in all the glass and polished steel that surrounded him. After he'd covered the distance, he had to vault over the Chevy Blazer.

And during all of it, James knew he'd have to pray that the Secret Service didn't miss his green armband, mistake him for another bad guy and blow his brains all over Pennsylvania Avenue.

Inching out from under the GEO, James rose silently to a squatting position. He took a deep breath, then rose higher to a crouch. The knife clenched in a saber grip, his thumb hidden behind the integral crossguard, he moved swiftly.

He had silently covered half the distance to the Chevy when the loud crunch sounded at his feet.

James cursed under his breath, knowing without looking that he had stepped on a pile of broken glass too small to have been seen from under the GEO. He darted forward, sprinting the last three steps to the Blazer and propelling himself off the ground with his right leg like a broad jumper.

His head and shoulders cleared the top of the Chevy just as the man squatting in the center of the barricade swung the barrel of the AK-47 his way. James looked down the long shaft, and imagined he could see the rounded nose of lead in the chamber.

With the reflexes of a cat, he twisted the knife downward in a vicious back cut. The sharpened edge of the clip point struck the rifle barrel, knocking it into the door of the Blazer. A lone 7.62 mm round exploded from the weapon, the sound echoing off the bodies of the vehicles and ringing through James's head like the bells of Notre Dame.

He fell on top of the man holding the rifle, his right arm still across his body on top of the rifle. Flipping his wrist, he drew the knife back in a reverse cut. The flat edge of the broad blade struck the shooter squarely in the nose, stunning, but not injuring him. His mouth opened wide in an ''O'' as the Phoenix Force commando raised the blade high over his head, then brought down the pommel on the gunman's skull.

The man who had shot at the White House fell forward, unconscious.

But alive.

Illinois

DOZENS OF SIMULTANEOUS rifle rounds from the
New Breedmen drove the Executioner back into the
thick leaves and vines behind the tree. He hit the
ground on his side and rolled. A split second later
another volley shredded the foliage where he'd disappeared. Particles of green leaves and twigs flew
through the air, then rained over the spot as if someone had just driven a giant thrashing machine
across the area.

The Executioner rose briefly, tapping the trigger
of the MP-5 and downing a New Breedman in a
camouflage baseball cap. He dropped into concealment again as the other gunmen pinpointed his new
position and turned their weapons that way.

Bolan crawled backward away from the clearing
as more bullets snipped the leafage from the vines
and branches. Lying flat, he could see nothing in
the dense surroundings. But as the new onslaught
died down, he heard a voice.

"Spread out!" it called. "Surround the son of a
bitch!"

Bolan couldn't see the speaker, but his instincts
told him it was the same man he'd seen wearing
the neatly starched BDUs and sitting in a folding
chair next to the beer keg; the man who appeared
to be the leader.

Running footsteps resounded through the forest
to both of the Executioner's sides. He knew what

they were doing. Some of the men would stay in front of him while others fanned out right and left. Still more would circle behind him, effectively closing off all avenues of escape. If there weren't already New Breedmen to his rear—and he had no assurance that the man who had crept up behind him was alone—there soon would be.

If there was to be an escape, it had to be to his rear. And it had to be now, before the men running past him on both sides had time to close the pincer.

Slowly the Executioner reversed his position until he faced the opposite direction. He slung the MP-5 across his back, cinching the sling tight to avoid any slippage that might disturb the leaves and give away his position. Behind him and to both sides, he could hear whispering voices. The men sounded as if they were merely yards away. And there was a hushed nervousness to their words. Each man knew if he was the first to stumble across the prey, he stood a good chance of dying before he could react.

Bolan crept on, straining his ears for any sounds directly in front of him. Depending on how large a circle the New Breedmen chose to deploy around him, there was still a chance he might slip through. But they were running and he was crawling, meaning each second narrowed the chances of that happening.

"He's got to be in here some place, Hank," a whispered voice not ten feet in front of the Executioner suddenly said. "He couldn't have got out. No way."

Bolan halted all movement. At least the question in his mind had been answered. Not the way he'd have liked it to be perhaps, but answered nonetheless.

He was completely surrounded. All chance of a quiet escape had been cut off.

It was time for Plan *B*.

The Executioner reached up, trying to shrug out of the MP-5. But to secure the swaying subgun, he had been forced to cinch the sling too tight and now there would be no loosing it without exaggerated movement. Movement—anything that would give away his position—was the last thing he needed.

Drawing his fighting knife, Bolan sliced noiselessly through the nylon sling. Carefully he pulled the MP-5 from his back and set it silently on the ground beside him. He could hear the men cautiously moving in on him from all sides. They moved slowly, brushing the undergrowth aside with their rifle barrels and dreading being the one to first encounter their quarry.

"Find him, dammit! I'll have the ass of any man who allows an escape!"

Again the Executioner reversed directions, crawling back toward the clearing where the New Breed leader's voice came from. A conventional escape was no longer a possibility.

But that hardly meant Mack Bolan intended to

give up. For years he had faced the most capable enemies—well-trained terrorists and drug dealers, KGB and the Iraqi Republican Guard, to name a few. He had fought them man-to-man and always emerged victorious.

The thought of death or capture at the hands of a group of beer-bellied good-ol'-boy bigots playing soldier was unacceptable.

Bolan crawled forward until he sensed, more than heard, the presence of another man just ahead. Slowly he raised his head through the thick foliage until he could peer through the leaves. A New Breedman stood less than six feet away, his AR-15 pointed at the ground. The man wore ragged black jeans, a chewing-tobacco-stained white T-shirt and a floppy boonie hat. The fumes of stale alcohol drifted through the underbrush as the man exhaled.

Bolan watched the New Breedman take a tentative step forward, sweeping vegetation aside with his rifle barrel. He froze in place, his trigger finger tightening slightly. Anxious eyes softened to relief as he realized another step hadn't brought death. Then his eyes returned to the same apprehensive state as the man's scuffed work boot moved forward again.

The Executioner remained still until the New Breedman had swept away the foliage over his head. Then the hand grasping the fighting knife shot up, slicing across the carriage of the AR and into the man's trigger finger. The finger fell to the forest floor as the gunner's eyes and mouth opened wide in disbelief.

Rising only far enough to grasp the New Breedman by the throat, Bolan jerked him down into the ground cover and drove the blade of the knife deep into the rifleman's carotid artery. He twisted the blade, then drew it across his throat severing the windpipe, voice box and everything else in the New Breedman's neck.

Bolan waited, listening. Only his camouflaged arms had been visible and them just for a second. Still, there was always a chance that one or more of the other men had witnessed the event. But when thirty seconds passed with no response, he wiped the blade of the knife on the New Breedman's T-shirt, left him lying hidden in the undergrowth and crawled on.

The swish of more rifle barrels disturbing the foliage sounded ahead. Again Bolan froze in place. There were two men this time, working side by side. He rose once more, just enough to squint through the thin greenery at the top of the leafage. He could see the heads of two men working his way. And less than ten yards behind them was the clearing that held the rifle range.

The Executioner took a deep breath. He had no doubt he could kill both New Breedman before they had time to react. But doing so without creating a disturbance that would alert the others was unlikely. He had been lucky with the man lying behind him.

He would have to be double-lucky with two men, and that wasn't likely to happen.

Bolan's jaw set firmly as he formulated the details of the next step of his plan. If silence was out of the question, he would have to put his faith in speed. Sheathing the fighting knife, he drew the sound-suppressed Beretta 93-R and flipped the selector switch to semiauto. Not as quiet at the knife, it was still preferable in this situation to the eardrum shattering .44 magnum Desert Eagle still holstered on his hip.

Again, the Executioner waited, letting the men brush the undergrowth to the side, check, move closer and repeat the process. Once he took out these two gunmen, the others would pinpoint his location. He'd have no choice but to make a mad dash for the clearing. If there were other New Breedmen in the immediate vicinity, he'd have to deal with them on the run. He would play the cards as they were dealt him, running and shooting. But if he could reach the firing line still on his feet, he stood a good chance of putting the last element of his escape strategy into motion.

Bolan saw the leaves directly in front of him stir as the two men neared. He tightened his grip on the Beretta and shot out of the underbrush.

Sudden shock covered the faces of the two gunners directly in front of the Executioner. Their rifle barrels still pointed downward into the foliage, and both pairs of eyes widened in disbelief.

Bolan raised his arm and got off the first shot, sending a 9 mm hollowpoint round angling into the man's brain.

The quiet cough of the sound suppressor was muffled by the proximity of the New Breedman's face. But the contact shot sent the gas from the round, as well as the bullet itself, blasting into the gunman's features. Blood, teeth, tissue and bone fragments burst back from the wound to fly through the air on all sides.

As the body collapsed to the ground, the Executioner turned the Beretta toward the other New Breedman who stood a short step to his left. The man began to recover from his shock and attempted to raise the barrel of his AR-15. It was a futile effort.

The Executioner swung his weapon toward the man, staring into the still-startled eyes. He saw a look of recognition, then resignation, replace the surprise as he pulled the trigger once more. Then all expression vanished as half the man's face disintegrated under the blast of another 9 mm round.

Bolan didn't wait. As the dead man fell to the ground, the Executioner pushed past him and sprinted toward the clearing ten yards ahead. The thick foliage forced him to raise his knees almost to his chest, like a football player running through tires laid out on the practice field. In his peripheral vision, he saw a man in khaki coveralls a few yards to his right. Twisting at the waist as he ran, he brought the Beretta to shoulder level and fired a couple of rounds into the New Breedman's chest.

Shots rang out from behind him, and the Executioner dived forward into ground cover. He landed on one shoulder as bullets shredded the leaves in his wake, then rolled to his feet. He passed the tree trunk where he had taken cover earlier and emerged into the clearing on the rifle range firing line.

Two men stood staring at him, open-mouthed. One wore navy blue fatigues and a matching drill sergeant's cap, looking more like a police SWAT officer than a bigoted drugstore soldier. He had a SIG-Sauer pistol in his hand but his arm appeared frozen.

The hesitation cost him his life.

Bolan raised the Beretta again as he ran forward, point-shooting two more rounds that caught the blue man in the chest and throat.

Rifle rounds blew from the trees, flying past the Executioner and perforating the dirt on both sides of his running feet. But as he neared the other man still in the clearing, they stopped abruptly.

The second man was the leader in the ironed and starched OD BDUs. He raised a Colt Gold Cup .45 automatic as Bolan raced toward him.

The Executioner had an easy shot, but killing the New Breed leader wasn't part of his strategy—at least at this point. If he did, he would find himself in the open with close to twenty rifles firing at him from the cover of the trees.

Bolan dived forward as a .45 round exploded. Heat scorched his back as the bullet skimmed his skinsuit. Rolling onto his side this time, he slammed his legs into the shins of the New Breed leader and swept the man from his feet.

The New Breed leader fell forward onto his face with a loud grunt, the Colt Cup falling from his hand. Before he could reach for it, the Executioner jumped to his knees, leaned over the man and grabbed a handful of hair. Jerking the leader away from the gun, Bolan pulled the man into his chest and rammed the Beretta's sound suppressor under his chin.

The rifle fire from the woods had stopped when the Executioner neared the New Breedman. The fanatics in the trees knew the chance of hitting their leader was too great. With the Executioner using the man as cover, they had no chance whatsoever.

"Okay!" Bolan shouted, pulling the man in the BDUs even closer. "Here's the deal! Everyone drops their weapons where they are, then moves around that elm over there!" He swung the Beretta briefly away from the leader's throat to indicate a tall tree that stood just inside the clearing twenty yards to his left. "When you get there, put both hands on your head."

The orders got no response from the men still hidden in the trees.

Bolan leaned in and spoke into the leader's ear.
"I suggest you tell them to do what I said. Otherwise, your brains are going to be pouring out the top of your skull."

The Executioner could feel the New Breed leader trembling in his grasp. "Who are you?"

"That's not much of a priority at the moment," Bolan growled. "The question is, are you going to tell them to drop their weapons or do we see how far the inside of your head will shoot into the sky?"

The man took a deep breath. "Do what he says," he called out. "Drop your guns."

Bolan heard the sounds of objects falling into the underbrush. "Now tell them all to gather around that elm, like I said."

"Go to the tree," the New Breed leader said.

"But Colonel Morris," a voice called out. "We can't just—"

"Yes you can, Bernard!" the man in Bolan's arms shouted. "Just do it!"

Movement began in the forest. Bolan watched flashes of camouflage, khaki and denim appear and disappear among the leaves. Gradually the militiamen began to take shape around the elm. Bolan counted fifteen men. They had all clasped their hands to the tops of their heads.

"Anyone still hiding out there?" the Executioner called.

He got no response.

"I'll give anyone still in the trees fifteen seconds

to make it to the elm. If I find anybody later, I'll kill this slimebag first, then them."

Ten seconds went by. Then two more figures stepped out of the woods into the clearing next to the tree.

"For your sake, let's hope that's all of them," the Executioner whispered into the ear of the man called Colonel Morris. The Beretta still jammed under Morris's chin, the Executioner turned back to the New Breedmen. "Now, single file, I want you to start walking toward the other end of the range. The first man who drops his hands gets a bullet. Move out."

The men around the elm looked at one another for a moment. Then a New Breedman wearing a green plaid jacket started downrange. Another man, dressed in brown canvas overalls, followed him. Gradually the rest of the men fell into line.

Keeping Morris in front of him as a shield, Bolan turned toward the marching men. His eyes stayed in the center of the line, watching the ends with his peripheral vision. As the group drew even with where he knelt, a New Breedman in an ear-flapped hunting cap suddenly dropped one hand to the back of his belt.

A nickel-plated Smith & Wesson Model 29 glimmered in the sunlight.

Bolan jerked the Beretta away from Morris's throat long enough to put a lone 9 mm round into the New Breedman's chest.

The line of walking men froze in place.

"Anybody else want to save your king?" the Executioner called out. He waited a few seconds in silence, then said, "Then move out again!"

Bolan kept turning Morris, keeping the New Breed leader between him and the men as they made their way downrange. When the man in the front had passed the two-hundred yard target, he rose to his feet, jerking Morris up with him. As the men moved on, the Executioner began to pull his hostage into the woods.

He stopped long enough to retrieve the MP-5 and sling it over his shoulder, then continued. His foot hit what he thought was a rock. But when he looked down, he saw a walkie-talkie evidently dropped by one of the New Breedmen.

The Executioner was twenty yards down the footpath that led to the parked vehicles when he felt the cold steel of a gun barrel in the back of his neck.

"Don't move."

Bolan halted in place.

"Slowly, one hand at a time," the voice said, "let Colonel Morris go."

Bolan nodded slowly. "Anything you say." He unwrapped his left arm from around Morris's neck.

"Now the gun hand," the voice said. "Slow, or you're a dead man."

Bolan began to pull the Beretta from under Morris's chin. But at the same time, his freed left hand moved to the knife attached to his vest. His fingers curled around the grip.

As the Beretta came away from Morris's throat, the Executioner brought it around, sweeping the gun at the back of his neck to the side. His left hand shot the knife up, driving it into the throat of the New Breedman to his rear.

Before the man could hit the ground, Bolan had whirled back to Morris, the Beretta again under his chin. As he sheathed the knife, he whispered, "That was a nice little break in the monotony, Morris. But we don't have a lot of time for more diversions."

Morris knew what to do without being told. "Anyone still out there," he called at the top of his lungs. "Let us pass. Repeat—do not interfere. Let us pass!"

If any of the New Breedmen were still hiding in the trees, they followed the colonel's orders. Bolan dragged the man in his arms to the clearing where the vehicles were parked. After determining which vehicle was Morris's, he shoved the man behind the wheel.

A few moments later, the blue Suburban was churning down the dirt road, heading toward the county blacktop.

[faded text from previous page bleeding through]

CHAPTER SIX

Texas

The Alamo Tavern's lunch and early-afternoon crowd had thinned, leaving a few scattered patrons at the tables. The Alamo was quiet; the band hadn't arrived yet to set up for the night, and the after-work crowd, that would stop for a few quick ones on the way home, had yet to come.

Lyons, Schwarz, Blancanales and Cube sat at a table in the corner. The manager had appeared a few minutes earlier from the side door off the dance floor. Lyons assumed it led to an office. None of the men of Able Team had been invited back to see.

The portly manager dropped a handful of paperwork and pens on the table. The men made small talk as they filled out their employment and social security forms.

"Damn federal government," Cube said, biting on a fresh cigar that protruded from his flabby lips.

"Work half the year for Uncle Sam before you see a penny of your own."

Blancanales looked up and grinned. "You do it all by the book, I'm sure, Cube," he said with a chuckle.

Cube answered the chuckle with a shifty grin of his own. "Some of it, anyway. Doesn't do to have an IRS pencil-neck gettin' too snoopy. Opens up all kinds of worm cans that don't need openin'."

The front door of the Alamo opened and three women walked past the statues in the foyer onto the dance floor. Their high heels clicked loudly across the tiles as they made their way toward the bar. All three wore exaggerated hairstyles, tight skirts and dark hose. The large breasts of the blonde leading the pack threatened to spill over her plunging neckline, the second woman wore an almost transparent blouse with no bra and the third, a skimpy halter top.

The blonde hiked herself onto a bar stool, her skirt riding high up her thighs to reveal the straps of a red garter belt. She glanced over to where Lyons and the other men sat and smiled.

Cube nodded.

"Hookers?" Schwarz asked.

Cube nodded.

"Not bad," Gadgets said. "You run them?"

Cube shook his head. "Not really. They pay a monthly fee to work out of here. And we—that's *you*—look after them in case somebody gets too rough. But they take their johns to the motel down the road.'' He paused and snorted through his nose. ''That's as involved as I get. I've run whores before. Nothing but a royal red pain in the ass.''

''Well, like I said,'' Schwarz repeated, ''not bad.''

''You want one?'' Cube asked. ''Get you a cut-rate deal with Delores. That's the blonde waving her ass at you.''

''Maybe later,'' Schwarz said. ''Right now I've got enough trouble trying to figure out what to put down as my last place of employment.'' He tapped the paper in front of him with his pen.

Cube frowned, the cigar angling toward his descending eyebrows. ''How's that?''

Blancanales took over. ''Well, Cube,'' he said, ''it's kind of like what you said about the IRS getting snoopy. What we were doing last…we'd just as soon nobody got too interested.''

''Yeah, okay, I get it,'' he said. ''So what was your last *legal* job?''

Lyons, Schwarz and Blancanales exchanged glances, then Blancanales said, ''The service, I guess.''

''Well, hell,'' Cube said. ''Put that down. What branch you guys in?''

''Army,'' Schwarz said as all three men wrote on their forms. ''Fifth Special Forces Group.''

Cube perked up. ''Green Berets? Hot damn, I got me a trio of Green Beanies workin' for me.'' He took the cigar from his mouth and looked from Lyons to Schwarz to Blancanales. "I shoulda known it, the way you moved."

The door opened again and a young man in a black cowboy hat, black jeans and black denim Western shirt strutted across the dance floor to the bar. As he entered the better lighted area, Lyons saw that his clothes could stand a cleaning. They looked like ashes had been poured over his head.

"Ah, fuck," Cube said. "The continuation of another perfect day."

"Who is that?" Blancanales asked.

Cube shoved the cigar back into his mouth and spoke around it. "Jared Justin. Daddy's an oil man—got lots of money. Though you'd never know it by the kid's bathing habits. Drug problem. Out smokin' that crack with anybody who'll have him every night."

"This Jared a problem?" Lyons asked.

Cube shrugged. "Sometimes. Runs with the whores. Likes to get rough and kinky." He pulled the cigar from his mouth and pointed toward the bar. "Those three, Delores, Sugar and Betty, they know him. And they won't have nothin' more to do with him for any price."

Lyons watched Jared Justin amble to the bar and take a seat next to Delores. The blonde stared straight ahead, ignoring him.

"Cube," Blancanales said, "don't get what I'm about to say wrong. We all appreciate the jobs. We really do. We're broke. But what you're paying us, well, it's not bad for bouncing. But we're worth more. We can do other things.''

Cube grinned again. ''Overpaid for what you do and underpaid for what you're worth, huh?'' he said around the cigar.

Blancanales nodded. ''That's about it.''

''So what did you have in mind?'' Cube asked.

Schwarz took over the conversation, shrugging. ''We don't know, Cube,'' he said. ''But all that talk about the IRS and everything. Seems like you must have some other action going we don't know about. Something where we'd be more valuable.''

''I've got my fingers in a few pies,'' Cube said.

''Well, how about cutting us a small piece of one of them?'' Blancanales asked. ''Afraid we can't handle the heavy stuff?''

Cube laughed out loud this time. ''No, like I said, I've seen you in action. I'm not afraid you can't handle it. I'm afraid I don't trust you yet.''

The table fell silent for a moment. Then Cube said, ''Look boys, don't take it as an insult. We just met each other. Give it a few weeks. Let me get to know you. There's bigger money for you down the line, but first I have to make sure you aren't cops.''

''Damn,'' Schwarz said with a smile. ''Cops? And we aren't supposed to take that as an insult?''

The men around the table laughed.

''I mean, do we look like cops to you, Cube?''

Cube shook his head. ''No,'' he said. ''You

don't. But good undercover cops don't look like cops, right?'' He nodded toward a table in the opposite corner of the room where a tall lanky man sat. The man had shoulder-length brown hair hanging to his shoulders beneath a brown cowboy hat and wore tiny purple sunglasses. "*He* doesn't, does he?'' Cube didn't wait for an answer. "And I know for a fact he's from the San Antonio PD vice squad.''

"You sure about that?'' Lyons asked.

"I got friends in blue places,'' Cube said without hesitation.

"So it's a dope operation you're running,'' Blancanales whispered, his smile widening. "You're in luck, Cube. You just hired three guys with a lot of experience in that field.''

Cube's eyes narrowed, and Lyons hoped Blancanales would let it drop. He was pushing things too hard, too fast. And that was the easiest way to arouse suspicions. Slowly, so Cube wouldn't notice, the Able Team leader raised a boot under the table and nudged it against Blancanales's shin.

"No,'' Cube finally said, "I don't run dope out of here any more than I run whores.'' Lyons noticed that his tone was a little less friendly than before. "But I'm sure the Alamo's no different than any other place like it. There's small-time deals going down on the premises that I don't know about.'' He put both hands on the table in front of him and pushed himself to his feet. "You boys finish up the paperwork. I got work in the back." He turned to go, then turned back. "The narc's probably watchin' our buddy Jared," he said quietly. "You do the same. I don't want him worryin' Delores and the other girls. I don't make much off them, but they bring in customers." Without another word, he waddled across the dance floor and through the door.

No sooner was he gone than Justin looked over at the table, then did a full 360 of the Alamo. Lyons knew what he was looking for—Harley and the other bouncers. When he didn't see them, he grinned a stoned grin and stuck his hand between Delores's legs.

Delores gave a little shriek and slapped Justin across the face. A split second later, Justin had both hands around the prostitutes' throat.

"You damn whore!" he cried in a high-pitched voice. "*I* do the hittin', not you!"

Lyons stood and walked through the tables to the bar. "Hey," he said softly.

Leaving his hands around the woman's neck, Justin said, "Who the fuck are you and what do you want?"

"I'm one of the new bouncers, and I want you to take your hands off Delores and vacate the premises."

"*Vacate?*" Justin said mockingly. "*Vacate?* You got any more ten-dollar words in that big mouth of yours?"

"A few," Lyons said politely. "How about *wristlock?*" He stepped in and grabbed Justin by the hand. Sliding his other arm through the man's, he bent Justin's wrist over it.

He squealed as Lyons pulled him to his feet. "You're breakin' my damn arm!" he cried.

"No," Lyons said quietly, "*you're* breaking your own arm. Quit fighting it, come with me and in a few more seconds it'll all be over." He led the man to the door, opened it and stepped out into the sunshine.

"You son of a bitch!" Justin swore, rubbing his arm when Lyons had released it. "Rest assured my daddy's gonna hear about this."

"Hope he enjoys the story," Lyons said, and shut the door in Justin's face.

The Able Team leader returned to the table but didn't sit down. Instead, he scanned the bar to make sure there were no curious ears within hearing, then whispered. "Cube said give him a few weeks to trust us. We don't have that kind of time."

"So what do you have in mind, Ironman?" Blancanales asked.

"Another phone call to the Farm," Lyons said. "This time, to Cowboy Kissinger."

Washington, D.C.

THE ATMOSPHERE on the floor that housed the Oval Office was tense when McCarter and James returned. Two dozen Secret Service suits lined the hallway outside, with an equal number of the agency's uniformed personnel. An American expression crossed McCarter's mind, something to do with closing the barn door *after* the horse was gone.

The Phoenix Force leader could hear the First Lady's angry voice even before he stepped into the reception area.

"This is what you call a protection team? How did that man get those cars arranged in a circle like he did without anyone noticing? For that matter, how did he even get onto Pennsylvania Avenue with a gun?"

McCarter led James into the Oval Office as the First Lady paused for air. But she wasn't through. "Where did you find these clowns?" she demanded of the President.

"Look, sweetheart..." the President began.

McCarter and James took up standing positions against the wall next to Encizo, Manning and Hawkins. The Secret Service agents—George, Howard and William—were still there whispering among themselves. The President's son stood next to his mother, but Kelly had squeezed in between Hawkins and Manning and was holding on to Hawkins's forearm.

McCarter decided to wait until things had settled down before he spoke. After a few more outbursts from the First Lady, they finally did.

The President turned to the Phoenix Force leader. "See what I mean?" he said. "There's a plot to kill me. A conspiracy. I know you were skeptical before, but do you see now?"

McCarter cleared his throat. "With all due respect, Mr. President," he said, "there may very well be an assassination conspiracy in the works." He paused. "But if there is, the man we just subdued across the street isn't part of it."

The President's eyebrows lowered in anger. "Really."

McCarter remained calm. "Mr. President, let's look at this logically. You were here in the Oval Office when the man began to shoot. His shots were scattered across the front of the building. They show no pattern, nor do they indicate that he was aiming at any particular window or a specific target of any kind. I doubt very seriously that the gunman knows where the Oval Office is located, or whether you were even in the White House this morning."

The President's frown softened slightly as he listened to McCarter's reasoning. "So what are you trying to say?" he asked.

"That this wasn't an assassination attempt," McCarter replied. "It was a political statement. The guy quite simply doesn't like you or your policies."

"Where did this guy come from?" the First Lady demanded. "Scotland Yard?"

McCarter ignored the remark. "Let's look at it another way, Mr. President. Considering the man's crude strategy, what possible chance of success did he have? Shooting at the front of the building?

Snipers could have taken him out almost immediately if we hadn't wanted him alive for questioning. And if there had been any real threat to you or your family, they would have. If he was really trying to kill you, wouldn't he have at least tried to *see* you before he revealed his hand by opening fire?''

When no one responded, McCarter summed up. ''No, sir, Mr. President. I think the investigation will uncover the fact that the man is simply a lone mental case trying in his own perverse way to be heard.''

The President nodded. ''Where is he now?''

William spoke up. ''He's been taken to our offices for questioning.''

''Then I suppose—'' the President began when the phone rang. He punched two buttons on the control panel on his desk. ''Hello,'' he said into the speaker-phone.

Eileen's voice came from the outer office. ''Mr. President,'' the secretary said, ''Mr. Taft on line four.''

The man behind the desk punched another button. ''Yes, Ted.''

The voice that came over the speaker-phone was a mixture of anger and anxiety. ''Mr. President, this is what happens when amateurs are sent to do the job of professionals,'' Taft said. ''As I stressed before, we don't know who these men you've brought in even are. Furthermore—''

The President's face turned crimson. His jaws

tightened. "Ted, shut up! *I* know who these men are, and I'm telling you for the last time I requested them and they are staying. Is that clear?"

McCarter fought the urge to chuckle out loud. He had heard rumors that the president's outbursts sometimes bordered on temper tantrums. It appeared they were true.

There was a long pause at the other end of the line. When Taft's voice came back it was softer. "The decision is yours, Mr. President," he said. "But I must go on record once more as advising that these men be removed."

"Ted, another call like this one could very well result in your being removed. Now is that clear, too?"

Another long pause followed. Then the Secret Service director said, "Good day, Mr. President."

The man behind the desk jabbed the button with a forefinger ending the call. He stared silently at the desk, apparently trying to regain his composure.

McCarter felt sorry for the Secret Service director. He could understand the man's frustration at having five unknown men from an unnamed agency forced upon him. And the President had no understanding of military or police work of any kind. He had been a career politician since leaving law school and had no experience whatsoever with the problems the Secret Service faced.

The President finally looked up at the Phoenix Force leader. "We've wasted a lot of everyone's valuable time this morning,'' he said, his voice even again. "Is it safe to resume our schedules?"

"As safe as usual," McCarter said. "The gunman is no longer any threat."

"Good," the president replied. "The children have missed too much school today already. Let's get them to classes."

McCarter turned to James, who nodded and crossed the room to where the President's son stood next to his mother. "Ready to go, big guy?" he asked.

The boy's sandy hair bounced as his blue eyes looked up at the former Navy SEAL. Wallace smiled, then reached out and took James by the hand.

Accompanied by Special Agent George, James and the boy left the office.

"See you later, Daddy," Kelly purred as she squeezed Hawkins's arm. The Phoenix Force commando's face looked as if it had developed chronic sunburn as he and Howard escorted the young lady away.

"I'm late," the First Lady practically spit. "Which one of these guys goes with me?"

McCarter cleared his throat again. "You may have your choice," he said. "I have to remain with the President, but I'm sure either Mr. Manning or Mr. Encizo would be delighted to escort you to your engagements."

The looks on Manning's and Encizo's faces didn't necessarily confirm that assumption.

The First Lady turned to face the two men, sizing them up as if she might be choosing a pet for the children. Finally she said, "I'll take the big one. Let's go." Without another word she pivoted on her heel and strode out of the Oval Office.

Manning followed, looking for all the world like a man on his way to the gallows.

Illinois

BOLAN RODE SHOTGUN, keeping the Desert Eagle trained on the side of Morris's head. With sound no longer an issue, he had traded the Beretta for the more fearsome looking .44 Magnum pistol, and watched Morris's eyes widen in direct correlation to the increase in caliber.

"When we get to the blacktop, turn toward Kankakee," the Executioner ordered.

Morris twined the wheel to navigate around a curve in the road. He had regained some of the composure he'd lost earlier.

"Who the hell are you?" he demanded.

"That's not the issue," Bolan said, shaking his head. "Who the hell are *you?*"

Morris straightened in his seat. "Colonel Jackson W. Morris of the Illinois New Breed Militia, that's who," he said as he drove.

"And how exactly did you get the rank of colonel?" Bolan asked. "Did you ever serve in the military?"

Morris's face colored slightly. "No. My men elected me."

"That's what I figured. Exactly what is New Breed's purpose?"

Morris straightened the wheel as they came out of the curve. "We're training. Preparing for the war."

"What war?"

"The coming war," Morris said. He glanced briefly at the Executioner. "Don't you have eyes? You can see it all around you. Escalating crime. Overcrowded prisons. Oppression from the federal government. We've got a third generation of professional welfare recipients and every time we threaten to jerk them off the tit, they start burning everything." He glanced up at the roof of the Suburban, then back down. "It's only a matter of time—a short time now—before all hell breaks loose. We're going to be ready. We're going to be prepared. We're going to live through it."

"Looks to me like you're creating it," Bolan said. "And it sounds to me like you think it's going to be fun."

"What makes you say that?"

"Look at you. Running around playing soldier, drinking beer and shooting your guns at targets you can't even hit. That's training? And look at the targets themselves. That's not preparation. That's a bunch of fat bigoted slobs having a party and telling each other how tough they are."

Morris shook his head. "'There are none so blind as those who will not see,'" he quoted.

"Exactly what I was trying to tell you," the Executioner said.

The Suburban started into another curve, and Bolan knew they were nearing the blacktop. Then suddenly, the hum of other vehicles sounded ahead of them.

Just as suddenly, a black Jeep CJ-5 appeared, coming toward them. Behind it on the narrow one-lane road were two pickups.

Morris slammed his foot on the brake as the Jeep skidded to a halt in front of them. The pickups ground to a halt behind and to the sides. Four men stood in the open Jeep and aimed rifles at the Suburban. A second later, the windshield exploded as a dozen .223 rounds shattered the glass.

"Stop, you fools!" Morris shouted. "It's me!" His words were drowned by the gunfire.

Bolan remembered the walkie-talkie on the ground and knew what had to have happened. As soon as he'd taken Morris hostage, one of the surviving gunners in the trees had radioed for reinforcements.

And here they were.

The Executioner grabbed the handle and tried to open the door. But a bullet, or perhaps several, had struck the mechanism and the lock jammed. As he shoved harder with his shoulder, another volley of fire blew into the Suburban.

"Stop!" Morris screamed again. "It's me you—" His words were cut off midsentence.

The Executioner glanced over his shoulder to see Colonel Jackson W. Morris of the Illinois New Breed Militia staring sightlessly ahead. A third eye had opened in his forehead, and blood dripped over his eyes and face.

Bolan drove his shoulder harder into the door and it gave way. He dived from the Suburban as more rounds ripped into the seat where he'd been a second earlier. Hitting the ground, he rolled to face the militiamen with the Desert Eagle in front of him.

The Executioner aimed at the man standing behind the wheel of the Jeep. A single .44 Magnum round twisted through the rifling in the barrel and drilled into the New Breedman's heart. The windshield of the CJ-5 had been lowered, and the gunman fell forward over the hood, his rifle bouncing off the vehicle and into the weeds at the side of the road.

Bolan swung the Desert Eagle slightly to his left, squeezing the trigger again. The big pistol jumped in his hand as his second round caught the man riding shotgun in the throat, sending a geyser of blood spraying into the air.

The men in the back of the Jeep leaped to the ground. Bolan took out the one on the right with another big .44 bullet. But the man to the left dropped out of sight behind the vehicle.

Both pickups behind the Jeep had transported

two men and none of the quartet had remained idle. Zeroing in on the Executioner's position, a firestorm of .223 rounds forced him to roll off the road into the weeds. He kept rolling as round after round peppered the vegetation in his wake, finally making it to the woods and curling up behind a thick tree trunk.

Having lost sight of their target, the New Breed men ceased fire.

Bolan crawled to the tree, sat with his back against the bark and took a moment to catch his breath. Dropping the partially spent magazine from the Desert Eagle, he reloaded with a full box. He hadn't had time to grab the MP-5 from the back seat of the Suburban, and he could have put it to good use now. But he wasted no time thinking about it. Wishing wouldn't make it magically appear.

"You! In the trees!" a voice called out. "Drop your weapon and come out with your hands up!"

The Executioner didn't answer. Drawing the Beretta with his left hand, he dropped the selector to 3-round-burst mode, then peered around the tree. The man speaking stood foolishly in the open, his AR-15 aimed in the direction of the trees.

Bolan leaned to the left of the tree trunk and sent three 9 mm hollowpoints boring through the man's chest.

The rounds brought a volley of return fire from behind the vehicles. Bolan rode it out, pressing his back against the thick bark and feeling the vibration each time one of the bullets struck the tree. Mentally he subtracted the New Breedmen he had shot from those he'd seen arrive. Four in the Jeep, another four in the two pickups. Three of the men in the CJ-5 had fallen to the Desert Eagle. The last man—from one of the pickups—had gone down to the Beretta's 9 mm rounds.

Eight up. Four down. Four to go.

The Executioner heard movement across the road to his right and leaned that way, peering around the tree. He saw no one, but the grass on the other side of the road, just inside the tree line, was moving. Leaning slightly farther, he tapped the Beretta's trigger once more and sent another trio of rounds at the spot.

A loud scream issued from the trees. A second later, a New Breedman wearing blue jeans and a green fatigue jacket hopped into sight holding one foot. Three more 9 mm bullets ended his hopping.

Three to go.

Bolan waited. He had planned to interrogate Morris, but that was no longer a possibility. The next best thing to the militia leader was to learn what his men knew. He needed one of these guys alive. But he had no idea how he was going to make that happen and remain alive himself.

More sounds came from the left of the tree again. The Executioner risked a quick look. The two pickups had stopped at angles behind the Jeep, and just above the tailgate of the nearest truck he saw the crown of a baseball cap sticking up.

Cover and concealment were two entirely different things, Bolan knew, but that fact evidently wasn't part of Morris's "preparedness" training. The man in the baseball cap apparently thought the latter was the former. And he wasn't even doing a good job at the latter.

Reaching around the tree with the Desert Eagle, Bolan lined up the sights on a spot in the tailgate directly below the crown of the baseball cap. He squeezed the trigger, and once more the Eagle boomed.

The gray-edged hole that appeared in the tailgate was nearly a half-inch in diameter. The velocity of the round knocked the cap off the New Breedman's head and sent him sprawling to the dirt a good ten feet behind the pickup.

Two to go.

Again, the Executioner paused. A plan was starting to form in his mind; a way of keeping one of the men alive for questioning. It would require taking out one of the remaining two, and it would be risky. But he could see no other alternative.

Bolan took another glance around the tree but saw no signs of the remaining two militiamen. Slowly he moved away from the trunk and onto his belly. He slid silently through the grass, creeping toward another tree ten feet closer to the pickups and Jeep. When he reached it, he moved in and raised his head high enough to see the parked vehicles. Again, he could see no sign of the men.

The Executioner frowned. He knew they were still behind the Jeep or the trucks. None of them so far had moved without his hearing them, and he had no reason to believe the remaining men were any better trained in the art of stealth.

From his current angle, he couldn't see beneath the vehicles. There would be no scanning the ground for the men's feet, but he had several advantages.

First, they weren't particularly well-trained. Second, they still thought he was ten feet to the left, behind the first tree. Third and most important, they would be expecting him to stay behind that tree and try to pick them off. They certainly wouldn't envision his coming to them.

The Beretta still in his left hand, the Desert Eagle in his right, Bolan rose suddenly from the tall grass behind the tree. He sprinted forward, sacrificing silence for speed as he raced directly toward the parked vehicles. His eyes darted left and right as he angled past the Jeep toward the nearest pickup. But he saw no sign of the remaining two New Breedmen.

Five feet from the nearest pickup, the Executioner shoved off with his right leg, vaulting over the side rail and into the bed of the truck. He landed on both feet with a loud clang, stepped to the opposite side and peered down.

Directly below him, a pimple-faced man in his early twenties aimed his Springfield Government Model upward. Bolan had no choice but to shoot. The .44 Magnum round drilled down into the New Breedman's face, through his neck and exited his back, with blood, bone and tissue following in its wake.

In his peripheral vision, Bolan saw the final New Breedman behind the other pickup to his left. The man was thin in the chest and shoulders but had a massive abdomen and posterior that stretched against the cotton khaki work pants he wore under a plaid shirt. As the Executioner turned that way, the man raised his AR-15.

Bolan clenched his teeth in disgust as he pulled the trigger, aiming low. He had hoped to take one of the men alive, but again, he could only shoot or die himself. Three more rounds coughed from the sound-suppressed Beretta 93-R, cutting through the New Breedman's flabby paunch.

The AR-15 fell from the man's grasp. His mouth opened as if to speak but instead, blood shot forth. He toppled onto his back.

Bolan jumped from the truck bed and hurried forward. Kneeling next to the man, he grabbed the front of the plaid shirt and shook it. "Who's Maestro?" he asked.

The New Breedman's chest rose and fell. A wheezing sound escaped his lips. His eyes stared straight up, unfocused, as if covered by some watery film.

"Maestro," Bolan repeated. "Who is Maestro?" Slowly, the man on the ground shook his head. "Don't know...any maestro."

"Who plans the bombings?" the Executioner asked. "Some guy on the Internet. Do you know who he is?"

He got no response.

Bolan shook the man by the shirt again. "Listen to me," he said. "Who is the brain behind the bombs?"

"I...don't know," the New Breedman wheezed. He closed his eyes. "Please...just let me...die...."

The Executioner shook harder. "Who would know?" he demanded. "Who would know who Maestro is?"

"Colonel Morris...maybe."

"Morris was in the Suburban with me. He's dead. You and your men killed him."

The man's eyes flickered open again. "Morris dead?"

Bolan let go of the man's shirt. The eyes were clouding. He didn't have much time. "Who else would know Maestro?" he asked. "Any of the other men back at the range?"

"No," the New Breedman said. Shaking his head was an extreme effort now. "Nobody...but Morris."

Bolan leaned close to the man's ear. "Who else

might know? Somebody from another militia? Another group, maybe?''

The man on the ground gave out a deep sigh. He wheezed again, then mumbled something.

The Executioner leaned in, his ear almost touching the man's mouth. "What?" he said. "Tell me again."

"Fred," the dying man whispered.

"Fred who?"

"Fred...Daley...."

"Where do I find Fred Daley?" Bolan asked.

A series of choking sounds spluttered from the New Breedman's throat. He coughed and more blood ran from the side of his mouth.

Bolan could see he was fading fast. Grasping the man's shirt with both hands now, he shook him harder. "Talk to me! Who is this Fred Daley? Tell me where I can find him."

"Fort...Wayne," the New Breedman breathed. "Indiana Militia..." The rest of the air left his lungs.

And no more went in.

CHAPTER SEVEN

Virginia Beach, Virginia

On the other side of his apartment building the sun had almost fallen, leaving the Atlantic coastline outside his window an amalgamation of colors. Desmond Click's brain recognized that the sight was beautiful, but the resplendent spectacle brought no joy to his heart.

Click turned away from the window, glanced at the watch on his scarred wrist and rolled his wheelchair to the computer. Sliding the mouse across the pad, he clicked the left button twice to access the Internet, then on the keyboard typed the code to search for Zulu.

As he waited, Click's mind wandered back over the years to his childhood. In most ways it had been little different than anyone else's, he suspected. Certainly, during the many times he'd reviewed it in his mind, he had never found any clues as to what had made him different from other boys and girls. He had had a loving mother and father who treated him well. They had never been wealthy, but they had never been impoverished, either. He had done well in athletics, playing baseball, football and basketball through grade school, junior high and high school. If anything had been peculiar, it was that he had never been successful at dealing with the ridicule other adolescents heaped on him. Looking back now he could see that, at least at first, he wasn't tormented any more than other kids. Children were cruel; in their immature search for their own identities they ridiculed one another. That was the way of things. If a child could focus attention on the shortcomings of another, their peers were too busy to notice their own imperfections. If the scapegoat took his turn well, it would soon be over and the taunting passed on to another.

But Click knew he hadn't passed the test. He had let the mockery get to him. Worse yet, he had let how it affected him show to his classmates. This transparency of emotion had left him vulnerable— a favorite laughingstock whose discomfort bolstered the shaky egos of other insecure children searching for their own self-worth.

The man in the wheelchair turned his attention back to the monitor screen. Where the hell was Zulu? He knew that this was the night. Perhaps he was busy taking care of some of the last-minute details Click had assigned him. If so, there was a definite problem in the division of labor—Zulu should be assigning trivial tasks to subordinates.

Click's mind moved from childhood to his teenage years. It was then that he had first suspected something about him was different. Really different. Maybe something even wrong.

Click stared ahead at the computer screen. His eyes remained open but unfocused as he drifted in recollection. It had been late junior-high school when he'd realized he didn't feel the attraction to girls that seemed to preoccupy all waking thoughts of his male classmates. At first, this difference didn't bother him. Only late in the game had his voice started to change, and hair begun to grow under his arms and on his pubic area. So Click had assumed that the longing to touch members of the opposite sex would eventually do the same, simply coming to him later than it had to his friends.

By the first year in high school Click had known something was wrong. Trying to force it, he spent most of his money on magazines and other pornography in a futile attempt to stimulate desire. That desire hadn't come. He looked at the pictures of nude women with the same curiosity he might have felt examining the formerly unseen parts of a car engine. But they hadn't generated lust in his heart or soul.

Click closed his eyes now, leaning back against his wheelchair as his reverie deepened. He remembered the dates he had forced himself to endure, and the nausea even the prospect of a good-night kiss had brought.

In particular, he remembered the hayrack ride.

Each year around Valentine's Day, Roosevelt High School had hosted an event called Sadie Hawkins Week. Activities such as movies, dances and hayrack rides were sponsored, and in contrast to the usual custom of the times, the girls invited the boys. Having spent the week dateless, Click finally accepted an invitation from Sandy Lee to be her date on the Saturday night hayrack ride that climaxed the week's activities.

Sandy was a well-known girl about school—not for her looks, or her grades or extracurricular activities. Unless you considered the time she spent with boys in the backseats of cars, often with several other boys waiting their turn, to be an extracurricular activity.

Getting a date for the hayrack ride hadn't been easy for Sandy. While she had been with most members of the football, basketball, and track team at one time or another, it had always been on the sly. None of them wanted their regular girlfriends to know they even knew Sandy Lee.

Since Click had no girlfriend, Sandy had finally asked him.

The same humiliation he had experienced that evening so long ago now returned to invade Click's chest. He closed his eyes tighter, sweat breaking out on his forehead. He remembered the horses pulling the wagon slowly down the moonlit road while boys and girls paired off, kissing and fondling each other beneath the hay. When Sandy had stuck her tongue in his mouth he wanted to gag. But he hadn't. He was determined to overcome whatever problem he had, convinced that the excitement and pleasure the others felt from such activities had to be an acquired taste.

Arriving at the bottom of a dry river, the students and faculty chaperons bailed out of the wagons to build a bonfire. Hot dogs and marshmallows were roasted and consumed, then the teenagers' thoughts returned to other appetites. In spite of the warnings from the sponsors, many couples drifted off into the trees. Desmond and Sandy had been one of those couples.

Click heard a series of beeps from the computer, and his eyes shot open. But there was still no reply to his search for Zulu, and he closed his eyes again.

Sandy Lee had done her best to excite him as they lay hidden in the trees near the bonfire. She used both her hands and mouth, then taken the risk of undressing completely and rubbing her body over him. She took him by the hand, showing him how to massage and stimulate her most secret places, and moaned in passion as his fingers moved below her own.

Click felt nothing except the same nausea he experienced when she'd kissed him. Until he'd rolled to his side and his eyes took in the blazing bonfire.

Someone had to have thrown more wood on the fire because it was the sudden crackling that had drawn his attention that way. Through the leaves and vines that hid them from view, Click saw the flames rising into the air. A change in wind wafted smoke into his nostrils, replacing Sandy's womanly scent and causing him suddenly to come erect.

Click's eyes closed again as the memory played across the back of his eyelids like a movie he had watched many times before. He remembered the excitement he suddenly felt when one of the unseen girls still around the fire squealed into the night. The squeal could have been one of surprise or delight, and probably was. But in the mind of Desmond Click, it had been one of pain; the pain of feeling her hot flesh on fire. As his hunger for release rose, he pictured Sandy Lee tied to a stake in the middle of the flames.

Feeling the change in her hand, Sandy had guided him toward her. But her realization had come too late, and he shot his fluid over her inner thigh. Click would never forget her words. "What a lot of work for nothing," she said as she slipped back into her clothes. They were the last words she ever spoke to him.

Click heard more noise from the speakers next to his monitor. He opened his eyes and stared at the screen.

Zulu had found him.

Status? Click typed simply with his keyboard and watched the word appear on the screen.

Ready, came back.

Click knew better than to take Zulu at his word. Bernell Dixon was a charismatic leader who could literally sell ice water to Eskimos. But he was no detail's man. He tended to overlook the small but imperative details of an operation, the technicalities that meant the difference between success and failure, escape and arrest.

Click began a sequence of questions he knew would irritate Zulu, but there was no way around them. He couldn't trust the FAN man to take care of the details himself.

Click's first inquiry was whether the Free African Nation leader had assigned men to take out the security guards in case they noticed the man planting the bomb.

Yes.

Had the FAN men who constructed the device from the components Click had had shipped to them double-checked his list of "Dos and Don'ts"?

Yes, of course.

Had the FAN surveillance team noticed any changes around the building? Had anything been different this day than the previous three days they had watched their site?

No, dammit. NO.

After several more queries that brought more annoyed responses from Zulu, Click typed in *Any final questions?*

Yes. Why this site? It seems unimportant.

Soft target, Click replied.

Other soft targets are more important.

I have my reasons, Click returned, mildly irritated himself this time. He had worked well for FAN, already setting up several fire bombs and never asked anything in return. Perhaps that was what made Bernell Dixon suspicious. He couldn't imagine what Maestro was getting out of the whole thing and couldn't believe he was getting something for nothing.

Click smiled. If only Zulu knew.

Why the odd method of detonation? Zulu demanded.

I have my reasons, Click responded once more.

Why should we trust you?

Have I led you wrong yet? Maestro answered.

For several seconds, no more questions or answers appeared on the screen. Then Maestro tapped the keyboard once more.

Are you ready?

Ready, Zulu answered.

Click took a deep breath. He felt a throbbing begin under the blanket that covered his legs. He had enjoyed watching the results of his bombs on the news. But what was about to happen would be even better.

Slowly Click's fingers began to stroke the keyboard. When he'd finished, he sat back against the chair. There would be a thirty-second delay after he sent the message before the code triggered the electronic impulse that would set off the bomb. It would give him just enough time.

Like a man watching his lover undress, Click eyed the monitor. Then, his breathing coming in shallow pants, he tapped the Enter key and sent the code across the lines.

Breathing even harder now, Click whirled his wheelchair toward the sliding glass door behind him. He rolled frantically across the room and reached up to grasp the handle.

"Dezzie? Dezzie, may I come in for a moment?" came his mother's voice behind the closed and locked door to the hallway.

"No! Not now! Leave me alone!" He heard her footsteps pad off down the hall as he almost ripped the glass door from its track.

Click wheeled his chair over the track and onto the balcony, feeling the breeze snake into the collar of his pajamas. But he didn't feel cold this time; his skin was warm, hot. A trickle of sweat even ran down his forehead.

His arms rolling the wheels at his side furiously, Click guided himself across the balcony to the railing, then turned to face the buildings along the shore. The tallest was Baptist Hospital, a medical center that specialized in the treatment of burn victims.

In a brief moment of conscience, Click felt the need for rationalization. "I am doing good as well as evil," he said out loud. "These patients—these scarred and mutilated victims of my mistress—will never experience the long-term pain I have had to endure.''

His words were cut off as the top four floors of the eight-story hospital suddenly exploded.

Click's mouth fell open as, a mile away, debris flew through the air. Smoke rose from the top half of the hospital, and he imagined he could hear the screams. He closed his eyes.

His body began to shake. He had experienced nothing like this since he had been in the wheelchair, since the days when he had been able to physically witness the fires he set rather than simply seeing them on television. He opened his eyes once more and stared at the flames down the road. As he shook in the ecstasy of sweet release, the memory of Sandy Lee and the hayrack ride bonfire played in his mind once more.

Texas

LYONS WATCHED the steel guitar player drop his instrument into the leather case and flip the catches closed. The man pulled the black cowboy hat off his head and wiped his brow with the sleeve of his fringed rhinestone-studded shirt. The stones sparkled and bounced under the lights as he left the stage and followed the other band members out of the Alamo to the parking lot.

The Able Team leader sat alone at a table sipping a cup of coffee. Blancanales had disappeared into the men's room and Schwarz stood at the bar, talking to the bartender.

The side door off the dance floor opened, and Cube waddled through. He had been scarce during the night, sticking his nose through the door only once or twice to check out the action, then mysteriously disappearing again into what Lyons assumed was his office.

Earlier, on the pretense of needing to ask Cube a question, the Able Team leader tried to open the door.

It had been locked.

"Quiet night, eh?" the fat man in the rancher's hat mumbled around his cigar as he crossed the floor to Lyons's table.

Lyons nodded. "Couple of drunks got a little out of hand. Nothing like this afternoon."

"Good," Cube said, the cigar moving in time to the word. "Nice and quiet. Makes for a good image for the place."

Lyons took another sip of coffee. "So what now?"

"I need you boys to take me to the bank," Cube said. "Night deposit." The grin that covered his face was full of greed. "Brought in almost $15,000 tonight. I ain't gonna leave it here for the raccoons." He turned toward the front of the Alamo. "I better lock 'er up."

The Alamo owner ambled toward the entryway of the bar. Halfway there, he stuck a hand into his pants pocket and withdrew a key ring, fishing through the keys as he walked. He stopped when he reached the door, bent slightly and started to insert the key.

With a loud cracking sound, the front door of the Alamo flew open, striking Cube in the forehead. The fat man's hat sailed from his head as he was knocked back into the statue of Jim Bowie. He came to rest in a sitting position, his back against the stone figure, blood seeping from the blow to his forehead.

Four men wearing black hooded sweatshirts and matching black stocking caps barreled through the door. Each man carried a pistol in one hand, a black satchel in the other. The lead man, tall and lanky, stopped long enough to kick Cube in the stomach, then sprinted through the entryway onto the dance floor. The other three followed.

"Throw up your hands!" the tall man in the lead yelled in a crazed voice. "Don't move!"

All four men spread out across the dance floor, covering Lyons, Schwarz and the bartender with their pistols.

Lyons ignored the orders, spinning out of his chair and hitting the floor behind the table. As he fell he ripped open the snaps of his Western shirt and jerked the Colt Government Model from the Bianchi bellyband. In the corner of his eye, he saw Schwarz dive for another table as the bartender ducked behind the bar.

The first shot whizzed past the Able Team leader's head close enough for him to feel the pressure. Bringing the .45 in his fist to eye level, he looked past it to see that the round had come from a the tall thin robber's Glock 19.

The Government Model pointed at the man's chest, Lyons squeezed the grips tightly and pulled back on the trigger. The .45 jumped twice in his hand.

The tall man in the sweatshirt jerked twice, then froze in his tracks. The satchel and the Glock 19 fell from his hands. Blood spurted from holes in both the front and back of his black hooded sweatshirt as he fell to his knees, then forward onto his face.

The room was suddenly ablaze with muzzle-flashes and explosions as the remaining three robbers opened up. Rounds drilled into the table at Lyons's side as he and Schwarz returned fire. The Able Team leader tapped out another duo of .45 rounds, and a second robber went down, blood flying through the air as if caught by a sudden windstorm. At almost the same time, Lyons heard Schwarz's Beretta 92 pop three times and the third of the four robbers hit the floor.

The Able Team leader saw movement to his side and turned his Colt that way. He lowered it as Blancanales, his SIG-Sauer in hand, dived from the men's room and rolled across the floor. He came to a halt behind the table directly to Lyons's right.

The last robber dived back into the entryway and grabbed Cube, hauling the fat bar owner to his feet. Circling an arm around the shorter man's neck, he crouched, his Browning Hi-Power jammed into the folds of fat under Cube's chin. "Move and he dies!" the robber yelled.

There was a long moment of silence. Then the robber said, "Pick up the satchels off the floor! Now! I want everything out of the cash register and safe. Do it! Or fat boy here gets it in the head!"

Lyons looked at Cube. The man's crimson face was a mask of terror. "Do what he says," Cube said, his voice coming out a high-pitched squeal.

Lyons stood behind the table.

"Drop the gun!" the robber screamed.

Slowly Lyons shook his head. "I don't think so," he said.

Another moment of silence followed. Then the man in the black hooded sweatshirt said, "I'll kill him, you son of a bitch."

Even more slowly than he had shaken his head, Lyons began to raise the .45. The robber held Cube at the edge of the entryway, while Lyons stood at the far end of the dance floor. It was bull's-eye target-shooting distance and the available target— the top right quarter of the robber's face—was roughly the size of the ten ring. Under match conditions, Carl Lyons could hit the shot a hundred times out of a hundred.

A grim expression covered the Able Team

leader's face. These weren't match conditions. Bull's-eye shooting was slow fire. Precise work. He would have to fire fast, before the robber realized that his bluff had been called and put a bullet in Cube's skull.

A smile threatened to curl Carl Lyons's lips. No, these weren't target-match conditions. But they weren't exactly the conditions they appeared to be either.

In one swift movement, the Able Team leader raised the Colt the rest of the way and pulled the trigger.

A burst of crimson shot from the top of the robber's head. He dropped like a rock as gray matter and other substances made his face unrecognizable.

Cube fell forward onto his hands and knees, away from the robber. In a microsecond, his face changed from bright red to pale white. A moment after that, he leaned forward and emptied his stomach onto the dance floor.

The bartender finally stuck his head up from behind the bar. "Everything over?" he asked.

"Appears to be," Blancanales said.

The man came around the bar, twisting nervously at the ends of his handlebar mustache. His eyes took in the scene and he said simply, "Oh my God."

Lyons turned to Blancanales. "Take Cube into the rest room and get him cleaned up."

Then to Schwarz, he said, "Check to make sure

these guys are dead. And get their guns.'' He headed for Cube, who was still retching on the floor.

By the time the Able Team leader had reached the Alamo owner, Cube had stopped vomiting. Pulling a handkerchief from the breast pocket of his jacket, he wiped his mouth.

Blancanales gently took the man by the arm to guide him to the men's room. Cube shook off the hand. Only now what had happened seemed to sink in to the Alamo owner.

"Oh, shit," he said.

Lyons looked down at the fat man. "Nothing to worry about. It's obvious they were trying to rob you. The cops'll call it justified homicide. No problem."

Schwarz cleared his throat loudly.

Lyons turned to face him. "Oh yeah," he said. "There is the little matter of an arrest warrant out on my friend here." He paused, then turned to Blancanales. "You didn't shoot anybody, did you?" he asked.

He shook his head. "Got in too late."

Lyons nodded. "Trade guns with Jake here," he said, using Schwarz's cover name. "Have him fill you in on the details of what he did so our stories match up."

The two men exchanged weapons.

Cube was still coming out of shock. But he was beginning to catch on. "No!" he said. "We can't play it that way. I don't want the fuckin' pigs snooping all over this place. I can't have it.''

Lyons, Schwarz and Blancanales traded glances. Then Lyons said, ''Well, there's only one other way to play it, Cube.'' The Able Team leader hooked a thumb at the bartender. ''Can he be trusted?''

Cube nodded. ''How do we handle this?''

''We'll have to get rid of the bodies,'' Lyons stated.

Cube was on the verge of hysteria. ''How?'' he asked. ''Where? Where do we get rid of them? Do you know a place?''

''We know a place,'' Blancanales said. ''A good place.'' He paused and glanced at Lyons. When Lyons nodded, he went on. ''We've used it before, Cube. It's safe. No one will know.''

Still pale-faced, Cube nodded. ''No one will know,'' he repeated weakly. ''Whoever these guys were, they'll just disappear.'' He sounded more like he was trying to convince himself than the men of Able Team.

''Cube?'' Lyons said softly.

The Alamo owner looked up.

''We'll help you. But if we do, we'll want a better piece of your action than being Alamo watchdogs. Understood?''

Cube nodded almost violently. ''Look, get rid of these bodies and I'll trust you,'' he said. ''If you do that I can trust you with anything.''

Lyons just smiled. As the smile faded, he turned

to the bartender. "Find a mop and bucket and get this mess cleaned up. I want the floor clean enough to eat off."

The statement made Cube look like he might throw up again.

"Roger," the Able Team leader went on, addressing Blancanales by his cover name, "you and Jake go out back and find me four trash cans."

He turned to Cube. "You've got some out there, don't you?"

Cube nodded, frowning, trying to figure out what was going on. "What do you want me to do?" he asked meekly.

"We won't be able to get all the bodies, and us, into our Suburban," Lyons said. "You got a vehicle?"

"Well, yeah," Cube said, wiping sweat from his cheeks with both hands. I've got a panel van. Blue. Parked out front."

"Perfect." Lyons held out a hand. "Give me the keys."

Cube fished into his pocket and came out with a key chain. A solid gold cowboy-boot fob bobbed below the keys as he handed it to the Able Team leader. "Anything else I should do?" he asked.

"Yeah," Lyons said. "Relax. The night is just beginning."

He turned to Blancanales. "Change of orders," he said, handing Blancanales the gold cowboy boot and keys. "You come with me."

The two Able Team warriors walked past Cube, glancing down at the three men on the dance floor. None of the bodies stirred. Lyons and Blancanales moved into the entryway where the last robber had fallen, stopping to look down at the chaos that had once been a face. The entire right side appeared to be gone. The left, however, had been untouched.

As Lyons and Blancanales looked down, the man's left eye opened.

And winked.

Lyons suppressed a smile as he and his teammate pushed through the front door of the Alamo and out into the parking lot.

John Kissinger and the Stony Man blacksuits had come through again. The blood bombs—similar to those used by Hollywood stuntmen—had been detonated without flaw. Even the one hidden in the stocking cap of the blacksuit who had taken Cube hostage had worked perfectly. And unbeknownst to Cube or anyone else, the men of Able Team had loaded their weapons with blanks during the course of the evening. The only real rounds fired, in case Cube came out of his trauma to look for bullet holes, had been those fired by the blacksuits themselves.

Those rounds had come dangerously close, Lyons remembered as he and Blancanales stopped next to the van. But then, Able Team's job description didn't say anything about being safe all the time. Any of the time, for that matter.

Blancanales inserted a key, climbed behind the wheel of the van and rolled down the window. He had a worried look on his face as he said, "That went down easy, Ironman."

Lyons nodded, knowing full well what concerned his Able Team comrade as he walked to the Suburban and started the engine. Pulling behind the Alamo, he halted next to the back door where Schwarz and Cube were waiting with the trash cans that contained "bodies."

Lyons exited the Suburban and helped the other men load the cans into the van. He took a hard look at each container as it was lifted up and into the vehicle.

Yes, what had gone down so far this night had been the easy part. What they were about to do would be far trickier.

That was, if they wanted the blacksuits crammed into the trash cans to live through the night.

Slamming the tailgate, Carl Lyons walked back to the Suburban and opened the door again.

CHAPTER EIGHT

Fort Wayne, Indiana

Bolan had the cab pull over in front of a large white two-story house that looked to have been built sometime in the 1930s. He handed two twenty-dollar bills over the seat to the driver, and opened the door.

"Late night meeting, eh, bub?" the cabbie said.

"You got it," Bolan replied, playing the part of the well-dressed businessman in his beige Hart, Shaftner and Marx suit. "Not enough hours in the day."

"I hear you on that," the cabbie said as the Executioner exited the vehicle.

Bolan walked to the curb in front of the house and began to fumble with the briefcase, slowing his pace as the man drove away. As soon as the cab was out of sight down the street, the Executioner changed course from the front porch and circled around the side, stopping between the white house and a similar brick dwelling next to it. It, too, looked to be fifty to sixty years old, as did all the other residences in the neighborhood. This upper middle-income area of Fort Wayne, Indiana, was well seasoned, yet still fashionable.

Quickly Bolan turned the briefcase upside down and emptied the contents onto the grass, using the full overhead moon for illumination. His jacket, slacks, shirt, tie and shoes came off in a flash, leaving him standing between the houses in a form-fitting blacksuit. From the ground, he lifted the shoulder system bearing his Beretta 93-R and extra magazines, and slipped it over his arms. Next came the black waist belt toting the .44 magnum Desert Eagle, the Applegate-Fairbairn fighting knife, and other equipment. He slid his feet into combat boots, tied the laces and reached for the last piece of gear he would wear for the soft probe he had planned a few houses away.

John Kissinger had removed the hard plastic belt loops from the belt pouch and refitted it with Bianchi clips. It slipped easily over the waist belt, and Bolan positioned it just to the left of the plastic snap-buckle, where he could reach it quickly with a cross-draw movement.

A bolt of lightning flashed distantly in the sky as the Executioner stuffed his suit into the briefcase. Thunder followed overhead as he cached the bag in a hedge separating the dwellings, then moved into the backyard.

A six-foot wooden fence separated the white

house from the home behind it, and Bolan pulled himself over it. He dropped next to a goldfish pond. Circling the pond, he moved to the front of the house, then knelt at the corner of the garage.

Across the street, he could plainly see his target site, and the iron fence that circled it.

A call to Stony Man Farm had found no Intel on a Fred Daley in Fort Wayne. But a quick computer cross-reference by Akira Tokaido had come up with the name Fred *Bailey* as the top dog of the Indiana Militia.

Bolan's trained eyes scanned the street between him and the Bailey estate. There were still lights on in many of the houses up and down the block, but no activity outside. It was too early for many of the residents to be in bed, but not too late to be winding down the day inside. No one was likely to be watching the street.

The Executioner moved away from the house, crouching as he sprinted across the pavement to the fence. He surveyed the iron bars, looking for the alarm wire Tokaido had warned him he would encounter. He spotted it three inches from the top and reached into the belt pouch for the wire cutters. A moment later there was a quick burst of sparks at the top of the fence.

The first droplets of rain fell on Bolan's face as he climbed the bars, squeezed between the spear points at the top, then lowered himself on the other side. He dropped to a squatting position, his eyes skimming the grounds. Intermittent trees, a hundred years old or more, speckled the grounds. The house in the distance, though well kept, looked just as old.

The estate was on an island of earth, surrounded by streets on all sides. This led the Executioner to believe that the house had once stood alone, probably as the central focal point of an Indiana farm. As the city of Fort Wayne grew, the land around it had to have been developed, and the newer homes Bolan had encountered had sprung up.

The Executioner rose and advanced slowly, his eyes searching the ground in front of him. The Stony Man computer file on Bailey and the Indiana Militia had stressed that the estate was well-fortified and secured. Bolan saw the next sign that the Intel was right when he came to the knee-high trip wire ten feet inside the fence.

Carefully stepping over the wire, he moved on, still searching for traps. He saw a small red glow in his peripheral vision and came to a halt just in front of a laser detector mounted in the fork of a tree. Dropping to his belly, he crawled under the beam, then returned to his feet.

He had gone only ten more steps when he heard the barking.

In the distance, the Executioner saw two Doberman pinschers round the house and sprint toward him. Ducking behind the nearest tree, he jammed his hand inside the belt pouch and came out with the tranquilizer gun. Leaning around the tree, he braced a forearm on the trunk and sighted down the barrel.

The lead dog was twenty feet in front of his partner, his teeth bared as he ran. Bolan let him get within ten yards of the tree, then dropped him with a single dart to the chest.

The second dog yelped as he stumbled over the first. For a second, he was disoriented. Bolan took advantage of the time to manually work the slide of the tranquilizer gun. As the second Doberman turned toward him, he caught the animal in the side, high near the heart.

Both dogs went to sleep. The animals were doing only what they'd been trained to do, and Bolan always thought it senseless to kill needlessly—human or animal.

By now, the raindrops had become a light drizzle that fell over the Executioner's head and shoulders. He tucked the tranquilizer gun into his belt pouch and walked on.

The trees stopped twenty yards from the house. Directly in front of him, Bolan could see an Olympic-sized swimming pool surrounded by a redwood deck. To one side stood a cabana-style pool house. The entire area was illuminated by overhead lights. Keeping to the trees, he circled the pool until he could see a back door into the dwelling.

If the house was built like most residences of its age and station, the door would be a servants' entrance into the kitchen. It should be deserted this time of night, the best place to enter.

Again, the Executioner examined the grounds between him and the house. There was no cover until he reached the door, but no apparent traps, sentries or outer guard, either. He shot from the trees at full speed, his eyes searching for any final trip wires. He saw none and reached the back door, his hand darting into the belt pouch again and coming out with a pick gun.

Bolan had inserted the pick device into the lock when he felt the hard steel of a gun barrel jab him in the ribs.

"Something I can help you with?" the voice said over his shoulder.

The Executioner froze in place.

A moment later, the voice said, "Raise your hands and turn around. Slow."

Bolan did as ordered, his hands moving to shoulder level. In front of him he saw a broad man in his midforties with thinning brown hair. The guard wore OD fatigues, a brown campaign hat and held a .357 magnum Smith & Wesson Model 66 an inch from the Executioner's chest.

The man looked Bolan up and down, taking in the blacksuit, weapons and other equipment. "Who the hell do you think you are?" he asked. "Batman?"

Shaking the pick gun in his hand, the Executioner said, "Would you believe the locksmith?"

The guard's eyes involuntarily drifted to the pick gun. Bolan let the device fall from his hand. Following his natural instincts, the guard reached to catch it.

Bolan dropped his right hand to the barrel of the .357. At the same time, his left slapped the back of the man's wrist behind the gun. The trigger guard caught the man's index finger, snapping it like a dry twig as the weapon twisted out of the guard's grip into the hands of the Executioner.

The guard let out a yelp as Bolan twirled the revolver into his palm and took a step back.

The guard grabbed his broken finger with his left hand and held it against his chest. He looked up into the eyes of the Executioner, his face a mask of disbelief. It had all happened so fast he wasn't sure it had happened at all. When he finally came to his senses, his eyes fell to the .357-caliber bore of his own weapon pointed at his head.

Sweat broke out on the man's forehead. "Hey," he said in a tiny frightened voice, "I'm just doing my job. Don't shoot me."

"Sorry," Bolan said, reaching into the belt pouch with his left hand and pulling out the tranquilizer gun. "I've got to. That's *my* job." He squeezed the trigger and sent a tranquilizer dart into the center of the man's chest.

The guard went to sleep like the dogs.

The Executioner shoved the Smith & Wesson into his belt behind the belt pouch and drew the

Desert Eagle. He found a set of keys on the guard's belt and opened the back door. No alarm sounded, but that didn't mean there wasn't a silent alert somewhere. Speed was called for now—he had to reach his objective before other guards or the cops showed up.

Shutting the door behind him, Bolan saw he had predicted the design of the house correctly. He was in a large kitchen. He crossed to a swing door in the opposite wall and pushed through, finding himself in a long hallway. From behind a door at the end of the hall came the faint sounds of 1940s swing music.

The Executioner's jaw set tightly. According to Stony Man Farm Intel, the founder of the Indiana Militia was in his seventies. The music fit.

Bolan hurried silently down the carpeted hall and pressed his ear to the door. The music was louder now and he recognized, but couldn't name, an old Tommy Dorsey tune. He could hear no other sound above the music.

Twisting the knob slowly, the Executioner found it unlocked. He pushed the door open, stepped into a den and saw an old man sitting in a reclining chair, his feet and legs covered by a multicolored afghan.

The old man looked up in surprise, his eyes taking a moment to refocus through the top half of his bifocals. When he saw what was before him, his

hand shot with surprising speed toward a Heckler
& Koch USP pistol on the lamp stand next to him.

Bolan took a step forward and cleared his throat.
"I wouldn't recommend it," he said quietly.

The old man's hand froze around the grip of the
pistol. Then slowly he opened his fingers again and
pulled them back. His hand dropped into his lap on
top of the book he'd been reading. Looking back
to the Executioner, a smile spread across his face
that surprised Bolan.

"Well, you obviously have the drop on me,"
Fred Bailey said. "So I guess you call the shots."
He paused, then glanced toward a coffee mug next
to the pistol on the lamp stand. "Would you care
for a cup of decaffeinated? I was just about to get
some more myself."

Texas

LYONS DROVE quietly in the early-morning hours
north of San Antonio, the road dotted with sporadic
traffic. The Able Team leader kept just under the
speed limit; not fast enough to be stopped for
speeding, not slow enough to give the appearance
of being an overly careful drunk.

Cube rode shotgun in the Suburban, sweating
like a pig in the tropics beneath his rancher's hat.
Periodically the Alamo owner would grab the brim
and remove his headgear, dab at the balding crown
of his head with a soaked handkerchief, then place

the hat back on his head. The fat man did it so often Lyons couldn't figure out why he didn't just leave the hat off.

"You guys seem to know what you're doing," Cube said.

Lyons nodded. "These aren't the first bodies we've made disappear."

"You've taken others up here? Wherever it is we're going tonight?" Cube asked. He was still nervous, but had come out of the shock he'd experienced earlier.

"A few."

"And they were never found, right?" Cube said, his tone of voice encouraging an affirmative answer. "Nobody ever found them?"

"No, Cube," Lyons said in a bored tone, letting the words slide over his teeth with his breath. "Nobody ever found them."

Lyons glanced into the rearview mirror. A quarter mile back, he could see the headlights of Cube's van. Blancanales was behind the wheel, with Schwarz in the passenger's seat. The Able Team men would have let the blacksuits out of the trash cans for a breath of fresh air as soon as Cube had gotten into the Suburban, and were probably helping their Stony Man brothers back into the metal containers about now.

A long gentle curve appeared in the road ahead, then a green road sign announced Canyon Lake in ten miles. Lyons drove in silence, finally saying,

"So. You think when this little party is over you'll be able to trust us, Cube?"

"Son of a bitch, after all this, if I can't trust you, who the hell can I trust?"

"Good. Because we can help you Cube. Whatever action you've got going, we're the men for it."

"I believe it," Cube said. "I believe it."

The two men lapsed into silence. A few minutes later, a sign announcing a camping area appeared. Lyons guided the Suburban past it, then past another sign that pointed toward the boat dock. He maintained his speed for another two miles, slowing when he saw the side road ahead on the other side of the pavement that followed the lake.

The Able Team leader killed his lights as he turned off the highway and bumped the Suburban over a cattle guard. Behind him, he saw Blancanales douse the van's headlights. Both vehicles drove on in the moonlight, following the grassy path that led through pastureland. They topped a hill, then descended into a valley.

At the bottom of the valley, Lyons could see the moon reflecting off the pond as clearly as if it were a mirror. He slowed further, bumping down the rocky track that led almost to the edge of the water. When he came to the end of the road, he pulled off to the side, killed the Suburban's engine and said, "Okay, get out."

Lyons and Cube stood to the side of the road as Blancanales pulled up, turned the van and backed

PLAY TIC-TAC-TOE

OR FREE BOOKS AND A GREAT FREE GIFT!

Use this sticker to **PLAY TIC-TAC-TOE.** See instructions inside!

THERE'S NO COST ✦ NO OBLIGATION!

Get **2** books and a fabulous mystery gift! **ABSOLUTELY FREE!**

Turn the page to play!

Play TIC-TAC-TOE and get FREE GIFTS!

HOW TO PLAY:

1. Play the tic-tac-toe scratch-off game at the right for your FREE BOOKS and FREE GIFT!

2. Send back the card and you'll get hot-off-the-press Gold Eagle books, never before published! These books have a cover price of $4.99 each, but they are yours to keep absolutely free.

3. There's no catch. You're under no obligation to buy anything. We charge nothing — ZERO — for your first shipment. And you don't have to make any minimum number of purchases — not even one!

4. The fact is, thousands of readers enjoy receiving books by mail from the Gold Eagle Reader Service™ before they're available in stores. They like the convenience of home delivery, and they love our discount prices!

5. We hope that after receiving your free books you'll want to remain a subscriber. But the choice is yours — to continue or cancel, any time at all! So why not take us up on our invitation, with no risk of any kind. You'll be glad you did!

YOURS FREE A FABULOUS MYSTERY GIFT!

We can't tell you what it is… but we're sure you'll like it!

A FREE GIFT —

just for playing

TIC-TAC-TOE!

NO COST! NO OBLIGATION TO BUY!
NO PURCHASE NECESSARY!

First, scratch the gold boxes on the tic-tac-toe board. Then remove the "X" sticker from the front and affix it so that you get three X's in a row. This means you can get **TWO FREE** Gold Eagle books and a **FREE MYSTERY GIFT!**

PLAY TIC-TAC-TOE

YES! Please send me all the gifts for which I qualify. I understand that I am under no obligation to purchase any books, as explained on the back of this card.

(U-M-B-10/98)

164 ADL CJAH

Name

(PLEASE PRINT CLEARLY)

Address _____ Apt.#

City _____ State _____ Zip

Offer limited to one per household and not valid to current subscribers.
All orders subject to approval.
© 1997 GOLD EAGLE

PRINTED IN U.S.A.

DETACH AND MAIL CARD TODAY!

The Gold Eagle Reader Service: Here's how it works:

Accepting free books places you under no obligation to buy anything. You may keep the books and gift and return the shipping statement marked "cancel." If you do not cancel, about a month later we'll send you four additional novels, and bill you just $16.80 — that's a savings of 15% off the cover price of all four books!* And there's no extra charge for shipping! You may cancel at any time, but if you choose to continue, then every other month we'll send you four more books, which you may either purchase at the discount price...or return to us and cancel your subscription.

*Terms and prices subject to change without notice. Sales tax applicable in N.Y.

If offer card is missing, write to: Gold Eagle Reader Service, 3010 Walden Ave., P.O. Box 1867, Buffalo NY 14240-1867

BUSINESS REPLY MAIL

FIRST-CLASS MAIL   PERMIT NO. 717   BUFFALO, NY

POSTAGE WILL BE PAID BY ADDRESSEE

GOLD EAGLE READER SERVICE
3010 WALDEN AVE
PO BOX 1867
BUFFALO NY 14240-9952

NO POSTAGE
NECESSARY
IF MAILED
IN THE
UNITED STATES

it toward the water. Blancanales and Schwarz jumped from the vehicle and opened the rear doors. All of the men except Cube began to unload the trash cans.

"Gather up some rocks to weigh them down," Lyons ordered as he began lifting the lids from each can. He looked into each receptacle as he opened it, seeing the still form of a Stony Man Farm black-suit. Blancanales and Schwarz dropped heavy rocks into each of the cans, then Lyons replaced the lids and began securing them with duct tape.

Frogs croaked along the shore of the pond and crickets clicked their nighttime chants. Somewhere in the distance, a coyote howled, adding to the ghostly mood.

The sounds however, seemed to have calmed Cube. Or maybe he had just finally had time to put it all into perspective. "Yeah," he said to no one in particular, "you guys have done this shit before. I can tell."

When he got no answer, he said, "Who you worked for before? The Mob?"

Lyons and Schwarz began to roll the cans toward the stony edge of the pond. According to the Intel Kurtzman's computer had come up with about the pond, there was a fifteen-foot drop directly over the side of the rock shelf at the end of the road. Lyons hoped he was correct. It was going to be obvious to Cube that they *hadn't* done this before if the first trash can hit bottom a foot beneath the surface.

With a deep breath, Lyons and Schwarz rolled the can over the edge and watched it hit the water. It submerged for a moment, then popped back to the surface, floating briefly as water seeped into the nooks, crannies and flaws in the metal. Then, slowly, it began to sink until the moon reflecting off the steel disappeared altogether.

The Able Team leader breathed a sigh of relief as he and Schwarz rolled the rest of the cans over the edge. He stood, stretched his back and turned to Cube. "By the time the containers work open the men inside will be in parts," he said. "Fish-bite-sized parts. You and the world have seen the last of these guys, Cube."

Cube pulled his hat from his head and used his handkerchief again. "Damned if I don't believe you. Like I said, you've done all this a time or two before. But you never did answer me. You guys worked for the Mafia, didn't you?"

Blancanales chuckled as the four men walked back to the van and Suburban. "Cube, you don't want to know about that," he said. "It would just cause you problems you don't need."

Cube stood in awe under the moon.

The van bumped back out of the valley and toward the highway with Lyons and Cube behind it in the Suburban. Lyons had noticed again the tinge of uneasiness in Blancanales's voice as he'd spoken. He was worried about the men in the trash cans.

Well, Lyons thought as he followed the van off the road and back onto the highway, so was he. But it was all part of the game. Anyone associated with Stony Man Farm had to be ready to accept all risks of the job.

The Able Team leader couldn't resist a glance over his shoulder as he straightened the steering wheel. He didn't know how long the air in the trash cans would last; it couldn't be long. But that didn't matter, really. Long before the oxygen supply was exhausted, the containers would fill with water, drowning the blacksuits.

Lyons stepped on the accelerator. He, Schwarz and Blancanales had done all they could do.

From here on in, the fate of the blacksuits was in other hands.

THE CHOPPER LANDED in the pasture, staying on the ground only long enough for the six men to drop and unload their gear. Then, without further ado or formalities, it rose into the sky once more.

Leo Turrin, grabbed the heavy canvas bag and slung the thick strap across his shoulder. "Let's go," he said to the other five men, and turned away. Turrin's mind raced as he hurried across the pasture. He glanced up at the full moonlit sky and twinkling stars, silently praying that God was paying attention.

Considering what Carl Lyons had set up earlier

in the day, the men of Stony Man Farm would need all the help they could get this night.

Turrin lugged the heavy bag around cactus and over tumbleweeds, wishing for a moment that he had Calvin James and Rafael Encizo of Phoenix Force with him. James was a former Navy SEAL and as good in the water as anyone Turrin had ever seen. Encizo, an expert in underwater operations himself, hadn't been given the nickname Pescado, or "Fish," for nothing.

The Stony Man operative glanced back over his shoulder at the five men with him. These men would be okay, he told himself. Four were blacksuit trainees rather than Stony Man regulars, but each had come to the Farm already boasting extensive scuba experience. The fifth was Yakov Katzenelenbogen, David McCarter's predecessor as leader of Phoenix Force. Now semiretired from the field in his role as mission adviser, the aging Israeli had insisted on being part of Turrin's mission due to its sensitivity.

Katzenelenbogen, or simply Katz as he was called by the Stony Man personnel, had only recently turned over the reins of Phoenix Force to McCarter. Time ignored no man, and even though the seasoned warrior had taken the less physically demanding consultant's position, he was still in better shape and sharper of mind than many men half his age.

Turrin glanced over his shoulder and saw Katz

jogging along with the others, his gait showing no signs of his advanced age. Turrin could think of few men he'd rather have with him when the going got tough.

Reaching the edge of the valley, Turrin stopped. Below, he could see the pond. The shoreline nearest him was a mixture of sand and dirt. Across the pond, on the other side, he could easily see the rocky ledge and the rough road leading away from it.

He frowned. The ledge was longer than it had seemed on the graphic map Kurtzman had called up on his computer monitor earlier that evening. It wouldn't have hurt to bring a couple more divers to completely cover the area. Still, the road from the pasture on the other side of the pond led almost directly to the center of the ledge. If he centered his men on that, then spread them out along the rocks, they should have no trouble.

Katz moved in to join Turrin at the edge of the valley. The former Phoenix Force leader frowned, and Turrin could see he was thinking the same thing. "You and I better take the flanks," the Israeli said. "I'd put Schaeffer in the middle and Taylor and Riel on either side."

"That's why they pay you," Turrin said.

Katz turned to him, his frown of concern becoming one of bewilderment.

"To advise, Katz. To advise. And I'll damn sure take that advice."

The two Stony Man operatives led the way down the hill to the pond, stopping at the shoreline and unloading their equipment. The blacksuits did the same, then all of the men took their scuba bags back out onto the prairie, hiding them in the darkness.

Returning to the shoreline, they began to suit up. Turrin slipped into his black wet suit and began hooking up hoses and other devices. "I want everybody double-checking his regulators," he said. "Both regulators. Seconds are going to count...no, split seconds are going to count on this op. We can't afford any foul-up." He slid into his fins and clipped the depth gauge and other monitors to the belt of his buoyancy vest before attaching the air tank. Leaning over, he twisted the valve at the top of the tank and stuck the primary regulator into his mouth.

Pure oxygen, rather than the usual compressed air, flowed smoothly into his lungs as he drew in a breath. Turrin reminded himself to go easy. The oxygen was necessary—it would prevent telltale bubbles from rising to the surface. But it could cause problems if the diver forgot what he was dealing with.

Turning his attention to the orange hose also attached to the tank, he ran his fingers along the length checking for any flaws. Except for the color, his second regulator was identical to the one he had just tested. Sometimes called "octopuses," such devices were usually carried as backup or emergency mechanisms in the event that another diver had problems. They were rarely used.

This night there was no maybe about it. The octopus would definitely see use. Turrin checked it with the same keen eye he had used on his primary unit. He was happy to see it was functioning just as well.

He and the other men waded into the water carrying their tanks and buoyancy units. When they were deep enough to float the devices on the water, they slid into the vests and finished hooking up. Turrin pulled the mask over his face. "Schaeffer," he said, turning to a tall lanky man. "I want you in the middle, right where the road intersects the ledge. Taylor, to Schaeffer's right. Riel, you go to his left." He paused as the three blacksuits nodded. "Katz and I will take the flanks." He paused once more to take the last breath of natural air he'd be taking for a while. "Once we submerge, go to the bottom and spread out the length of the ledge. We don't want to lose any of these boys, so keep your eyes open."

Five heads nodded their understanding.

Turrin stuck the regulator in his mouth and tapped the control to his buoyancy unit until he floated easily on top of the water. He swam across the surface toward the rocky ledge, watching the road until it disappeared overhead behind the overhang. When he had reached the rock wall, he grasped onto a small outcropping for stability, then waited for the others to take up their positions.

From here on, Turrin knew he would be able to see nothing above him. But in the quiet Texas night, he would be able to hear Lyons and the others approach, even over the clamor of the frogs and crickets.

Thirty minutes had passed before Turrin heard the Suburban come down the road into the valley. What sounded like a Chevy engine was right behind it, and the Stony Man operative guessed it to be some model of van or panel truck Able Team had acquired to transport the trash cans. He turned down the line of men at his side and whispered, "Everybody down," then watched as the five other divers submerged beneath the surface.

Turrin made sure the other men were invisible before tapping the control to his buoyancy unit again, this time bleeding air from his vest. He descended to the muddy floor of the pond and tried to remain motionless as mud and silt floated up around his fins. Visibility in the pond was bad already; he couldn't even see Taylor who he knew had to be less than ten feet away. He lifted his hand in front of his face. He could see only a shadowy spider-shaped outline.

Turrin waited, hearing semidistinguishable sounds through the water above him; what sounded like vehicle doors slamming shut, voices, metal scraping against rock. Finally a splash sounded somewhere down the line of divers. Then another splash came, closer by.

Good. Though they hadn't discussed it, Lyons had guessed that he, Katz and the other divers would spread out along the ledge. And the Able Team leader was dropping the trash cans accordingly, making sure each container fell far enough away from the last that there would be room for them to maneuver.

Another splash sounded, and the water rippled toward him from only a few feet away. A few seconds later, Turrin felt something hit the water directly above his head. He looked up to see a dark oblong object descending on top of him.

Turrin moved slightly to one side, letting the trash can descend to the bottom on its side. He righted it, then reached down to his left calf and drew the stainless-steel dive knife from the rubber sheath. Slicing through the duct tape at the top, he used the blunt tip of the blade to pry the lid off, then reached in and pulled the blacksuit-clad body from inside.

The Stony Man operative shoved the octopus into the blacksuit's mouth with one hand, holding on to the trash can with the other. The blacksuit breathed in and out, then lifted his hand in front of Turrin's face. Making the universal diver's okay sign with his thumb and index finger, he nodded.

Turrin made sure the trash can had filled with water and wouldn't float back to the surface before hooking a thumb down the line. Nodding again, the blacksuit swam along at his side, both men linked to the same tank like conjoined twins with one set of lungs. Turrin came to where Taylor and another blacksuit were waiting, nodded and moved on. Schaeffer and Riel had teamed up to get the third man out safely, and Turrin and his man gave them the okay as they passed.

Above, through the water, the men below the surface heard vehicle engines start up.

The undercover man and his blacksuit partner swam on, looking for Katz and the final trash can. They had gone twenty feet when Turrin realized he had to have somehow missed them.

Something was wrong. He didn't know what. But something.

Grabbing his blacksuit swim partner by the arm, Turrin pulled the man's face close to him. By now, the Suburban and whatever other vehicle Able Team had arrived in should be gone. It would be safe for him and the other men who had been in the cans to surface.

Turrin pushed his hand close to the blacksuit's face, his index finger pointing up. The blacksuit nodded as he took a last breath of oxygen from the octopus, then dropped the regulator from his mouth and started toward the surface.

Clipping the octopus to his side again, Turrin started back through the water. He bumped into Riel and Schaeffer, a blacksuit breathing from

Riel's orange backup. Sending the blacksuit to the surface, the mission leader jerked a small plastic pad from his belt and wrote on it with a waterproof pen.

Katz and last can?

He drew the dive light from his side, aimed the beam onto the words and shoved the pad toward the men.

The two blacksuits held both hands out, palms up.

Turrin's hands shot out, his finger's apart, silently ordering the men to spread out and search. He moved back along the ledge, frantically trying to pick up any clue as to where Katz and the last man might be. He reversed direction twice, then finally moved ten feet out from the rock wall and began swimming back and forth.

The tiniest trickle of current caught the side of Turrin's neck, and he turned toward it. It could be anything—water moving around a boulder at the bottom, a large fish swimming a few feet away. But it was the only clue he had so far, and instinctively he swam toward it.

The mission leader bumped into Katz before he saw him. Moving back, he saw the Israeli frantically trying to pry open the lid of the last trash can. Somehow, the can had drifted much farther from shore than any of them could have guessed. Maybe it had hit something and rolled—maybe even one of the other cans. Whatever it was, it mattered little now. What did matter was that Turrin could see Katz had already cut the tape but the lid was still sealed. Somehow, a vacuum had formed, welding the lid to the can and creating what in seconds would become a corrugated underwater coffin for the blacksuit inside.

Turrin got Katz's attention and held out his buoyancy control for the Israeli to see. He pointed toward the surface, indicating that they should grab the can and inflate their vests, hauling the man to the top.

Katz shook his head, drawing his own hand across his throat, indicating the blacksuit didn't have enough air to make it. Even on the surface, the can would be filled with water. The man inside would drown while resting on dry land.

Turrin nodded, knowing the Israeli was right. They were dealing with seconds, now. If the man inside the can hadn't already drowned, he would soon. They had to get him out and get the regulator into his mouth *now*.

Turrin and Katz had the same idea at the same time. Drawing their knives, they thrust them into the can just under the lid and used the sawbacks to begin opening the top. Halfway around, Turrin saw the blacksuit's face. His eyes were closed. The mission leader jammed his octopus through the hole.

The blacksuit didn't respond.

Both men sawed furiously on, finally opening the hole enough to drag the blacksuit out. Katz reached out, opening the man's mouth and shoving his orange-hosed regulator between the parted lips. Turrin pushed on the man's chest, attempting to force him to breathe as they inflated their vests and shot upward through the water.

Reaching the surface, Turrin and Katz towed the man to the ledge where the other blacksuits hauled him up onto the rock. By the time the two Stony Man operatives had slipped out of their tanks and crawled up to join the party, Taylor and Riel were performing CPR.

A few moments later, the blacksuit opened his eyes. First he coughed. Then rolling to his side, he threw up a mixture of half-digested food and pond water onto the rocky ground. He'd live.

CHAPTER NINE

Washington, D.C.

Gary Manning was bored, which had made the Phoenix Force commando's brain kick into full alert. As a seasoned warrior, he knew that boredom was a perilous state of mind. It could lull a man into distracted thinking to alleviate the monotony. It also encouraged digression, lethargy and passivity. Boredom could lure a man into the oblivious state of mind known as the white zone in which he missed subtle signs of danger around him.

Indirectly, boredom could kill a man as quickly and surely as a shotgun blast to the face or a dagger to the heart.

Manning glanced to his right and saw Rafael Encizo. The little Cuban member of Phoenix Force leaned against the wall on the other side of the door leading into the Oval Office's reception area. Manning knew Encizo had to be as tired of this tedious baby-sitting job as he was. The shorter man's eyes kept darting up and down the hallway, himself fighting the invisible enemy named listlessness.

Manning's eyes followed his partner's gaze down the hall, letting them fall on the uniformed Secret Service agents up and down the passageway. Many of these men had given into the temptation to divert their attention. Some were chatting in low voices that, regardless of volume, drifted down the hall in the late-night silence of the White House. Two others had pulled paperback books from secret hiding places and were whiling away the midnight hours reading. One guard sat in a wooden chair at the table near the metal detector, his SIG-Sauer in pieces before him as he ran the white patch at the end of a metal cleaning rod in and out of the weapon's barrel.

Manning glanced over his shoulder at the closed door to the reception area. The President had decided to work late into the night, saying he needed to catch up on the reading of some upcoming Senate bills. So they, too, were working late.

Encizo turned to look at Manning. The Cuban shook his head. "You get the feeling we're the only ones still awake?" he whispered, nodding at the uniformed men farther down the hall.

Manning chuckled but didn't answer. As the chuckle faded, a frown replaced the wry grin that had accompanied it. He wondered if he should report the unprofessional behavior of the men in the hall, and the question posed a moral dilemma.

While they weren't on full alert, it still bothered him to think that these men were taking the job of protecting the President of the United States so lightly. On the other hand, no soldier, least of all Gary Manning, liked snitching on his comrades in arms.

Encizo interrupted Manning's thoughts again, saying, "Hey, Gary? I been thinking."

The barrel-chested Canadian turned to his partner once more and grinned. "Make your head hurt?"

Encizo's return smirk was his only answer. He went on. "What I meant," he said, "is maybe this is good training. Maybe we should change careers. Become security guards."

Manning nodded solemnly, adding to the parody routine, "Maybe that's not such a bad idea. Pinkerton's, you think? We could guard hospitals, shopping malls...." His voice trailed off.

Encizo's face turned to serious now, too. "You think too small," he said. "I was thinking more along the lines of our own company."

"Manning and Encizo Security, Inc.?" Manning asked.

"No, Encizo and Manning."

"I can see we'll have to compromise," Manning said. "How about Phoenix Force Security?"

Encizo shook his head and tsk-tsked his partner, making the clicking sound parents employ to scold small children. "Again, you're thinking too small. We might want to hire away some of the guys from

Able Team. How about Stony Man Rent-a-Cops, Ltd. It has a nice ring.''

''I like it. From hospitals and all that we could branch into the big time. Roving patrols in broken-down jalopies that check the lots of car dealerships, rattle the doors of businesses—''

''Don't forget the personal protection end of things,'' Encizo said. ''Plenty of wealthy paranoids these days think they need bodyguards.''

The banter was broken suddenly as the bell on the elevator at the end of the hall rang. Both Phoenix Force commandos looked down the passageway as the doors rolled open. Another uniformed Secret Service agent hurried out of the car and passed through the metal detector, his gun and other equipment setting the sensors buzzing. Manning recognized the gray-haired supervisor Brognola had called ''Henry'' earlier in the day. The Canadian stepped in front of the door to the reception area before the Secret Service agent could enter. ''We have orders not to let anyone disturb the President,'' he said.

Henry stopped abruptly. ''I've got an important message for—''

After the way they had been treated that morning, Manning couldn't resist. Grabbing the man by the shoulders, he spun him around and pushed him into the wall next to the door.

''Wha—'' Henry choked out.

Manning drew the man's side arm from his holster and jammed it into his belt. He ran his hands up and down Henry's ribs, around his Sam Browne belt, then down his legs. He found a .357 snub-nosed Ruger in an ankle holster and jerked it from Henry's leg.

It had all taken place too fast for the Secret Service agent to react. But now, as Manning stepped back, Henry spun violently around. "You son of a bitch!" he said. "What the hell do you think you're doing?"

"Can't be too careful." Manning smiled. "Especially after what happened this afternoon."

"Don't be such an asshole," Henry said through clenched teeth. "Where do you think I got this uniform?"

"Blauer?" Encizo said innocently. "Hatch?" Both were well-known manufacturers of police supplies.

Manning pulled Henry's SIG-Sauer from his belt and extended it and the Ruger butt-first. "Just thought it might do you some good to learn how it feels to be treated like a second-class cop," he said. He stepped past the angry uniformed man and knocked on the door.

"You're both bastards," Henry said, snatching back his guns from Manning and replacing them in their respective holsters. His face softened. "But your point is taken."

George, Howard and William had been occupying the reception area, creating yet another layer of defense between the President and whatever evil he thought was trying to get him. William answered the door, with a face like milk gone sour. "Yeah?" he said.

Manning hooked a thumb toward Henry. "Says he's got an important message for the President," he said.

William stepped back. Henry entered the reception area followed by Manning and Encizo. William eyed the uniformed man up and down as if he were appraising some inferior life-form. "What is it, Henry?"

"I was sent to give the President some news," Henry said. He was still slightly ruffled by Manning's surprise search.

"So tell me what it is. I'm the one who decides if it's worth disturbing him."

Henry took a deep breath. "There's been another fire-bombing," he said. "Big one. Hospital."

William frowned, his face telling Manning he was debating whether the news warranted a disturbance. Evidently it did. William walked to the door of the Oval Office and knocked lightly.

"What is it?"

"Sorry to bother you, Mr. President, but there's something of which you should be aware."

The President opened the door. "What is it?"

Henry repeated what he had told William and the President's face turned grayish. He stepped back, motioning for the men in the reception area to enter, then crossed the room to the large-screen television mounted in the wall.

The scene that appeared as the screen lit up was one of total carnage. Flames still shot from the top of the Baptist Hospital. Multicolored smoke filled the air surrounding the structure. Fire trucks surrounded the building with antlike men in fire-resistent suits climbing ladders and running in and out of the building's ground floor. Horns honked, machinery ground and screams added to the chaos.

"The bomb, which detonated at approximately 10:14 this evening, emitted a near-white illumination that temporarily blinded several nearby witnesses," the voice of an unseen newscaster said. "Fire officials state they have already lost two men to the blaze. The number of patient deaths is so far unknown."

The men in the Oval Office watched in disbelief as the scene progressed. "My God," the President said quietly. "What next?"

As if to answer his question directly, the television camera suddenly zoomed in to a window on the eighth floor of the hospital. A blurry figure behind the glass was beating on the pane with a white shoe. The smoke around the woman made it almost impossible to make out her features, but Manning could see that she wore a nurse's uniform. Behind her, red-and-orange flames flickered through the smoke, growing ever closer to the window.

Unable to break the glass, the nurse disappeared

into the smoke, returning a moment later with a metal chair. She raised the chair overhead with the strength of the adrenaline rush in her veins.

Manning heard Enzico beside him. "No," the other Phoenix Force man said softly. "Don't..."

Enzico had been an insurance investigator in the past, and while he had specialized in maritime claims, many had involved fire. The Cuban knew and understood this faceless enemy better than anyone else on Phoenix Force.

"Don't do it..." Enzico breathed again.

Manning had no time to wonder what he meant. The nurse slammed the chair through the window and the glass shattered. For a moment, she stood in front of the opening, a smile of relief on her face. Then the smile became a mask of shock and torture as flames engulfed her body.

Manning didn't have to ask what had happened. The sudden opening in the window had sucked new oxygen into the room, feeding the fire behind the nurse and drawing the flames around her.

A sick feeling filled Manning's gut as he helplessly watched the woman clumsily crawl out onto the ledge of the window.

A second later she was plummeting to her death on the sidewalk below, a trail of flame and smoke following her like some eight-story tail.

Fort Wayne, Indiana

THE DRIZZLE that had started while the Executioner was still outside the house suddenly evolved into a powerful torrent, pattering down on the roof and skylight of Fred Bailey's den. Bolan stared at the man in the reclining chair. The book Bailey had been reading was still open in his lap.

The surprise on Bailey's face had faded as his hand inched away from the pistol on the lamp stand. In its place, a friendly smile had etched itself into the man's lips and eyes. He repeated his question. "Would you like some coffee?"

Bolan didn't know what kind of man he'd expected to find secluded behind the fence and walls of the large estate. But whatever it had been, it wasn't what he saw before him now.

"No," the Executioner said. "I don't want any coffee."

Bailey shrugged as Bolan crossed the room, lifting the Heckler & Koch USP from the lamp stand. He shoved it into his belt next to the guard's .357, and saw Bailey's eyes follow the movement.

"I see you've already met Mike," the man in the chair said.

Bolan glanced down at the two pistols and nodded.

"Is he all right?" Bailey asked, his face frowning in concern.

"He'll wake up in the morning," the Executioner said. "He'll need a splint on his trigger finger but other than that, he'll be fine." He paused, then added, "So will your dogs."

The pleasant smile returned to Bailey's face. "Good." He took a deep breath, then said, "So, since you didn't come for my coffee, how else can I help you Mr....?" The sentence trailed off in a double question.

"Belasko will do if you want to call me something," Bolan said.

"Well," he said, "that beats Smith or Jones now, doesn't it? So, Mr. Belasko, what can I do for you?"

Bolan's eyes fell to the afghan covering Bailey's legs. For all he knew, the man might have another weapon hidden beneath it. That might explain the unusual friendly attitude he was exhibiting to a stranger who had obviously injured one of his men, broken into his home, and now held him at gunpoint.

"You can toss the afghan on the floor and stand," Bolan said. "Slowly."

Bailey lifted the book from his lap with one hand, throwing back the afghan with the other. He let the knitted blanket fall to the floor, then grasped the arm of the chair and chuckled amiably. "I'm glad you said slowly," he said, using his free hand to help drag himself to his feet. "I'm afraid that's the only way I can manage standing at all at my age."

The Executioner stepped forward. Bailey wore a plaid flannel bathrobe so ragged that loose threads dangled from the cuffs and collar. The pajama legs that extended beneath the robe were equally worn, and seemed incongruous with the obvious wealth the estate bespoke.

Bolan kept the Desert Eagle trained on Bailey as he took the book from the man's hand. He tucked the thick hardback under his arm and patted down the bathrobe, finding no evidence of other weapons. "Okay," he said. "Sit back down."

"Thank you, I will," Bailey said as the Executioner holstered the Desert Eagle. The leader of the Indiana Militia nodded toward a small study hutch built into the wall of the den. "Pull up a chair for yourself."

Bolan kept one eye on the man in the recliner as he crossed the room. He glanced down at the book Bailey had been reading as he set it on the work surface of the hutch and pulled out the chair. It was entitled *Unintended Consequences,* and had been written by a St. Louis investment broker named John Ross.

Bailey caught the Executioner's gaze. "You're familiar with Mr. Ross's work?" he asked.

Bolan nodded as he dragged the chair in front of Bailey's recliner. *Unintended Consequences* had become something of a cult classic among members of America's gun culture. Much in the same vein as Ayn Rand's *Atlas Shrugged,* it forewarned of a time when Americans might finally scream "Enough!" to government restrictions and use armed violence to restore the freedoms they once had.

"And you've read it?" Bailey asked, his face brightening.

Bolan nodded again. He had perused the text during downtime at the Farm. The story ended with otherwise honorable citizens assassinating federal agents from the Bureau of Alcohol, Tobacco and Firearms, the Internal Revenue Service and other federal agencies that had abused their powers. The book's message, contrary to what gun-control supporters would lead one to believe, was not to advocate or defend violent actions, but to warn that such occurrences were inevitable if the federal government didn't back off.

"So what did you think of it, Mr. Belasko?" Bailey asked.

"I hope Mr. Ross is wrong," the Executioner said. "I hope things never come to that."

"So do I," Bailey said, dropping his eyes and shaking his head wearily. "Every sane man does. It would hardly be the romantic adventure that some morons seem to think. Martial law would be imposed. The federal government would turn an even blinder eye to the murder of dissenters by federal agents. They would sanction searches without warrant…" He looked up suddenly. "But I'm sure you didn't go to all this trouble to discuss Mr. Ross's book any more than you came here for a cup of coffee. So I will ask you again, Mr. Belasko. Just how *can* I help you?''

Bolan's gaze circled the room, taking in the collection of antique firearms, swords, spears and other primitive weapons that decorated the walls before returning to Fred Bailey. He tried to stare past the man's eyes and into Bailey's brain. The man's incongruities went far deeper than a worn-out bathrobe inside a multimillion-dollar house. Bolan had been led to believe by the dying New Breedman that Bailey was the leader of a similar right-wing terrorist group. Yet what the Executioner saw before him now appeared to be the antithesis of the witless, bigoted beer-guzzlers he had just left in Michigan. Bailey was obviously intelligent and not prone to thoughtless response; he had proved that when he halted his lunge for the pistol on the nightstand, and had seemed to immediately sense that Bolan wasn't there to kill him unless he provoked such action.

The Indiana Militia leader had been the archetype of courtesy ever since, and the Executioner didn't sense that fear had been the catalyst for his good manners.

Bolan's eyes narrowed. ''I want to know exactly what you and the Indiana Militia have to do with the fire-bombings going on around the country,'' he said.

Bailey's smile widened. ''How rare it is to be asked a question so easily answered,'' he said.

"The answer is nothing. We have nothing to do with them, Mr. Belasko. We are not responsible for such actions in any way, shape or form, nor would we ever condone them."

"But you know who is responsible?" the Executioner asked.

"Ah." Bailey smiled. "Another easy question. No."

Bolan paused. He wasn't sure why—maybe it was Bailey's tone of voice, or pleasant demeanor or body language—but the Executioner believed the man in the reclining chair. Nevertheless, he pushed on. "That's not what I was told," he said.

"I'm not surprised." Bailey started to reach toward the lamp table again. His hand stopped halfway there and he looked back to Bolan. "Do you mind?" he asked, indicating a pipe and jar of tobacco with a sideways dip of his head.

Bolan shook his head.

Bailey opened the jar and began to stuff the pipe's bowl with tobacco. "The newspapers, the TV networks, all are conspiring with the federal government to take away what few liberties remain for the individual in this country, Mr. Belasko. As part of that conspiracy, they are doing their best to portray me, the Indiana Militia and similar groups of patriots as dangerous right-wing lunatics." He rolled the wheel of a marble lighter with his thumb and held the flame over the pipe bowl as his cheeks puffed in and out.

"I didn't get my intelligence from the newspapers," Bolan said. "I got it from one of your own kind."

An expression of genuine shock fell over Fred Bailey's face. "Who, may I ask?" he said.

"I didn't catch his name before I killed him," Bolan said. "He was a New Breedman."

The shocked look was now replaced with the first sign of anger the Executioner had seen since entering Bailey's den. "The New Breedmen are *not* 'our own,' as you so eloquently put it, Mr. Belasko. They are a bunch of uneducated, racially prejudiced, dim-witted cretins who aren't associated with me or the Indiana Militia. In fact they are the fools I had in mind earlier when I said that some morons believe the portrait of what may come painted by John Ross in *Unintended Consequences* would be fun."

"Then why did the man give me your name?" Bolan asked.

Bailey stared the Executioner in the eye. "You say he was dying?"

"I'd shot him, yes."

"Well," Bailey said, "it wouldn't be the first time a dying man lied. Some men use their last breaths to clear their consciences, Mr. Belasko." He paused. "Others take advantage of the supposed validity a dying declaration suggests to take a final stab at their enemies."

Bolan sat back in his chair. "The New Breedmen are your enemies?" he asked.

"Not officially," Bailey said, puffing on his pipe. "But they tried several times to align with us. Perform joint training exercises and the like. I wanted nothing to do with them." His pipe had gone out, and he stopped talking long enough to relight it. "The Indiana Militia isn't a racially bigoted organization. We have members of all races, classes, religions, creeds...what have you. Nor are we trying to overthrow the government of the United States as the press would like you to believe. We simply believe that the federal government runs more of the individual's life than they should. We want to return to the days when Americans were citizens, not subjects."

Bolan glanced at the walls surrounding him again. "Nice collection of primitive weapons," he said. "But I'm sure you have more modern firepower at your fingertips, too."

Bailey didn't hesitate. "Of course," he said. "AK-47s, M-16s, you name it." Now, he paused. "And every last one is legal. All full-autos have the appropriate tax stamps. Regardless of how silly, no, make that immoral, I believe such government impositions to be, I still comply with the law of my country, Mr. Belasko. You are welcome to search the house if you don't believe me. The key to the gun safes upstairs are in that drawer." He nodded toward the hutch again.

Bolan ignored the invitation. "You comply with the law," he said. "But you'd like to change it?"

"You're damn right I would. And so would many other patriotic Americans who love their country but don't trust their government anymore."

All of the Executioner's senses told him that Fred Bailey was an honorable man. Still, he was skeptical. "You mentioned that New Breed wanted to join you in training. What kind of training are we talking about?"

Bailey opened his mouth to answer when the door behind Bolan suddenly burst open. "Don't move!" a gravelly voice commanded.

The Executioner turned slowly to see three men enter the room and spread out along the walls. Each was dressed similarly to the guard Bolan had left unconscious outside the house. Two carried British Sterling submachine guns. The third sported a 12-gauge Winchester pump shotgun.

Bolan suddenly understood why Bailey had appeared so relaxed. A silent alarm had been tripped when he'd entered the house, and the Indiana Militia leader had known it was only a matter of time before his security personnel would come to save him.

But Bailey had more surprises in store. "Joe," he said, "your response time was admirable and will be duly noted. But this isn't necessary. Mr. Belasko and I are having a very pleasant discussion."

"But Mr. Bailey—" one of the men started to say.

Bailey waved a hand, indicating that the men should leave. "Mr. Belasko simply has an unusual way of entering a house to visit," he said. "Now, if you'll excuse us please…"

The three men left, closing the door behind them.

Bolan looked back to Bailey. "Why did you do that?" he asked. "How do you know I don't plan to kill you? You don't even know who I am."

Bailey shrugged as he lit his pipe again. "Call it intuition if you like," he mouthed around the stem. "But I don't believe you're from the federal government." He frowned slightly. "At least in the conventional sense." The frown disappeared. "Besides, what if you were? What would I do with you? Have you killed? I've already told you, that's not what the Indiana Militia is all about. You were asking about our training. We include firearms, of course. Close quarters combat, tactics, squad maneuvers, things of this nature." He sighed again. "It's military training, Mr. Belasko. Of which you've had your share yourself, unless these ageing eyes are missing more than I think they are." He sighed as if he had said what he was about to say many times in the past. "Military training," he repeated. "But without the far right-wing-nut spin the media adds to it."

Bolan continued to stare at the man. "What are you training for?" he asked. By now he knew what

Bailey would say. But he wanted to hear the man say it.

"In case we're needed," Bailey said. "And there are any number of reasons why we, and other groups like us, might be. Invasion by a foreign power. Civil insurrection that goes beyond what police and National Guard can handle." He paused, again meeting Bolan's stare. "Or in the unfortunate event that our own government doesn't see the error of its ways before it is too late."

"Then you can foresee a time when you might battle American troops?" the Executioner said.

"It's always possible," Bailey replied without hesitation.

"When?"

Bailey smiled sadly. "Not yet. Not now, and not in the immediate future. But I'm sorry to say I believe we are closer to a time when such unpleasant and unfortunate actions might be necessary than we have ever been before in the history of this nation."

The Executioner sat back in his chair. For several moments, neither man spoke. Then Bailey said, "Mr. Belasko, I, and others like me, fear that this nation is about to face problems the like we have not seen since the Civil War. Oh, this war will be different. There won't be blue and gray uniforms to identify the enemy. What we will see is guerrilla warfare, riots such as those in Los Angeles after the Rodney King fiasco, and the fire-bombings that concern both of us so much right now. Only the smart and prepared will survive, Mr. Belasko. I intend to be one of those."

Bolan stood. "You're right," he said and turned toward the door.

"You agree that a war is coming?" Bailey asked.

Bolan shook his head. "No. I don't know. I hope not. What I meant is that you were right about some men using their dying breaths to lie."

"My words haven't convinced you?" Bailey asked, struggling to his feet.

"No. Words never convince me. Words mean nothing. You could simply be a very good liar. But that wasn't what I meant. I believe you."

"Then what—"

"I don't know for sure why I believe you," Bolan said. "You called it intuition, I call it instinct. And that instinct suggests to me that you're on the level. I've met a lot of skilled liars in my time, Bailey. I could always be wrong, but I don't think you're one of them." He started toward the door.

Fred Bailey smiled. He shuffled across the den, stopping in front of the hutch. Opening the drawer, he produced a note pad and pen and wrote quickly on the paper.

Bailey was still smiling when he met Bolan at the door. "Thank you for listening," he said. "Few people will. Fewer still understand the differences that make the goals of groups such as mine unique from those of imbeciles such as the New Breedmen." He extended the hand that held the piece of paper. "I can understand your reluctance to accept the spoken word at face value, Mr. Belasko."

He glanced at the paper Bolan had just taken from him. "I feel the same way," Bailey said. "But if spoken words can't convince you of my sincerity, perhaps the written word will."

Texas

THE BRIGHT SOUTH Texas sun that had caused Carl Lyons to pull down the Suburban's visor became masked behind a cloud. The Able Team leader relaxed the squint that had helped shield his eyes.

Things had gone well the previous night. A quick phone call to Stony Man after they had dropped Cube at the Alamo confirmed that all of the blacksuits had been rescued from what might have become their underwater graves. And Cube himself was now convinced that the new men he had hired could be trusted. Enough, at least, that he'd sent Lyons to pick up a package at the Lone Star Brewery.

But not enough to tell the Able Team leader what was in the package or who his contact would be.

The former detective saw the brewery ahead and slowed the Suburban. He adjusted the Government Model .45 in the Bianchi bellyband rig beneath his plaid Western shirt, making sure it was in place for a quick presentation once he'd ripped open the pearl snaps that served as buttons. His hand drifted down to the cuff of his faded jeans, tapping them once to make sure the Velcro fasteners on the Kydex sheath were still secure.

The green handle of the Newt Livesay "Company" knife, originally designed for the CIA, was held upside down outside Lyons's brown cowboy boots. In this position, the Able Team leader could draw the thick, double-edged six-inch blade quickly in either a natural or reverse grip. He didn't think he'd need it or the .45 under his shirt this morning. All he was doing was making a pickup.

On the other hand, one never knew.

Lyons turned off the road onto the gravel strip that led into the brewery, coming to a halt in the parking lot. A small ticket booth stood halfway between him and the series of buildings that held the Buckhorn Museum operated by Lone Star. The museum consisted of the Hall of Horns, Hall of Feathers, Hall of Fins and various other exhibits.

Lyons's boots crunched on the gravel as he sauntered casually to the ticket booth. He dropped a ten-dollar bill on the counter and picked up his change and one of the wooden nickels that served as entry tokens. Good For One Free Beer Or Soft Drink was printed on the wood.

The Able Team leader moved into the shade under a roof between two buildings, checking his watch. He was a few minutes early, but that was okay. Cube had given Lyons an overly complex series of actions to go through that would serve to identify him to his contact. The first step was to trade in the wooden nickel for a Dr Pepper soft drink.

Lyons shook his head in disgust as he opened the door on his left and stepped into the Hall of Horns. That was only part of the little identification drama Cube had related as if he thought he were James Bond. Next, Lyons was to wait for another man who'd be wearing a tan cowboy hat to come in and get his own Dr Pepper. Then he was supposed to walk through the Hall of Horns which, according to Cube again, consisted of several rooms. He would stop at the gazelle heads mounted on the wall, directly in front of the third head from the left.

And the silliness went on and on, far past what any self-respecting intelligence officer would put anyone through. But the Able Team leader would put up with it—he had to. While Cube had proved he was definitely a small link in the chain to the bombings, he was the only link Able Team had.

Lyons had to hope that link led to a bigger link, and finally to the end of the chain. Cube had to be part of a bigger picture, a picture that featured the fire-bombings somewhere on the canvas.

Lyons stepped into the bar area that led to the Hall of Horns. Along the wall to his right was an elaborate Old-West-style bar, complete with a bartender wearing bloused shirt and sleeve garters.

"What'll you have, sidewinder?" The man asked, smiling.

The Able Team leader dropped his wooden nickel on the bar. "Dr Pepper," he said. He waited as his soft drink was drawn from a brown wooden keg, eyeing the framed pictures and other items on the walls around the room. A few mounted animals were scattered about the walls, evidently a spillover from the Hall of Horns proper.

Lyons sipped the soft drink and watched tourists come and go. A family of five—all three children too young to enjoy or even remember the outing in the years to come—drank their soft drinks and moved on. A middle-aged couple wearing shorts and multipocketed safari vests came in. The man was slightly taller than average and muscular. He wore a tan straw hat with a beaded Indian hatband. Lyons watched the couple in the mirror behind the bar. Cube had said nothing about a woman, but that didn't mean there couldn't be one involved. And while the man looked harmless, the Able Team leader didn't miss the fact that the cane he carried had a side-handle like the PR-24 police baton. It wasn't being carried as a walking aid but rather as a weapon. As was the knife clipped inside the right front pocket of the man's denim shorts.

The former LAPD detective's suspicions vanished when both the man and woman ordered beers.

Five minutes later, a short skinny man wearing jeans, a cutoff sweatshirt and a tan cowboy hat opened the door. Ignoring Lyons, he strode to the bar, asked for a Dr Pepper, and struck up a conversation with the middle-aged couple.

Lyons thanked the bartender for his drink and moved off into the Hall of Horns. In the first room he passed several mounted animals of both African and North American origin, then found the gazelles in the third row of the second room. Stopping in front of the third, he waited until he saw the tan cowboy hat appear in the doorway.

The Able Team leader's instructions sent him next to a ram in the corner of the room. Feeling the eyes of the man behind him on his back, he repeated the words Cube had told him to say. "Damn big ram." He felt like a little kid playing spy as he walked through another open door into the last room.

Lyons found the Topperwein display in the farthest corner of the room. Through the glass he saw photographs, rifles, pistols and other memorabilia. He had always held the Topperweins in high esteem, and knew that the point-shooting system for both pistol and rifle—which he used himself in combat—was a direct outgrowth of their shooting style.

Adolph and Elizabeth "Plinky" Topperwein had been the most famous husband and wife exhibition shooting team in U.S. history. Sponsored by Winchester, the couple toured the North American continent for twenty-nine years giving demonstrations, breaking shooting records and representing the Winchester Company. Plinky, Lyons remembered, earned her nickname while Ad was teaching her to shoot shortly after their marriage. "Throw up another and I'll plink it," she would often say. The term "plinking," still used to describe casual target practice, had come from her.

Lyons saw movement at his side and turned toward the man in the tan cowboy hat.

"You ever read Topperwein's book *Fast and Fancy Revolver Shooting?*" the man asked.

Lyons suppressed a sigh. It was the final stage in Cube's silly routine, and he would be relieved to get it over with. "I've read *Fast and Fancy Revolver Shooting,*" he replied, "but it was written by Ed McGivern, not Ad Topperwein."

The man in the hat glanced around nervously, then whispered, "Let's go." He turned on his heel and headed out of the Hall of Horns.

The Able Team leader followed him through the various rooms, past the bar and out the door again. The man led him to a bright green Jeep Wrangler, pulled a key ring from the pocket of his jeans and unlocked the door. With another key from the same ring he opened a lockbox bolted to the floor between the seats and removed a package roughly the size of a shoe box and wrapped in plain brown paper.

The man kept the package hidden inside the Wrangler while he took another look around the parking lot. Satisfied that no one was watching, he handed it to Lyons.

The Able Team leader frowned at it. "What is it?" he asked.

"Damned if I know," the other man said. He had already slid behind the wheel of the Jeep and was starting the engine. "All I know is I did my job and now I'm goin' to go collect my money." He threw the vehicle into gear and was gone.

Lyons memorized the license plate of the Jeep as it drove away, knowing even as he did it would be a phony. He walked back to the Suburban, started the engine and pulled out of the parking lot, guiding the vehicle back along the road to the Alamo.

The tavern hadn't opened yet, but the front door was unlocked and he found Schwarz, Blancanales and Cube waiting for him in the entryway.

Cube was leaning against the statue of Davy Crockett. He smiled when he saw what Lyons had in his hands. Turning away, he waved for the other men to follow him and walked across the dance floor to the bar.

Lyons set the package on the bar and stepped back.

"What you waitin' for?" Cube said. "Let's get it open."

The Able Team leader shrugged, dropped a hand to his boot and drew the knife from its sheath. The tape at the corners of the package snapped as the razor-edge made contact.

A moment later, Cube stepped in and jerked away the paper. It *was* a shoe box, but there were no shoes inside when Cube lifted the lid.

Lyons, Blancanales and Schwarz looked into the box.

What they saw was a thermal charge detonator. The charge itself wasn't in the box, but that mattered little. Simple thermal charges that would burn at temperatures of up to 2,400 degrees centigrade could be manufactured easily in the most basic workshop. The detonators were the tricky part, but once the two components were combined the charges could be used to weld or burn through metal. Mixed with gasoline, diesel or other oils, the bomb could do even more damage. The horrible flame weapon had dreadful effects.

"Son of a bitch," Cube said, grinning. "There'll be a hot time in the old town tonight."

CHAPTER TEN

Washington, D.C.

Calvin James glanced around the living room of the presidential suite as he, McCarter and three of the Secret Service's presidential protection team waited for the First Lady to finish her morning rituals. They had been ordered to be at the suite at 0500 hours, prepared to escort the President's wife to a breakfast speaking engagement.

The Phoenix Force commando glanced at his wristwatch. It was 0650 now, and they hadn't seen sign of the First Lady.

Across the room from James, seated on a small love seat, David McCarter cleared his throat and turned to Charlie Yeager, the Secret Service agent next to him.

"She always this slow?" McCarter asked.

Yeager glanced toward the hall door leading to the bedrooms before nodding. "Always," he whispered.

James saw McCarter grin at the agent's discomfort. "What time is the breakfast meeting?" he asked in a voice just a little too loud.

"Seven thirty." Yeager's whisper was even softer than before, as if it could somehow make up for McCarter's louder voice.

"Well, tell me this, Special Agent Yeager," McCarter said. "If she doesn't have to be there until 0730, why did she send orders for us to show up at 0500?"

"Because I *can*," came a voice from the hall.

The Secret Service agents jumped to their feet. James stood and turned to see the First Lady standing in the doorway, rummaging through her purse. She wore an austere navy blue skirt suit, black flats and no makeup. Her hair was tied back so tightly it stretched the skin around her eyes.

"Let's go," she said, closing her purse and striding purposefully toward the front door of the suite. She stopped at the door and waited, sighing in disgust and impatience sigh as Yeager set a new world speed record from the love seat to the door. He turned the knob and the First Lady darted through.

Two members of the protection team broke into a trot in order to pass her in the hallway before she reached the elevator. The one who was called Simpson punched the button.

A few minutes later, the procession exited one of the rear doors of the White House. McCarter fell in stride next to the First Lady. James followed. When they reached her limo, the Phoenix Force leader opened the door and helped her in.

"I hope you aren't planning to get in next to me," she said, looking up at the Phoenix Force leader.

"Yes, ma'am," McCarter said pleasantly.

"Well, don't." She pointed an index finger at James. "I want him with me."

"Madam First Lady," McCarter said patiently, "the security details have already been worked out and the division of labor agreed upon. If we have to change roles now, it will—"

"I don't give a damn what you have to do. The group I'm addressing is the African-American Professional Women's League," she said. "I want an African-American escort." She hooked the finger she'd been pointing at James and beckoned him.

Calvin James bristled inside. He didn't like being a "token," getting special treatment because of his color. Nevertheless, he had a job to do—protect the First Lady. He circled the limousine and got into the back seat.

The lead Secret Service vehicle pulled out, and the First Lady's car pulled in behind it. "Thank you," the woman next to James said, her voice filled with fake earnestness. "I do appreciate your riding back here with me, and I'm sure you understand. I need an African-American."

James wanted to get along with her but there was

only so much he could take. "I'm afraid I don't fit the bill," he said, smiling.

The First Lady frowned.

"My ancestors were African," James said, still smiling. "But I was born in Chicago. That makes me an American, pure and simple." He thought he heard a low, chuckle from the front seat.

"Yes, of course," the First Lady said, nodding. "I certainly didn't mean—"

James couldn't resist another light jab. "And there's one other thing."

"Yes?" The First Lady was suddenly all ears, fearful that she might be labeled a racist in spite of her politically correct exterior.

"Just seems funny, you ordering me to sit in the back," James said, "when the Civil Rights movement started so black people could sit in the front of the bus."

"Oh, please don't misunderstand," the First Lady said as the procession left the White House and started down Pennsylvania Avenue. "Your people fought long and hard for equality. You're still fighting for it." She puffed up like a pompous toad. "And we intend to continue helping you achieve it."

The procession moved on, the limo's occupants silent for several minutes. Then, as they turned onto a freeway, McCarter turned and rested an arm over the seat. "Madam First Lady," he said, "in view of the recent problems, I'd like to recommend that you speak, then answer any questions from behind the podium.'' He paused and drew in a deep breath. "I'm given to understand that you like to mingle with the crowd afterward. Under normal circumstances, that would be fine. But I don't think it's a very good idea today. It's very hard to insure your safety in the middle of a crowd.''

The First Lady was smarting from James's subtle needling and decided to take out her frustrations on McCarter.

"May I remind you that you work for *me*, Mr.... What was your name? MacArther?''

"McCarter, ma'am.''

"You work for me, Mr. MacArther,'' she said briskly, getting his name wrong again. "I will do what I want to do and you will do what I want you to do. If I decide to mingle with the crowd, you will be expected to act accordingly and keep me safe. And I don't care how hard it is. Is that understood?''

McCarter didn't answer. He just grinned and turned back around.

The lead car pulled off the freeway onto an exit ramp and then up to the front door of a Holiday Inn. The First Lady's limo and the trailing vehicles followed. James saw more Secret Service agents, as well as uniformed Washington PD officers, stationed around the parking lot and the perimeter or the motel. Today, everyone wore red armbands.

The First Lady was all smiles for the cameras as

she hooked a hand through the crook of James's elbow and let him escort her into the lobby. Flashbulbs popped and a thousand questions from health care to gay rights were thrown at her. She had the face of a cherub as she moved through the throngs of reporters and photographers toward the conference room.

James escorted the First Lady into the conference room where she was greeted by applause and a standing ovation from the women of the African-American Professional Women's League. A platform had been set up at one end of the conference room, raising the head table a few feet higher than the others. James helped the woman on his arm step up, found the seat with her name on a place card in front of it, then pulled her chair out and seated her. He took the seat next to her and looked out over the crowd.

He didn't know why, but he was getting a bad feeling.

A smartly dressed black woman of around fifty-five greeted the First Lady, then stepped up to the microphone at the podium in the center of the table. "Ladies," she said after tapping the mike twice to make sure it was working, "please allow the First Lady to be the first through the buffet, then we'll all go through and get some breakfast."

McCarter had dropped into the seat on the other side of the First Lady. Leaning back slightly, he turned to James.

James nodded and the two men stood.

The buffet table stood against a side wall, and James and McCarter followed the First Lady through, watching her select several items and put them on her plate. James grabbed only a cup of coffee for himself when they reached the end of the table, carrying it in his left hand to keep his gun hand free as he and McCarter walked the First Lady back to her seat.

While the First Lady ate her breakfast, James scanned the crowd of women lined up at the buffet. Again, the uneasy feeling crept over him.

Something was wrong, out of place. He didn't know what it was yet, but something caught his imagination. Some tiny discrepancy had registered in his unconscious mind and was trying to surface.

The Phoenix Force commando looked past the First Lady to McCarter. The Briton was frowning at the line himself. He caught James's glance and turned that way, shaking his head slightly, then shrugging.

Whatever it was, the Phoenix Force leader had felt it, too. But McCarter couldn't identify the problem yet either.

James sipped his coffee, his battle senses on red alert. Something was definitely wrong, and something wrong meant something was going to happen. He was ready.

When the First Lady finished her breakfast she turned to James. "So, Calvin," she said, "tell me about your plans for the future. What are your goals with...whatever bureau it is you're with?'' The sweet smile had returned to her face.

James saw that her eyes weren't really on him, she was trying to scan the crowd. She was striking up conversation not because she cared about Calvin James as a person. In fact he was surprised she had even remembered his name. The reason behind her attention was image, pure and simple. She wanted the black women to see her on friendly terms with a black man.

Before he had a chance to respond, the woman at the microphone earlier came down the table and tapped her on the back of the shoulder. ''Madam First Lady?'' the woman said. ''I know how very busy you must be. Are you ready?

The First Lady nodded.

The woman in charge of the meeting returned to the microphone. After tapping it again to get everyone's attention, she said, ''Ladies, those of you who haven't finished breakfast, please feel free to continue.'' She then gave a glowing introduction of the guest speaker, starting with the First Lady's birth and hitting the highlights of her career up to the present. Her husband, the President of the United States, wasn't mentioned.

The First Lady took the microphone, greeted everyone and began to tell the women seated at the tables what she'd been told they wanted to hear.

James's uneasiness hadn't left him. As the First

Lady spoke, he began to scan the audience again, trying as best he could to start at the left side of the room and focus briefly on each individual face. The task was impossible. Some of the women seated around the tables were hidden by others, and the AAPWL members against the far wall of the conference room were too far away to study closely.

The Phoenix Force commando heard the First Lady begin to wind down her oration and switched tactics again, focusing on the center of the room and watching the corners with his peripheral vision. He saw the women break into applause and stand. He turned suddenly as he felt the President's wife hurry past him and down into the audience. Before he or McCarter could even rise, she was seated between two elderly women at a table in the center of the room.

James shot to his feet and beat McCarter by half a step into the throng of women milling around the First Lady. He started to speak, realized it would be useless and resigned himself to watching the immediate crowd. A quick glance at McCarter told him the Phoenix Force leader had picked up on his strategy. McCarter began to scan the women farther away as they crowded toward the front table.

"No, the President has no plans to do away with that program," James heard the First Lady say. "Yes, the money will still be there if those mean-spirited congressmen don't vote it away. Did I mention that the opposing political party controls both houses?''

The last comment brought a round of laughter from the women, all of whom knew quite well which party controlled the Senate and House of Representatives.

James saw a dark-skinned woman, who looked eighty if she was a day, shuffling through the crowd, leaning heavily on a cane. She had been one of the women at the back of the room who had been too far away to scrutinize closely, and the Phoenix Force commando remembered her sitting by herself. She muttered something under her breath now as she walked, and looked as if she herself were her only listener.

He was about to dismiss her as harmless when suddenly, for no reason he could explain, something caught his attention and riveted his eyes on the elderly woman. The apprehension in his throat suddenly rose to eleven on a scale of one to ten.

The old woman was two steps in front of the First Lady when James made his move. With speed and dexterity that defied her age, she suddenly lifted the cane off the ground and gripped the shaft halfway down in her left hand.

James stepped in and caught the stick with his right hand. He drove a short left jab into the woman's midsection that doubled her at the waist. Wrenching the cane away, he followed with an uppercut that picked the gray-haired octogenarian off her feet and dropped her to the floor in a sitting position.

For a moment, the room fell into silence. Then the First Lady's scream echoed off the four walls. "What the hell do you think you're doing?"

James didn't answer. Stepping forward, he tucked the cane under his arm and pulled a set of handcuffs from behind his back. Twirling the old woman onto her face, flat on the ground, he cuffed her wrists behind her back. He used the chain between the cuffs to jerk her to her feet, producing a very unladylike scream.

A buzz of angry exhilaration went up from the women in the room. "Stop that! Stop that immediately!" the First Lady shouted.

James ignored the words again. Instead of answering, he spun the old woman to face the First Lady, hanging on to the woman's upper arm.

He finally knew what it was he had seen earlier, what had registered in his unconscious and made him know something was about to come down.

The old woman was neither old nor a woman.

James grabbed a napkin off the nearest table and began to rub off the thick makeup.

"What do you think you're doing!" the First Lady yelled, shooting to her feet and reaching out.

Before she could touch either James or his prisoner, the Phoenix Force commando had removed enough of the makeup to clearly show that the skin below was white. And that it belonged to a man in his late twenties or early thirties.

The First Lady froze in her tracks, both arms extended in the air. A collective gasp went up from the women of the AAPWL.

James dropped the napkin and ripped the gray wig off the man's head to expose a short brown flattop. The gasps of surprise from the women turned into petitions for immediate execution, not to mention a few endorsements of cruel and unusual punishment.

McCarter moved in and grabbed the man's other arm, and James dropped the one he'd been holding. Stepping to the side, he retrieved the cane from under his arm, gripped the handle with one hand and the shaft with the other, and jerked.

A gleaming stainless-steel blade, roughly fifteen inches long, glistened under the bright overhead lights and brought another round of gasps.

James held out the sword-cane, making sure the First Lady could see its tapered point and razor edges.

The First Lady's face turned the color of cigar ash. Her bottom lip fell an inch below the top.

"What am I doing?" James said, finally deciding to answer the woman's question. "Saving your life, Madam First Lady."

Above Arizona

BOLAN HAD LEARNED early in his career as a young soldier that it was wise to take advantage of any, and all, opportunities to rest.

A warrior never knew when the chance would present itself again.

The whir of the Learjet's engines hit the Executioner's ears even before he opened his eyes. When he lifted his lids, he looked out through the windshield and saw the bright morning light shining through the thick clouds.

"Good morning, sunshine," said the voice next to him. "I'd have your coffee and ham and eggs ready, but it's the chef's day off."

Bolan turned to Jack Grimaldi who sat in his usual place behind the controls of the plane. Grimaldi was dressed, also as usual, in a faded brown leather bomber jacket, suede Alaskan bush pilot's cap and mirrored sunglasses. The Executioner yawned around the smile the sight brought to his face. Life, particularly the warrior's life he had chosen, was unpredictable. There were only a few things you could count on.

Jack Grimaldi in the pilot's seat was one of them.

The Executioner stood and moved between the seats toward the plane's cargo area, bracing himself against the wall to catch his balance as the jet hit an air pocket. When the plane had leveled off again, Bolan continued on to the row of lockers bolted against the side of the plane. Opening one of the doors, he pulled out a navy blue blazer, khaki slacks and the appropriate accessories, and began to change out of the blacksuit. The Beretta's shoulder rig came off, then went back on again over a white Oxford shirt and paisley tie. He switched the Desert Eagle to a Helweg speed holster, traded the Applegate-Fairbairn commando dagger for the folding variety in a horizontal Kydex sheath, and slid both weapons onto his belt before covering them with the blazer. The blacksuit, and his other assault gear, went into a soft-sided suitcase.

Bolan dropped the suitcase behind his seat and rejoined Grimaldi in the jet's cabin. "How much farther?" he asked.

Stony Man Farm's number-one pilot shrugged. "Ten minutes. Maybe less with this tailwind."

The Executioner reached back between the seats and opened the suitcase, riffling through the contents until he found the blacksuit again. He unzipped one of the breast pockets and pulled out the note Fred Bailey had given him.

Liberty Arizona, it read in the old man's scribbly hand. John Wesley Needham. Phoenix.

The Executioner tucked the paper into his jacket pocket. Bailey had described the group as another of the violence-prone extremist organizations giving legitimate militias such as his own a bad name. The Indiana man had seemed as anxious as the Executioner to see them stopped, and offered to help in any way he could.

Bolan decided to keep that in mind. Bailey just

might turn out to have other connections that would prove useful.

The cellular phone mounted in front of the Executioner buzzed. Bolan leaned forward, tapped the On button, then another connecting the unit to the speaker-phone feature so Grimaldi could hear what was being said.

"Striker," he answered.

"How was your nap?" Stony Man mission controller Barbara Price asked in a pleasant voice.

"Not long enough," Bolan said.

"That's too bad. Because I don't know when you're going to get another one. Looks like you're going to have to do your own detective work once you set down."

Bolan frowned at the clouds in front of him. "Aaron didn't have a file on Needham or the Liberty Arizona group?" he asked.

"Oh, there's plenty on file," Price said. She took a deep breath. "All outdated."

Bolan's frown deepened. "That doesn't sound like the Aaron Kurtzman I know. Bear and his staff stay on top of things."

"Yes, they do," Price said. "But they're only human. It seems Liberty Arizona moved their headquarters recently."

"How recently?"

"Like yesterday," Price replied. "We had an address on them under the front of Ragtime Cowboy Joe's Shipping & Storage. Leo contacted a Farm-trained Phoenix PD officer—name's Devlin—to confirm. When Devlin drove out, the building was empty. The landlord was there. He told him.'' She paused. ''Before you ask, Hunt already tried the phone company. Records indicate the lines were cut yesterday. No transfer of service orders.''

''Which means they've opened up shop somewhere under another front,'' Bolan said.

''That's what it sounds like. And it fits their MO—the file indicates they relocate and get a new cover every couple of years or so.'' Price sighed. ''We just got unlucky with our timing.''

Bolan was a soldier, not a detective. He had neither the time nor desire to play Dick Tracy. He shook his head.

''Give me the old location,'' the Executioner said to Price. ''It's as good a place to start as any. And tell Aaron or whoever he's got working this end to keep trying. Chances are the group used a moving company. If they did, there'll be records of where they took everything.''

''That's affirmative,'' Price said. She read the old address to him over the phone. ''But the Phoenix detective who checked it out will be waiting for you,'' she added. ''He'll know the place and how to get there.''

Bolan nodded. ''I take it the Phoenix PD doesn't know what our former trainee is up to?''

''Affirmative again. He's taken some time off

and for all they know he's gone fishing. He'll meet you in the rental-car parking lot.''

The jet's engines whined as Grimaldi began the decent over Phoenix.

"What's the status of Able Team?" the Executioner asked Price, changing the subject.

"Lyons and company think they've made some headway at the Alamo," she said. "The blacksuits got out of the water all right, by the way. They're upstairs catching forty winks right now. Turrin and Katz are with them."

"How about McCarter and his crew?" Bolan asked. Even though Phoenix Force was engaged in a separate mission, he liked to stay abreast of things.

"As a matter of fact," Price said, "David just called in. He's not discounting the rumor that there's an assassination plot in the wind, but so far all they've encountered are kooks. James stopped an attempt on the First Lady this morning.

"Stay in touch, Striker," Price said.

"Always." Bolan hung up the phone in front of him. The jet broke out of the clouds, and he looked down to see the Theodore Roosevelt Dam in the distance. A few moments later, the jet's wheels hit the runway.

The Executioner shook his head, putting words to his earlier thought. "Jack, I don't have time to play detective. Stay close to the phone in case

Stony Man can come up with Liberty Arizona's new location.''

''I will,'' Grimaldi replied as the plane ground to a halt at the end of the runway. ''Stay safe.''

''I will.''

''I bet,'' Grimaldi said.

As Price had said, the Phoenix PD detective was waiting for him next to a late model Chevy Blazer. ''John Devlin,'' the man said as Bolan neared.

The Executioner eyed Devlin as he walked up. The Phoenix detective was a brick of a man, standing barely five feet seven inches, but carrying around two hundred pounds of what looked like power-lifting muscle. He wore black Wellington police boots with a painfully cheap brown suit. The jacket couldn't come close to buttoning around his broad chest, so he didn't even try.

Devlin's face was vaguely familiar, Bolan thought, as he extended a hand.

''I remember you from training. Belasko, wasn't it?''

''Still is,'' Bolan said as he shook the man's hand and threw his suitcase into the backseat of the Blazer next to a green canvas duffle bag. He got into the passenger's seat as Devlin slid behind the wheel. They left the parking lot, cruised off the airport grounds and onto the highway.

''The Chevy's rented,'' Devlin said as the Blazer picked up speed. ''But I borrowed a little police equipment that ought to save us some time. You mind reaching into that bag and getting it out?"

Bolan turned in his seat and rummaged through the duffle bag. He found a red magnetic "Kojak" light and handed it to Devlin. "This what you mean?"

Devlin nodded. He rolled down the window, stuck the light to the roof of the Blazer and plugged the other end into the cigarette lighter. A few seconds later they were weaving in and out of traffic toward downtown Phoenix.

Bolan glanced at the vehicles pulling to the side of the road as they passed. "You're off duty," Bolan said. "You going to catch any fire over this?"

Devlin laughed softly. "The Phoenix PD is like any other big bureaucracy," he said. "The right hand hardly ever knows what the left hand's doing." He turned onto an exit ramp into an old industrial area. "Besides, your people promised to throw water on the flames if I needed it."

Bolan smiled. He was remembering Devlin better now, and recalled him as a good man. A hard worker. But he had one misconception, and the Executioner decided to clear it up here and now. "You were Farm-trained, weren't you, Devlin?" he said.

The detective nodded, his face falling slightly in disappointment that the man beside him didn't seem to remember.

"Then you don't say *your* people when referring

to us," Bolan told him. "You're one of the family. It's *our* people, and we always look after our own."

The disappointment on Devlin's face blossomed into beaming pride.

The Blazer slowed and Devlin pulled to a halt a half block down from an old four-story warehouse. The Executioner looked down the street at the faded red brick. Several concrete steps led up to the front doors, and above them he could see where the letters of the company sign recently had been removed. The brick behind the characters was clean and less faded, and until the rain, wind and sun blended the area in with the rest, Ragtime Cowboy Joe's Shipping and Storage could still be read.

Devlin turned to face the Executioner. "Think we ought to leave the car here?" he asked.

Bolan nodded. "No sense sending out announcements that we've arrived."

Devlin threw the Blazer into Park and killed the engine. The two men exited the vehicle, walked casually down the street, then mounted the steps. The front door was locked.

"You got a key?" Bolan asked.

"Sure," Devlin said. He glanced quickly up and down the deserted street, then brought up one of his Wellington boots and smashed it into the door just below the lock.

Bolan followed him into the deserted warehouse, closing the door behind him. They stopped in a small office at the front, watching scattered paper and other debris blow across the tile in the breeze that entered with them. An old wooden desk, too crumbled and splintered to bother moving, stood on its remaining three legs in the corner.

"You been through all this already?" Bolan asked.

Devlin nodded. "Briefly, anyway. When the landlord was here yesterday. I flashed my badge and told him I was looking for one of the employees who was backed up on child-support payments."

The Executioner chuckled. He was liking Devlin and his unorthodox approach to police work more and more all the time. "Phoenix PD taking over the county sheriff's job of working civil law, are they?" he said.

"Hell, no. We let the deputies chase the deadbeats. But the landlord didn't know that." He kicked at a dirty yellow invoice on the floor in front of his foot. "Anyway, all I found yesterday were a few old receipts, stuff like that. Just enough to tell me that there was no more storage or shipping going on here than Liberty Arizona needed to keep up their front. Didn't find anything that would indicate where they've moved."

Bolan nodded. "You have a cellular?"

Devlin reached into the inside pocket of his coat and pulled one out.

The Executioner tapped numbers into the instrument and a moment later Grimaldi answered. "Have you heard anything from Price?" he asked.

"Negative," the pilot said. "Still waiting." In the background, the Executioner could hear the sounds of aircraft landing and taking off. He hung up and returned the instrument to Devlin. He was about to speak when a noise from the back of the abandoned warehouse echoed to the front.

Bolan and Devlin turned toward the sound. A door in the rear wall of the office area stood open, and through it the Executioner could see a two-story storage area. Holding a finger to his lips to silence Devlin, he drew the sound-suppressed Beretta.

Devlin nodded and pulled an AMT Hardballer .45 pistol from under his coat.

The detective's Farm training had stayed with him—the Hardballer certainly wasn't Phoenix PD-issued or even approved. But the man was working for Stony Man Farm today, not the police department, and he had wisely chosen to carry a weapon that couldn't be traced to him should he have to use it.

Bolan took the lead, walking softly to the door and peering around the corner. He could see nothing in the huge storage room, but subdued voices drifted out from some hidden area at the back of the warehouse. Staying close to the walls, he stepped into the room and began to make his way toward the sounds, carefully stepping over and around the rubble on the floor. Behind him, he could barely hear the squeaking rubber soles of Devlin's Wellingtons.

Halfway to the wall at the end of the storage area, the Executioner saw that the room took a twist behind the wall he was hugging. The voices grew louder as he neared. They were joined now by a few grunts and groans, and the screech of steel scraping across the concrete floor. He slowed his pace, moving silently to the junction where the room bent. He stepped over a bottle cap on the floor just before the corner, then dropped to one knee and inched an eye around the barrier.

Four short-haired men, dressed in blue jeans, T-shirts and leather jackets had just moved a steel filing cabinet away from the wall. The Executioner could see that a hole had been cut into the wall in the plaster and lath where the cabinet had been.

Bolan drew back around the corner out of sight. These had to be Liberty Arizona men returning to retrieve something they had left behind. And if they had gone to the trouble to hide it in the wall, that meant it was either valuable or illegal.

The Executioner would put his money on illegal over valuable. But whatever it was, it was probably both.

A few quick whispers were exchanged between the men, drawing half of Bolan's face around the corner again. As he watched, a tall gangly man reached into the hole and pulled out a package wrapped in brown paper.

Which was the exact moment that Devlin chose to plant his foot on top of the bottle cap Bolan had just stepped over.

The cap snapped like a gunshot under Devlin's bulk, then scraped the concrete almost as loudly as its sharp edges embedded themselves into his rubber sole and moved with his boot.

All four Liberty Arizona men turned, looked toward the sound and saw the Executioner.

A half second later, Bolan stared down the barrels of four guns.

CHAPTER ELEVEN

Virginia Beach, Virginia

Desmond Click stared in fascination at the television news show. Although her perky little face couldn't be seen, NBC newsanchor Anne Cormack's voice was narrating the story of the fire burning on the screen. The hospital bombing had been the top story on all three of the networks' early-morning news shows, with each featuring footage taken the night before. As Click watched, the nurse who had jumped to her death several hours earlier did so again.

The man in the wheelchair cursed silently, realizing he had forgotten to record the show. He rolled himself across the room to the closet, found a new video tape on the shelf and clawed the plastic wrapper off the cardboard case. But by the time he had rolled back to the VCR next to the television, Cormack's face had returned to the screen.

Click stuffed the tape into the front-loader anyway. He could catch the fire again on the midday news. He knew that, like the beating of Rodney King, the television stations would play the woman jumping over and over until everyone in America had the scene engraved in their memories for eternity.

A sudden sharp pain shot down Click's leg. He ignored it. Today he was happy, and he would stay that way. He had achieved his goal of the night before, and was another step closer to his master plan. Yes, the Maestro was nearing his virtuoso performance and nothing, absolutely nothing, was going to ruin the optimism he felt this morning.

"Police believe the hospital bombing is linked to other similar arsons perpetrated around the country in recent months," Cormack stated. "A combined task force of federal, state and local authorities is adding the hospital to its list in the ongoing investigation." Her serious expression faded and she smiled as she switched to a story about the rescue of a whale beached on the California coast.

Click's lips pursed in disgust. The woman was such a phony, able to turn her projected emotions on and off as if she had a switch mounted to her heart. He watched her bubble away about the whale, and began to wonder what she would look like naked. In his mind's eye he suddenly had her stripped, gagged and bound with ropes. Should he add a blindfold? No. It would be more fun to watch her eyes as she realized what he was doing to her.

Click closed his own eyes tightly. He felt the old

familiar stirring in his groin as the fantasy progressed. He would burn her most sensitive areas with a cigarette for a while, then slice open the belly of that beached whale and roll her perky little face in the blubber.

Blubber, like all fat, burned well he was sure.

The stirring in Click's groin continued as he reached for the remote control, checking the other major networks. But the fire was indeed the top story, and by now they had moved on to other subjects. He dropped the TV to channel 3 and began moving up the line, hoping to catch something about the bomb on one of the cable stations.

Finding nothing of further interest, Click pushed the Mute button to kill the sound, then wheeled back to his computer. He gazed at the monitor for a few moments, watching the fixed cloud formation on the right side of the screen, then glanced at the pad beneath the mouse. It was decorated with a colorful cartoon by S. Adams that showed a nerd with large spectacles in front of a computer.

Technology, read the words on the mouse pad. No place for wimps. His mother had picked it up somewhere in one of her many attempts to cheer him. But rather than make him happy, every time he looked down it angered him.

Technology *was* a place for wimps. The final and only frontier for invalids who could no longer get out and do anything in the real world. It was a place for people who had no friends, no life and no future.

Technology was the place for Desmond Click.

Click moved the mouse across the pad, directing the arrow to the America Online symbol in the bottom left-hand corner of the screen. He clicked the mouse twice and watched the clouds give way to a new screen. A few more clicks brought up his name, and below it the rectangular box for his password. He typed in the word *holocaust,* and watched asterisks representing the secret letters appear in the box.

He tapped the mouse button to sign on, and the screen changed once more. Over the speakers came the sound of a ringing telephone. A moment later, he heard a computerized voice say, "Welcome," and a moment after that, "You have mail."

Click checked his E-mail, finding a few short messages from faceless code names he recognized from a chat room. Each of them shared the same passions for fire as Click, and through the anonymity of cyberspace they were able to discuss these feelings and know they weren't alone in the universe. Some of the members in the unofficial club even related arsons they had committed.

The man in the wheelchair found their accounts boring by his standards. Small time. Part of him was tempted to send back messages of his own exploits just to let them know what losers they really were. But he refrained from giving in to the temptation. Click was taking no chances that he didn't have to take, regardless of how anonymous the world of cyberspace might be.

He was about to try contacting Zulu when he heard the knock on the door.

"Dezzie?"

Click groaned. His mother had impeccable timing—she always came knocking when he was in the middle of something. Turning to face the door, he said, "What is it now, Mother?"

"May I open the door?"

Click closed his eyes and shook his head. "Yes."

His mother appeared in the doorway wearing a white cotton housedress, her hair in curlers. "How about a nice hot cup of tea, Dezzie?" she said with a smile on her face. "I've just brewed a fresh pot."

"No, thank you, Mother," Click said irritably. He started to turn back to the computer.

"It's your favorite kind. Formosa Oo-long," Mrs. Click said. Like always, she drew out both syllables in the word "Oolong," and giggled. She continued to laugh at the way she'd pronounced the word as if it were the first rather than the ten-thousandth time she'd said it that way.

Click stared at her, taking in the frumpy housedress, the curlers, the varicose veins bulging from her calves beneath the hem of the dress. He stared at the legs. Ugly, perhaps. But not nearly as ugly as his own. And they worked. They took her where she wanted to go, and even the obnoxiously protruding veins didn't invite the stares that Click's own disfigurement assured.

A wave of malice toward his mother rolled through Click. "I don't want any fucking tea," he grated. "Now will you get the hell out of here, please?"

The smile on Mrs. Click's face fell away as if she'd been slapped. "All right, Dezzie. I'm sorry I bothered you." She closed the door behind her as she left.

Click turned back to the monitor, another bolt of lightning shooting down his thigh to his calf. This time, he jumped in his chair. It had been no worse than the earlier jolt but his good humor was ruined for the day—his mother had seen to that—and now the pain became almost unendurable.

The man in the wheelchair slid a CD into the computer and listened to Snoop Doggy Dog begin rapping as he called out electronically for Zulu. When he got no response, he left a message for the Free African Nation leader.

Click returned to the television set. On CNN he found a brief update on the bombing. Over seventy people had died with twice that many injured. He smiled at the news but the smile was superficial. The joy in his heart—a joy that came both from his love of fire and the pride of accomplishment that he had pulled off yet another successful bombing— was missing.

Again, something for which to thank his mother.

Click turned toward the door. Beyond it, he could hear the old woman puttering in the bathroom. Probably taking the damned curlers from her hair. The hatred he had felt for her earlier returned, but now he realized that his enmity wasn't directed solely at his mother. Click hated all people who could walk. He hated all of the beautiful people who hadn't been disfigured into mutant eyesores. And he hated all men and women who didn't share his lust for fire. Which meant, he realized, that he hated almost all of the human race.

But most of all, Desmond Click knew, he hated himself and what he had become.

"You have mail."

The computerized voice behind him rousted Click from his thoughts. Turning back to the screen, Click punched the mouse button and the message from Zulu appeared.

No deliveries yet, the screen said. *Worried. Must begin preparations.*

Click frowned. He went immediately into the chat room where he and Zulu always met and found the Free African Nation leader waiting. They entered a private room, and he typed *Neither delivery?* onto the screen.

No, came back.

The frown on the face of the man in the wheelchair deepened. He had purposely cut the timing on the final deliveries thin. The less time Zulu had the bomb components in his possession, the less chance there was of his being discovered. The diesel fuel was no problem—the FAN leader could pick up that without drawing any suspicion. But the other two components—the thermal device and the detonator—those things would be hard to explain. There could be no mistaking either for what they were.

Still, the two items should have arrived in Zulu's possession by now, and the fact that they had not meant Click needed to check things out.

I'll get back to you, he typed in to Zulu.

Hurry. I've got work to do.

Click tapped into the Form Mail function and typed the E-mail address of the Alamo Tavern in San Antonio into the upper left-hand box. The fat pig fascist who owned the Alamo was a member in good standing with the KKK, and before Click had realized that his true loyalties lay with FAN's black freedom fighters, Travis "Tex" Thompson had been the liaison between Maestro and the Klan. Cube still came in handy on occasion. Even now, the fat man thought the thermal detonator was going to another right-wing extremist group. Before he knew any better it would be too late.

Is there a delay? Click asked simply.

Cube had to be sitting in front of his computer because the response was immediate. *I just got the damn thing this morning!*

Then get it in the air, Click wrote back. *Now. Take it YOURSELF.* He thought a moment, then added, *You won't get the rest of the money until it's delivered.*

Click cut off the correspondence and sat back. He wiped a bead of sweat from his brow, a little surprised to see that for once he was too warm rather than too cold. Not to worry, he told himself. There was still plenty of time to get the components to Zulu.

Typing in a new set of coordinates, he sent a message to Arizona. *Where is your product?* he demanded.

There was a long pause before the response came back. When it did, he saw the words *Short delay. Nothing to worry about,* come on the screen.

A light bulb suddenly flashed in Click's brain. Something was wrong. He didn't know what. But he could sense it.

Type in identification code, he demanded.

Again there was a long pause. Finally the word *holocaust* appeared.

Now it was Click's turn to pause. The response had taken too long. Why?

Click closed his eyes. Because whoever had typed it in had had to ask someone else what it was. Someone was there who wasn't supposed to be there.

Someone was onto the Maestro.

Mission aborted, Click typed onto the screen. *Await further orders.* He cut off the transmission before he could get a response.

Click whirled in his wheelchair. He hadn't yet told the Liberty Arizona bigots where to deliver the thermal charge. But he had done enough work for the group in the past that John Wesley Needham hadn't questioned that fact, knowing he would get his orders when it was time. Consequently whoever it was that now sat at Needham's computer—local police, Feds, whoever—couldn't follow up on the stroke of luck they seemed to have had.

Click smiled now. He had a backup thermal charge. An emergency stash that he kept for just such an occasion. This new twist in the plot meant a few changes in the game. It meant he would have to take a more active role than he had planned, and—

A sudden realization chilled Click's mutilated skin to his brittle bones. In his hurry to find out about the delivery delays, he had skipped the usual chat-room procedures and E-mailed his messages to Cube and Needham. Cube had been there himself so that was no problem. But if cops really had taken over the Liberty Arizona computer, and every fiber in Click's body told him they had...

Click's return E-mail address would be listed on the correspondence.

The cops who were there now with Needham could trace him down. They would have to go through America Online, and that would mean a court order. It would take time, but eventually, they would trace the message right back here to his mother's apartment.

For the first time he could remember since the fire that had burned him beyond recognition, a consummate encompassing peace settled over Desmond Click. That the police would find the apartment made no difference. It would take them time—too much time. By then it would be too late.

He was nearing the end. This would be his last fire-bomb. But that no longer mattered. He could still pull it off before the authorities caught up to him.

Click let the new tranquillity envelope him, reveling in a sensation he had nearly forgotten existed. He was happy. It was different from the happiness he had experienced while watching the news that morning. Less manic. More subtle. And tinged slightly with an enjoyable pain. Like pressing lightly on a bruise—not enough to really hurt, just enough to feel good in a curious sort of way. It was a bittersweet exhilaration brought on by the knowledge that his pain would soon be over, and the world would understand Desmond Click a lot better than it did now. The general public could never know the depth of the suffering he had endured but soon—very soon—people would at least get a glimpse of the fiery hell that he had lived in for so many years.

And when it was over, his new hell could be no worse than the one he presently inhabited.

Click whirled in his wheelchair, almost tipping it over. He had work to do. He rolled across the floor to the desk, opened the lower right-hand drawer and lifted the backup thermal charge from the bottom. Carefully he set the unit on the desktop, closed the drawer again and slid out the one just above it. Inside, he found his father's old Colt Single Action Army .45-caliber revolver.

Yes, Click grinned. He had work to do. And the first item of business was something he had wanted to do for a long time.

Wheeling himself across the room to the hall door, Click opened it and called out, "Mother? Oh, Mother?"

"What is it, sweetheart?"

"Could you come in here a moment?" Click asked pleasantly.

"Certainly, darling."

Click heard her fuzzy slippers shuffling down the hall as he rolled himself halfway back into his bedroom. He lifted the .45 with both hands, aimed it at the open doorway and waited.

Texas

IT WAS MORE THAN apparent to Gadgets Schwarz that Carl Lyons was getting impatient. Of course, that was hardly an unusual emotional state for the man.

The sounds of old downtown San Antonio buzzed in Schwarz's ears and the mixed smells of vehicles, people and spicy Mexican cooking filled his nostrils. He glanced past a streetcar parked on the curb and saw the Alamo across the street from where he stood. The *real* Alamo—not the tavern. Even amid the tourists in shorts and T-shirts who turned the hallowed grounds into a sort of frontier Disneyland, Schwarz seemed to feel the kindred spirits of the brave Texans who had died within the walls a century and a half earlier.

Behind Schwarz, a family of five pushed its way into Ripley's "Believe it or Not!" Museum. He turned to watch them, then looked down at his wristwatch, feeling a bit restless himself.

Cube had sent them to meet a man in front of the museum over an hour ago. According to his watch, the man was now thirty minutes late. There had been no complicated series of codes or pass-words like Lyons had suffered through that morning at the Buckhorn. Cube had said only, "Pick up a package from a guy wearing a red shirt. He'll know you."

If you combined the cloak-and-dagger nonsense the tavern owner had insisted on earlier with the tardiness of their contact, things were starting to add up. Or not add up, depending on your point of view.

Schwarz glanced to Blancanales, who frowned and shook his head.

"Something's wrong," Lyons finally said. "None of this makes sense."

"Couldn't agree more," Blancanales said. "Think Cube sent us on a wild goose chase?"

"It's starting to look that way," the Able Team leader said. "The question is why?" He drew in a deep breath. "Okay. Pol, stay here just in case we're wrong. Gadgets, come with me. I think maybe it's time we leveled with our old buddy Cube."

"You mean leveled *with* him?" Gadgets asked. "Or simply *leveled* him?"

"I mean slammed him up against the wall and read him the riot act until we have some answers," Lyons said.

He turned back to Blancanales. "You got your cellular?"

Blancanales tapped his pocket.

"Call if anybody shows up."

"I will. But I wouldn't hold my breath."

Schwarz fell in next to Lyons as they hurried down the street to the parking lot where they'd left the Suburban. Schwarz slid in behind the wheel, took the keys from Lyons and pulled out onto the street. "What do you think's up?" he asked as he guided the vehicle back toward the Alamo Tavern.

Lyons shrugged. "I don't know. But this smells to high heaven, and I could kick myself for falling for it. My guess is that Cube wanted us out of the way while he took the thermal detonator some-place."

"So he doesn't trust us after all," Schwarz said. "After all that work."

Lyons shook his head. "He trusts us, Gadgets. His motive is greed, pure and simple. My guess is he's scoring some big bucks with this detonator. Why cut us in when he can deliver it wherever it's going himself?"

A few minutes later, they pulled up to the Alamo. Schwarz opened the door and led the way inside. They found the usual small afternoon crowd being waited on by Amy and another waitress, with the mustachioed bartender on duty behind the bar.

Schwarz and Lyons caught Amy on her way to a table with a trayload of drinks. "You seen Cube?" Gadgets asked.

Amy shook her head. "No, he took off like a whirlwind right after you guys left." She frowned. "Where's your sexy friend?"

Schwarz didn't answer. He followed Lyons to the bar. "Where'd Cube go?" the Able Team leader asked.

The bartender shrugged as he pulled a soapy beer mug out of the sink. "Beats me," he said.

Schwarz saw Lyons's eyebrows fall. "You got the keys to the office?" he asked.

The bartender rinsed the beer mug and picked up a towel. "Yeah, I got them," he said.

Schwarz saw Lyons's eyebrows lower.

So did the bartender. "I'm not supposed to—"

Lyons's hand shot across the bar and grabbed the

front of the bartender's shirt. "I'll be sweet the first time," he growled. "Sir, I'd like to have the keys, please."

The man behind the bar froze in place. In the brain behind his eyes, Schwarz could almost see a movie playing that featured the fights and shooting that had happened in the Alamo since Able Team's arrival.

The bartender reached into his pocket and came up with a key ring.

Lyons jerked it from his hand and led the way across the dance floor to the side door. A moment later, the mysterious barrier was open and Schwarz was following the Able Team leader down a dimly lit hall.

Two offices stood at the end of the hall. The smaller of the two had been converted into a storage room, and Lyons and Schwarz found nothing but restaurant and bar equipment, paper towels, toilet paper and other supply odds and ends inside. They moved quickly to the room that appeared to be Cube's base of operations.

The disheveled office was like an extension of the slovenly tavern operator himself. Half-chewed cigars overloaded the ashtrays and spilled over onto receipts, order forms and other papers. Piles of files were scattered across the desk, table and floor, and dust covered everything. The computer on the cheap plywood hutch in the corner was on, as was the printer next to it. A screen saver that showed a cowboy on horseback throwing a lariat around the neck of a bikini-clad cowgirl floated soundlessly across the monitor.

Schwarz found himself sneezing as he and Lyons sifted through the filth looking for any clue as to where Cube might have gone.

Finding nothing after fifteen minutes, Schwarz looked up. "Well, at least we know the detonator isn't here."

Lyons nodded. He pointed to the computer. "Take a look at that demon-machine, Electronics Boy," he said. "That's more your ballpark than mine. I'm still not convinced computers aren't the Antichrist."

Schwarz chuckled as he dropped into the chair in front of the screen. He took a few moments to study the setup, then clicked into the hard drive and began running through the files. They were titled with numbers and letters that made no sense to anyone who didn't know the system or have a key. With no clues to go on, he arbitrarily picked a file and called it up.

It contained the maintenance costs the Alamo had paid out to contractors over the past three years.

With Lyons watching over his shoulder Schwarz searched, playing hit or miss with the files. He came across what appeared to be an inventory of sorts that listed, among other things, diesel fuel and fertilizer. Both items could be used to make bombs and neither seemed necessary to the everyday operation of a tavern. But the list included other articles that appeared harmless.

"Think it's anything?" Lyons asked.

Schwarz shrugged. "Maybe something, maybe nothing. Cube might have been fertilizing the grounds and we know he has other business interests. Lots of things use diesel. On the other hand, my guess is some of these items are just red herrings. Something to throw off anyone casually looking through the files."

"Like us," Lyons said.

"Like us," Schwarz agreed. He sat back against the chair. "But the bottom line is we could waste a lot of time trying to figure this out and still come up with nothing."

"We don't have a lot of time." Lyons cleared his throat. "Can you link this crap to Stony Man?"

"Sure," Gadgets said. "Kurtzman can copy the hard drive."

"Good," Lyons said. "Maybe he and his team can make something of it." He found the telephone amid the office wreckage and lifted the receiver. "I'll call and tell them it's coming."

"Wait a minute, his E-mail program is running," Gadgets said. "Let's check and see what we find." He tapped the mouse a few times, and the mail center appeared on the screen. The mailbox icon's red flag was up. "Well, our fat friend has *something,* anyway."

A moment later, Schwarz had pulled up the new

mail and clicked onto a message that had come in shortly before Cube had sent them to the museum. *Is there a delay?* the message read.

Cube had written back. *I just got the damn thing this morning!*

Then get it in the air, had come the response. *Take it YOURSELF. You won't get the rest of the money until it's delivered.*

Schwarz turned to Lyons. "Cube's an idiot."

"What else is new?" Lyons asked.

"No, I mean he could have shut down his E-mail. Then we'd have needed a password to get in. I guess he got in a hurry and forgot."

"Are you telling me this is enough to make you believe in God?"

"I already believe in God," Schwarz said. "But He's working a double shift for us at the moment." He turned back to the screen. "We've got to assume this is all about the detonator. Whoever sent it, and my guess is Maestro, says get it into the air. Does that mean fly it somewhere?"

"Maybe," Lyons said. "But Cube's not likely to try to get the detonator onto a commercial flight. Too dangerous, and while he's an idiot, he's not *that* big an idiot. He'll go charter." He lifted the phone and dialed Stony Man. A moment later, Kurtzman was on the line. The Able Team leader handed the phone to Schwarz. "You do the computer talk," he said. "I'm getting a headache from it already."

Schwarz informed Kurtzman that they'd be linking Cube's hard drive to the Farm, then told him about the message.

"Hang on a second," Kurtzman said.

Schwarz listened to the sound of the Stony Man computer keys typing as he waited. A moment later, Kurtzman said, "Okay, I'm hacked into computers at San Antonio Airport. There aren't any charters under the name Travis 'Tex' Thompson, or anything close."

Schwarz relayed the message to Lyons, who cursed.

"Could he have used another name?" Kurtzman asked.

"Sure," Gadgets said. "But if he did, we have no way of knowing what it is."

"Wait a minute," Lyons said suddenly. "What if he owns his own plane?"

Schwarz relayed the question to Kurtzman.

"That would be in a different file," the Stony Man computer wizard said. "Hold on again."

More key tapping came over the line. A moment later, Kurtzman was back. "Bingo. Travis Thompson has a Cessna 425 Conquest. He filed a flight plan for Nashville an hour ago."

"Has he taken off yet?" Schwarz asked.

"Just a second."

Schwarz heard the sound of more keyboard keys. "Five minutes ago, Gadgets," came the reply.

Lyons had picked up enough from his end to

catch what was happening. Ripping the receiver from Schwarz's hand, he said, "Bear, have Barb get on the horn. Tell the Nashville cops to be at the airport." He paused. "Mott still here in San Antonio?"

Price came on the line. "Of course. You told him to stand by," she said. "Want me to tell him to get the plane warmed up?"

"Roger," Lyons said. He hung up and turned to Schwarz. "Get that hard drive thing sent—however you do it—and let's go get Pol," he said.

Schwarz linked Cube's hard drive to Stony Man Farm and sent the files across the line to Kurtzman. He knew that whatever was hidden in the documents would be deciphered. But how long would it take? Whatever Cube had going down was going down now.

And the only chance of stopping it was nabbing Cube himself.

By the time Schwarz reached the parking lot, Lyons had already started the Suburban.

CHAPTER TWELVE

Washington, D.C.

Seated against the wall of the reception area to the Oval Office, David McCarter crossed his legs impatiently. The clicking of computer keyboard keys was the only sound in the room. He glanced at the desk. Today, Eileen wore a tight white blouse and short red skirt that, like all of her clothing, showed off her assets to full advantage.

The Phoenix Force leader shook his head. The President's secretary was a true master of walking the line. Every outfit he had seen her in so far fell somewhere between professional and provocative, yet always seemed closer to the Victoria's Secret side than Lord & Taylor.

McCarter let his eyes move away from Eileen's desk to circle the rest of the room. Special Agents George and Howard were seated along the wall that intersected with his. The general attitude of the protection team had softened toward the men of Phoenix Force. McCarter doubted that they'd all be getting drunk or going to movies and baseball games together, but at least they were speaking. Right now, George and Howard looked as if sitting quietly were an activity in which they were well experienced. They stared ahead into space, lost in their thoughts.

Gary Manning and Rafael Encizo, however, were fidgeting in their chairs next to the Secret Service men with the same restlessness McCarter felt. The Phoenix Force leader envied Calvin James—at least James was getting to watch the President's son's soccer game. He didn't, he decided, envy T. J. Hawkins. Not at all. At least McCarter wasn't having to fend off the advances of an underage enchantress.

The Briton allowed a thin smile to play at the edge of his lips. His team, like all of the teams at Stony Man Farm, was made up of men of action. None of them had been excited about bodyguarding the President and his family. But they were, first and last, warriors. And *warrior* translated into soldier.

Soldiers took orders. They did what had to be done, whether they wanted to or not.

The hall door opened and Special Agent William entered the room, taking a seat next to McCarter without speaking. His face was a mass of worry lines. But that was nothing unusual for the head of the First Family's protection team. McCarter had noticed from the first that William showed the stress of the job more outwardly than his subordinates, and had chalked it up to the fact that ultimately, if anything went wrong, the buck stopped with him.

William sat silently for a few minutes, then suddenly turned to McCarter. "You know the President and First Lady are planning to have dinner out tonight, right?" he whispered.

McCarter nodded. It had been printed on the day's schedule issued to all protection team members every morning. He kept his voice low like William had as he answered. "Monique's Château," he said, naming the restaurant where all of the tables had been reserved to insure security. "At 2030 hours. On Elm Street."

William indicated agreement with a quick bob of his head. "I don't like it," he said. "In view of everything that's been happening, I'd rather they stayed here. Monique's could cater in."

McCarter shrugged. "So why not arrange it?"

William laced together his fingers and anxiously cracked several knuckles. "You should have noticed by now," he said, "that the President, and his wife, have no concept of what providing security entails. They don't understand that there are always loopholes—windows of opportunity, so to speak—for a would-be assassin." His head bobbed nervously again. "They think we can protect them under any circumstances." Now his head shook. "That's simply not the case."

The Phoenix Force leader uncrossed his legs. "Well," he said, "why don't you go in and talk to him about it?"

William took a deep breath. Then, with the reluctant mobility of a schoolboy about to enter the headmaster's office, he pushed himself up out of the chair and walked over to the secretary's desk. "Eileen," McCarter heard him whisper, "could you see if the President has a moment to talk to me?"

Eileen looked up from her typing and sighed, as if the interruption might cause major problems in her own schedule. She lifted the phone and spoke into the receiver. Then hanging up, she looked back to William. "It will be a few minutes," she said.

William sat back down. A few minutes turned slowly into an hour. McCarter studied the man next to him out of the corner of his eyes as William went through a series of knuckle-popping, seat-shifting and general wiggling and squirming that made the men of Phoenix Force appear to be happy with the inactivity they were enduring.

McCarter raised a hand and ran it along the stubble of his face. While William did indeed have a high-stress job, outward indications of strain were unusual for a man so highly placed. Most men with such responsibilities bore them silently. They never let others see them sweat. They just went on with their jobs, then went home one night and suffered a major coronary that surprised everyone.

Finally the phone on Eileen's desk buzzed. The woman lifted the receiver to her ear and said, "Yes, sir," then hung up again. She looked at William and nodded.

The Secret Service agent disappeared into the Oval Office.

No sooner had he left than McCarter saw Gary Manning turn to Agent George. "He always this uptight?" the big Canadian asked.

"William?" George said. "Yeah. Didn't used to be. Last few weeks, though, seems like it's really getting to him."

Manning nodded. "It could get to anybody," he said. "How long has he been in charge?"

George frowned, thinking. "Couple of years now, I guess."

The room fell silent again except for Eileen's typing. McCarter listened to the muted clacking as an uncomfortable feeling began to work its way slowly into his chest. Manning was right, of course. The type of assignment William had drawn could eventually get to anyone. Perhaps it was simply time to rotate the man off the protection team. Put him to work chasing counterfeiters, which was the Secret Service's other major responsibility. The symptoms William was showing had a simple explanation.

Too simple? Maybe, maybe not. But if so, why was McCarter suddenly feeling so troubled by it all?

The Phoenix Force leader crossed his legs again and watched a fly crawl up the wall across the room. He remembered a discussion he had once had with Bolan about the uneasiness that sometimes came over a warrior for no apparent reason. Some men claimed it was a mysterious sixth sense developed by years of experiencing danger. Bolan didn't think it was anything quite so ethereal. The Executioner simply believed that the battle veteran's subconscious often picked up hints of danger before the conscious mind could figure them out. McCarter wasn't sure. But whatever the answer was, both men from Stony Man Farm agreed that ignoring such gut-level instincts wasn't only dangerous, it could be fatal.

McCarter's mind traveled back to something the President had said during their first meeting. The man behind the desk of the Oval Office had suspected a leak from the Secret Service. At the time, McCarter had chalked it up to simple paranoia.

But what if he was wrong? What if there was a leak? What if someone on the President's protection team was dirty and helping arrange an assassination?

The Phoenix Force leader's eyes shot to the door of the Oval Office. George had said that William hadn't always been so high-strung; it had only started during the past few weeks. Could the grounds for this new anxiety be the fact that William had sold out?

McCarter stood. Part of him still said that this new theory was nonsense. But it couldn't hurt to check it out, particularly while he was forced to wait here in the office twiddling his thumbs. He was about to start for the hall when the door to the Oval Office opened again.

"Thank you for your concern," McCarter heard the President say from somewhere inside the office. "But it's necessary."

A very subdued Special Agent William returned to the outer office and closed the door behind him. He glanced at McCarter and shook his head.

The Phoenix Force leader nodded his understanding and walked toward the door to the hallway. "Lavatory break, mates," he said over his shoulder. "Hold the fort while I'm gone."

A moment later, McCarter was hurrying down the hall to the small office the protection team used as a command post. Slipping quietly inside, he found it empty. He lifted the phone from the nearest desk and tapped in the number to Stony Man Farm.

Price answered. "Hello, David," she said after he'd identified himself with his personal code.

"How goes the war?" McCarter asked.

Price blew air through her teeth into the receiver. "There may be a break," she said. "Ironman and his crew came across a thermal detonator. They're about to nab the guy transporting it to Nashville."

"Really," McCarter said. "They find the charge that goes with it?"

"No," Price said, "but Striker did. In Phoenix." She paused, then added. "We still don't know for sure if the two are connected, though. If they are, it would seem either the charge was going to the detonator in San Antonio, or the detonator was going to meet the charge in Phoenix. Nashville's the wrong way, either way."

McCarter nodded, then said, "Maybe both are headed for a third destination. What about Aaron and his people? They having any luck?"

"Not up to now. But they hardly had anything to go on. Let's face it, when the Bear has them searching libraries to see who's reading books on military strategy, well, it means they're working from scratch." Her voice brightened slightly. "But Able Team also intercepted some E-mail that may lead to the source of the thermal charge. I think our resident computer Houdini is tracing that right now."

"Let me speak to him, will you, Barb?" McCarter said.

"You've got it," Price said.

McCarter heard a click and a buzz, and a moment later Aaron Kurtzman picked up the line.

"Bear," the Phoenix Force leader said, "see what you can find out about a Secret Service agent named Richard William, will you? He's the head of the President's protection team."

"That shouldn't be too difficult," Kurtzman said. "But remember he passed one hell of an in-depth background investigation before they hired him. There would have been another before he got an assignment like that.''

''True,'' McCarter said. ''But he's been at it for two years now. A lot of changes can take place in a man in that length of time.''

''Okay,'' Kurtzman said. ''Anything specific you want?''

McCarter frowned, looked around the office to reassure himself he was alone, then said, ''Try the usual reasons people switch teams,'' he said. ''Blackmail and financial problems. Find out if William might be gay or cheats on his wife. Then hack into any bank accounts he has. Check his credit and find out how much money he makes.''

''That'll only take a second,'' Kurtzman said. ''Want to hold?''

''I will.''

McCarter kept the receiver against his ear, turning toward the hall as he waited. Through the translucent glass in the upper half of the door, he watched two blurry uniforms walk past and silently prayed they wouldn't enter the office. His prayer was answered, and a moment later Kurtzman was back on the line.

''I just tapped into his personnel file. No hint of philandering or any other sexual escapades that might lead to extortion. And his overall record is exemplary, which is why he secured this assignment, of course.'' He stopped, drew a breath, then went on. "But you may just have something on the financial end. You want specifics?"

"Just give me a summary."

"Okay, William was in debt up to his eyeballs until two months ago. Second mortgage on his house, credit cards maxed out, bank accounts lower than a four-year-old's piggy bank. He cashed in two CDs he had but that hardly made a dent in his bills. Looks to me like he was on the verge of bank-ruptcy."

McCarter felt the uneasiness in his soul suddenly multiply a hundredfold. "I've got a feeling the next words out of your mouth will be 'but then,'" he said.

"But then," Kurtzman said, "he suddenly pays off everything, and he's got a big bank account again. Then he sells the old house he was about to lose and buys a bigger one in Georgetown."

"Georgetown?" McCarter repeated. "That's a little upscale for his pay rate, isn't it?"

"Let's put it this way," Kurtzman said. "Hal Brognola couldn't afford the place William and his wife just bought and Hal's got a higher G-rating than William."

The apprehension McCarter had been experiencing was now replaced by a sick feeling. The Phoenix Force leader had never liked criminals, terrorists or any of the other malefactors of society. But dirty law-enforcement officers, men who used their position of public trust for their own selfish purposes, lay at the bottom of the heap. And even below them was anyone who would aid in the assassination of the President of the United States.

"Need anything else?" Kurtzman asked.

"Not that I can think of," McCarter said. "Ring me if something comes up, though."

"I'll have Akira check a few other angles," Kurtzman said. "Right now, I'm chasing down an E-mail address through America Online."

"So I heard," McCarter said. "Good luck." He quietly returned the receiver to the cradle and stared at the wall.

Had Richard William sold out or hadn't he? Everything Kurtzman had just discovered indicated that the man had rolled over to the enemy. Were there other factors that hadn't surfaced yet? Some legitimate explanation for the agent going from rags to riches over night?

The Phoenix Force leader wanted with all his heart to believe there was a good reason for the Secret Service agent's sudden financial turnaround. But if there was one, he couldn't imagine what it was.

McCarter opened the door and started down the hall toward the Oval Office. One thing didn't fit into the picture. If William was dirty, why was he so intent on keeping the President and First Lady at home tonight? An assassination attempt at the White House would seem to be picking the hardest of all possible targets.

The door to the reception area opened just as McCarter reached for the knob. He stepped back and let a smiling Special Agent Richard William step out into the hall. Glancing over his shoulder as he shut the door behind him, William looked down the hall to make sure the uniformed guards were out of earshot, then whispered, "Stroke of luck. The President has reconsidered. He's staying in tonight."

McCarter looked the man in the eyes, searching for the treachery he suspected lay behind them. "How'd you maneuver that?" he asked.

William grinned, obviously pleased with the success of whatever strategy he had employed. "Tried another approach," he said.

McCarter waited.

William glanced up and down the hallway once more, then lowered his voice even further. "I had Eileen go in and speak to him," he whispered. "Seems the man has decided the two of them need to work late tonight."

Special Agent Richard William gave McCarter a we're-both-men-of-the-world wink, and walked off down the hall.

Arizona

BOLAN'S FIRST TAP of the trigger sent a 3-round burst of 9 mm rounds sputtering from the sound-suppressed Beretta 93-R. Two of the hollowpoints found a home in the skinny chest of the Liberty Arizona man holding the package. The third drilled through the man's face.

As the guy collapsed in a heap of death on the concrete floor, the package skidded across the concrete to the wall.

Next to him, the Executioner heard a double-tap of .45s erupt from Devlin's pistol. At the same time, a Liberty man gripping a sawed-off 12-gauge Rossi "coachgun" cut loose with both barrels. The combined explosions were deafening inside the warehouse.

Bolan heard a muffled grunt from Devlin but had no time to check the man out. A third gunman swung a Colt pistol his way, shuffling his feet into a Weaver stance as he did so. Bolan saw him searching for the front sight of his weapon, trying to center it on his target.

In the split second it took the Executioner to repoint the Beretta, he saw the cylinder start to revolve as the gunner began to pull carefully back on the trigger.

A grim smile came over Bolan as he tapped the trigger of the Beretta again. The Liberty man had read too many books, seen too many training videos on proper stance and trigger control. All of that was fine for long-range shooting when there was time.

The problem was, the man had no time. And his proper form wasn't only unnecessary to effective close-quarters shooting, it proved fatal.

Three more full-auto 9 mm rounds sped from the 93-R and downed the man with the Colt.

The fourth Liberty gunner, middle-aged and sporting graying temples and a full beard, suddenly froze as if he'd turned to stone. His eyes took on a faraway look and the arm holding the .45-caliber Government Model pistol dropped to his side.

It was a rare stroke of luck. Holding his free hand out to stop Devlin from killing the man, he shouted, "Drop your weapon! Now!"

The Liberty gunner stared at him with unseeing eyes.

"Drop it!" Bolan shouted again. This time he fired another 3-round burst past the man's ear for emphasis.

The rounds didn't even seem to register in the man's idling brain.

The Executioner stepped forward and grabbed the barrel of the .45. The man offered no resistance as Bolan twisted the weapon from his fingers. Shoving the .45 into his belt, Bolan turned to face Devlin.

The Phoenix PD detective was inspecting a rip in the shoulder of his suit coat.

"You hurt?" Bolan asked.

Devlin's fingers came away from the tear lightly covered in blood. "Don't think so," he said. "Not bad, anyway. Looks like I caught a pellet or two is all." He raised his arm and rolled his shoulder several times, then shook his head. "No biggie."

"Then watch our new friend for a minute," Bolan said. He turned to the wall and dropped to one knee in front of the package. Opening his folding knife with his thumb, he sliced the paper from around the box.

The Executioner felt Devlin move in above him as he removed the lid. There was a moment of silence, then the PPD detective said, "What in hell's name is that?"

Bolan stared down at the apparatus. "It's a thermal charge," he said. "Homemade, a little crude, but highly effective." He looked up to see that Devlin had handcuffed the Liberty Arizona man's wrists behind his back and was holding him by an arm.

The Executioner's gaze returned to the box. He squinted harder for a moment, then stood and moved to the hole in the wall. Sticking his head inside, he searched the area top to bottom.

"What are you looking for?" Devlin asked.

"A detonator," Bolan said. "But I'm not finding one."

"Think they made one of those, too?" Devlin asked.

The Executioner shook his head. "I doubt it. The detonators aren't as easy to make as the charges themselves. They'd have to come by one somewhere else, is my guess." He turned back to the human statue next to Devlin. "Wake up," he said. "You know anything about a detonator?"

The man continued to stare into space as if in some catatonic trance.

The Executioner drew back his free hand and slapped the man across the face. "Wake up!" he ordered.

The slap had the desired effect. "Huh?" the man said, as if coming out of a deep sleep. His eyes scanned the bodies on the floor around him as if he wasn't sure where he was or how he got there. Then the dull orbs in the sockets began to slowly take on a new awareness.

Devlin continued to hold the man's arm with one hand, reaching around with the other to grab his throat. "What do you know about a thermal detonator?" he demanded as his fingers began to squeeze.

"A...what?" the man choked out around Devlin's hand.

Bolan reached up and pulled the cop's hand from the militiaman's neck. "He was probably sent to pick up the package without knowing what it was," he said. "He doesn't look like he has enough brains to be trusted."

The Liberty man proved the Executioner's words by letting the insult go over his head.

"It doesn't matter," Bolan said. "What he will know is where the new headquarters are." He grabbed a handful of the back of the Liberty man's jacket and shoved him toward the door.

Devlin hung on to the man's arm and guided him. Bolan fell in on the other side.

"This suit cost over a hundred bucks," Devlin growled. "And I'd rather spend my money on cheap bourbon. Now, like they say in the movies, take us to your leader."

"You got a name?" the Executioner asked as they made their way back through the warehouse.

"Chamberlain," the man mumbled. His voice sounded detached from the rest of his brain, as if he were still suffering at least partially from the shock that had turned him into an ice sculpture earlier.

Bolan and Devlin escorted Chamberlain down the steps in front of the warehouse and along the street to the Blazer. A moment later, they were pulling away, with Devlin behind the wheel.

The soldier noticed that the detective's jacket had soaked through with blood. "How bad you bleeding?" he asked from the backseat where he had the Beretta trained on Chamberlain.

"Not that bad," the detective replied. "But worse than I thought. My place is only about a mile from here. We got time for me to stop and take care of it?"

Bolan nodded. "We need to make a phone call anyway," he said.

Five minutes later, Devlin pulled into a parking lot outside a run-down two-story apartment building. "It's not much," he said apologetically, "but it's the best I can do with two divorces and child support.''

The Executioner jerked Chamberlain out of the back seat and towed him to a splintered ground-level front door. Devlin inserted a key and a moment later they were inside the one-room efficiency apartment. Bolan slammed Chamberlain onto a frayed divan and pointed to the phone on the end table next to it. ''Call your people,'' he said. ''Tell them you've just bumped into some old friends who are coming in with you.''

Chamberlain was still half out of the real world. But by now he was cognizant enough to speak. ''They won't buy it,'' he mumbled. ''Where am I supposed to know you from? What do I tell them?''

Bolan slid the Beretta back under his arm and drew the big Desert Eagle. Shoving the .44-caliber bore under Chamberlain's nose, he said, ''That's your problem. But you better make it convincing. Because the first round out of this thing will be for you if you don't.''

Devlin had disappeared into the bathroom and now emerged shirtless. He had washed the wound to his shoulder and pressed a towel over it. ''No bone, no ligament, no problem,'' he said. ''Pellet didn't even stay inside. But it's a bleeder.''

Bolan saw that his guess about the man's weight-lifting had been correct—Devlin looked like a thick, hairy block of concrete. The Executioner watched the man move to the kitchenette at the end of the room, open a drawer and pull out a tube of fast-acting glue. Dropping the towel, Devlin pried open the wound, squirted the epoxy into the laceration at the top of his triceps, then quickly closed his flesh again.

A grin crept over the Executioner's face. It was a trick he'd used himself from time to time. The alcohol in the glue acted as an antiseptic and the adhesive agent became makeshift field stitches.

Devlin walked to a closet on the other side of the room as Chamberlain picked up the phone and tapped in a number.

A moment later, the Liberty Arizona man said, "Yeah, let me talk to Needham." There was a pause, then he said, "Johnny? Chamberlain. No, everything's fine. The others are on their way now. But listen, I bumped into two old buddies from my Montana days." There was another pause while he listened. Then he said, "No, just saw them at the place we stopped this morning for coffee. Yeah, they were part of the group I was with up there. They need to relocate, if you get my drift. Mind if I bring them in? Okay." Chamberlain hung up and looked at the Executioner. "Needham said okay. But he's suspicious. He says if there's anything fishy about this it'll be my ass."

"It'll be your ass anyway," Devlin said. He crossed the room now wearing a red sweatshirt, faded jeans and the Wellingtons. The muscular detective looked far more at home in the casual clothes.

Devlin drove again with Chamberlain guiding him through the streets of Phoenix. They turned east onto Highway 60 and crossed into Tempe, took the exit for Arizona State University, and soon found themselves in a small shopping center near the school.

Students toting canvas backpacks and book bags came and went along the storefronts as Chamberlain pointed to a sign that read Books New and Used. "They're in there," he said. "That's the new headquarters."

Bolan had traded the Desert Eagle for the Beretta. Now, he jammed the sound suppressor into Chamberlain's ribs. "You saw what this thing did to your buddies back at the warehouse?" he asked.

Chamberlain nodded. His eyes glazed over as if his brain were about to take another vacation.

The Executioner poked him harder. "This is no time to go zombie on us," he said. "I want to get in and talk to Needham without creating a scene that will bring the cops. Some quick talking and thinking on your part just might keep you alive. You understand?"

"They'll kill me if I take you in there," Chamberlain said.

"I'll kill you if you don't," Bolan reminded him.

The Executioner tucked the Beretta under his jacket and got out. Devlin and Chamberlain followed, with the Liberty Arizona man moving to the lead as they neared the front door of the bookstore.

Three men far too old to wear Arizona State T-shirts were unloading used books and placing them on the empty shelves inside the front room. They looked up briefly, then went back to work as Chamberlain led the way to the back office.

John Wesley Needham, the leader of Liberty Arizona, sat at a desk in front of a computer as they entered the room. Like Chamberlain, he was nearing fifty. Bald on top, he had a close-cropped stubble of hair above his ears and a clean-shaven face. He looked up, scowling. "Where's Drake and the others?" he asked. "I thought you said they were on their way."

The Executioner glanced quickly around the small office. An exit in the opposite wall evidently led to the rear of the shopping center. He closed the door and pulled the Beretta from under his blazer. Turning to Needham, the Executioner said, "He lied."

Needham started to speak, but Bolan raised the pistol a little higher. "Keep your voice down."

Devlin drew his weapon from beneath his sweatshirt and said, "I'll cover the door." He moved back against the wall, listening for sounds from the front room.

Needham regained his composure quickly. "What do you want?" he said. "You got a warrant?"

Bolan ignored the second question, answering the first. "Where was the thermal charge going? To Maestro?"

Needham laughed. "Like I'm gonna tell you," he said. "Right." He turned to Chamberlain. "As for you, you son of a bitch—" He was interrupted by a voice from his computer speakers: "You have mail."

Bolan holstered the Beretta and grabbed Needham by the collar, lifting the man off his chair. He performed a quick frisk, finding a double-edged dagger that he stuffed into his belt next to the .45 pistol he had taken from Chamberlain, then pushed Needham onto the floor in the corner by the desk. "Stay put," he said, taking the chair in front of the computer.

"You keep him covered," he told Devlin.

The detective nodded, swinging his pistol that way.

The Executioner clicked the mouse to bring up the mail. *Where is your product?* appeared on the screen. He looked down at Needham on the floor. "They talking about the thermal charge?" he asked.

A grunt was Needham's only answer.

Bolan glanced up at the return address, memorizing the numbers and letters. There was nothing about them to lead him to believe that the communiqué was from Maestro. But every instinct in his soul screamed that it was.

The Executioner knew he wasn't likely to get another break like this. He had to stall and find out all he could before Maestro caught onto the fact that it wasn't Needham he was talking to. *Short delay,* he typed onto the screen. *Nothing to worry about.* He turned to Needham again. "Who am I talking to here?" he demanded. "Is it Maestro?"

Needham remained silent.

Type in identification code, appeared on the monitor in front of Bolan. "What is it?" the Executioner asked Needham. "What's the ID code?"

Needham just stared at him.

Bolan swiveled in the chair, grabbed Needham by the collar again and jerked him up to his level. Drawing Needham's own knife from his belt, he pressed the tip into the hollow just above the man's collar bone. "We don't have time to play games," he said in a low even voice. "You've got three seconds to give me the code word. Then your larynx becomes a shishkabob. One...two..."

"Holocaust," Needham said, a film of sweat breaking out on his forehead. "The word is *holocaust.*"

Bolan dropped the man back in the corner. He typed in the word and waited for a response. It took a full minute before it came.

Mission aborted. Await further orders.

The Executioner sat back. "He's on to us," he said. "He knows something's wrong." Picking up the phone next to the computer, he dialed Stony

Man Farm. Five minutes later, he had relayed the new developments, including the return address, to Kurtzman.

Needham spoke as Bolan hung up again. "Lot of good all this will do you," he said sarcastically. "You broke in here at gunpoint. You threatened me with a knife. You got no warrant, and you didn't advise me of my rights." He threw back his head and cackled. "You dumb bastards, is it any wonder our federal government is in the shape it's in? None of this will stand up in court. By the time my attorneys get through with you, it'll be *your* ass in the slammer, not mine."

Bolan sighed and shook his head. "Guess I screwed up," he said sadly. "But since I didn't advise you of your rights, tell me something. Was Liberty Arizona really responsible for that train derailment that killed all those people?"

Needham's chest puffed with pride. "You bet your sweet ass we were," he said.

"Innocent men, women and children died in that crash," Bolan said. "That ever bother you?"

Needham shrugged. "All wars have innocent casualties," he said without emotion.

The Executioner nodded. "The guys outside unloading the books. They help with the derailment?"

Needham cackled again. "Oh, yeah," he said. "They helped on that, and a half-dozen bombs and a lot of other shit you don't even know about. None of which you'll ever pin on any of us."

The Executioner turned his eyes to Chamberlain. "How about our new buddy here?" Bolan asked.

"He's done his share," Needham said. "But that's over now." His eyes narrowed in hatred. "Chamberlain's gonna pay for bringing you here."

"Thanks," the Executioner said. "That's all I needed to know."

Needham held out both hands. "So get the cuffs on and let's get down to the station," he said. "The sooner we get that out of the way the sooner I can bond out and start getting my lawsuit filed against you."

Bolan shook his head. "We're not going to arrest you, Johnny," he said. "We aren't the law."

A puzzled look came over Needham's face.

Still seated in front of the computer, Bolan drew the Beretta, flipped the selector to semiauto and pointed it at Chamberlain's face.

As Needham realized what was about to go down, he made a desperate lunge toward the desk drawer for the gun no doubt secreted there.

Bolan pulled the trigger, and drilled a hole in Needham's chest. A second round pierced Chamberlain's head, as the man attacked the Executioner.

The Executioner stood and opened the door.

The three men unloading the books stopped and looked his way.

As Bolan walked forward, raising the Beretta as he went, the men fumbled at their waistbands for their guns. The next hollowpoint struck a Liberty

Arizona man in the middle of the forehead. For a moment, it looked like he had grown a third eye.

Two quick shots took out the other two men.

The bookstore fell into silence.

CHAPTER THIRTEEN

Nashville, Tennessee

The wheels of the Learjet flown by Stony Man Farm number-two pilot, Charlie Mott, hit the tarmac without a bump. Carl Lyons looked over at the man in the frayed Kansas City Athletics warm-up jacket as the plane rolled to the end of the runway. "Stay loose, Charlie," he said. "And ready. We don't know what we've got yet."

Mott grinned as he turned onto the taxiway and crept to a halt. "This mean I won't be visiting that sweet young thing from Vanderbilt that I met at Ft. Lauderdale over spring break?" he asked as he guided the jet in.

"Not this trip," Lyons replied. Behind him, he could hear Schwarz and Blancanales gathering Able Team's gear bags.

"Charlie," Schwarz called from the back, "you're as bad as Pol with that barmaid back at the Alamo. Both of them are young enough to be your daughters, you old farts."

Mott feigned indignity. "Some of us old farts still got what it takes to attract the young ones," he told Gadgets. "Of course, Pol and I wouldn't expect *you* to understand how that works."

"Right on, Birdman," Blancanales called out as Lyons heard one of them slide open the rear door.

Lyons dropped to the ground and grabbed a bag handed down by Schwarz. Behind him, he heard the roar of a vehicle and turned to see a dark blue panel truck racing across the runway toward them. The crest of the Nashville Police Department was painted on the doors of the truck. On the sides, in bright white four-foot letters, read *SWAT*.

"Oh, great," Lyons said.

The truck screeched to a halt ten feet from the jet, and a tall wiry man with reddish-brown hair peeking out of the sides of his blue Ranger-style cap leaped from the passenger's seat. Lyons saw the gold bars on his navy blue coveralls. The captain held an M-16 by the carry grip and wore a combat vest complete with extra magazines, walkie-talkie, smoke grenades and other tools of his trade stuffed into the pockets. A Heckler & Koch USP pistol hung on one side from the black nylon belt around his waist. His name tag read *Lang*.

"Special Agent Lyons?" Captain Lang asked.

The Able Team leader nodded, quickly flashing the Justice Department credentials issued to him by Brognola. "That's right," he said. "I take it the Cessna hasn't landed yet."

The captain shook his head. "No, sir. But that's hardly surprising." He glanced at the Learjet behind Lyons. "Looks like you had a considerably faster unit. You didn't happen to spot him in the air, did you?"

Lyons slung the gear bag carry strap over his shoulder. "No," he said, "but that's hardly surprising either. Even knowing his flight plan it's a big sky out there." He frowned past Lang at the truck. Ten men dressed similarly to their captain had come out of the rear door and now stood around the vehicle. "Just exactly what did you have planned, Captain?" he asked. "Invading some small Third World country?"

Lang stood a little straighter. It was obvious he didn't like the comment. "No, *sir*," he said indignantly.

"I gave orders to have police standing by," he said. "Not mounting a charge up San Juan Hill."

"Sir—"

Lyons didn't let him finish. "Were you planning to just charge the plane, Lang? Didn't they tell you what was on board?"

Lang was matching Lyons's scowl now. It was clear he wasn't used to being interrupted or criticized. But he did a fairly good job maintaining a professional demeanor. "We were provided with information that a Cessna carrying an illegal thermal detonator would be landing, and that we were to prevent the pilot or anyone else on the plane from leaving the airport.'' His jaw set firmly as he continued to stare Lyons in the eye. "As I'm sure you must be aware, Special Agent Lyons, a detonator without a charge is fairly harmless.''

"Did whoever briefed you tell you there was no charge on the plane?'' Blancanales asked, stepping down from the Learjet and taking a place next to Lyons.

Some of the color left Lang's face. "No,'' he said. "They didn't specifically say that.''

"Then how do you know the Cessna doesn't have the whole she-bang on board?'' Now it was Schwarz stepping in to stand on the other side of the Able Team leader.

Lang's Adam's apple bobbed out then back in as he swallowed. "Are you telling me they *do* have all the components?''

"No,'' Lyons said, "we don't know that they do. On the other hand, we can't be sure that they don't. The pilot may have picked it up on the way for all we know. So I'd say this operation calls for a little more finesse then a dozen blue-clad Arnolds and Slys trying to recreate Entebbe, wouldn't you?''

Lang's face reddened with anger, then embarrassment. Then suddenly it relaxed. "Okay,'' he said, shaking his head and glancing at the ground. "I made a mistake. I assumed there was no charge since one wasn't mentioned, and we all know that old joke about making an ass out of *u* and me.'' He looked back up. "So. You have a plan?''

A rare smile lit up on Carl Lyons's face. All men made mistakes. Many couldn't admit them. Lang was a good man. "I'd like your boys close, but out of sight," the Able Team leader said. "We don't know yet if Cube—Travis Thompson, the man in the Cessna—is stopping here or just refueling and going on. If he deplanes, he'll be easy enough to take. If not…" He let his words fade, then indicated Schwarz and Blancanales with his head. "Can you get the three of us into some coveralls? Flight line, not SWAT."

Lang returned the smile. "It can be arranged. I'll take you to the locker room."

"Good," Lyons said. "But we better hurry. The Cessna could be landing any—"

"Captain!" a voice suddenly called out next to the truck.

Lang and the men of Able Team turned to see a SWAT officer holding up a walkie-talkie. "It's the tower," he said as the other men began to disappear into the back of the truck. "The Cessna just radioed in its coordinates and requested permission to land."

"Tell them to stall," Lyons said, starting toward the truck. "Make him circle once or twice." Schwarz and Blancanales hurried to join him at the rear door of the vehicle and the three Stony Man warriors jumped into the back with the SWAT team. A moment later, the panel truck was laying rubber down a service road toward the flight-line locker room.

The driver ground to a halt in front of a green concrete building next to the maintenance hangar, and Able Team piled out the back. Lang met them at the door, sticking his head briefly inside. "Lieutenant Steele!" he said. "Make sure the truck's out of sight and get the men hidden in the refueling area. We'll keep in touch by radio." He slammed the door shut and turned toward the building as the vehicle pulled away.

Lyons, Schwarz and Blancanales followed Lang into an office area. A lone desk stood in the middle of the spartanly furnished room. A name plate of cursive letters carved out of wood rested at the front edge. Betty Dickenson, it read. The middle-aged woman who went with the name looked up from behind the desk in surprise as the four men burst through the door. "What in the world—" she started to say.

"There's no time for explanations, ma'am," Lang said. "I'm Captain Lang with the Nashville PD, and I need a master key to the lockers."

Betty Dickenson's hand rose to a lock of hair, which she twisted nervously. "I don't...I mean, we don't...I mean, the men furnish their own locks. We don't have a—"

Lang and the men of Able Team didn't hear her finish the sentence. They had already sprinted through the door leading to the locker room.

Green metal lockers, similar to those found in any high school in any city in the country, lined the walls. Lyons hurried to the nearest one, drew his knife, and jammed the sturdy tip into the steel loop at the top of the padlock securing the door. He twisted right, then left. The padlock held firm, but the thin metal holding the door to the frame snapped like a dried twig.

Inside, the Able Team leader saw a pair of flight-line coveralls, boots and other gear.

Lyons moved down the line, cracking open another half-dozen of the lockers, all of them empty. The next two held similar equipment to the first he had tried, and he shoved the knife back into his sheath.

His teammates were already pulling off their shoes. "I take it we shouldn't expect a tailor's fit today," Blancanales said as he ripped a pair of the coveralls off the hook and stuck a leg inside.

Thirty seconds later, the men of Able Team had hidden their weapons beneath the coveralls and tied the laces of their boots. The walkie-talkie on Lang's belt suddenly squawked, and the captain jerked it from its nylon carrier. "Go ahead," he said.

Lyons recognized the voice of the man who'd manned the radio earlier. "Radio tower just advised that the Cessna has requested refueling. He's planning to call in another flight plan and go on."

"They say where?" Lang asked.

"Negative. And they won't know until he files

the plan,'' the voice came back. The man on the other end cleared his throat. ''But they've already circled him twice, Captain. Unless he's a stone-cold fool he's going to get suspicious pretty soon. There's not that much traffic out here. He'll be able to see that.''

Lang turned to Lyons, who nodded.

''Tell them to bring him in,'' Lang said.

''Ten-four, Cap.''

Lyons and the others hurried back out into the office where the elderly woman still sat, wide-eyed. ''You have a car?'' Lang asked.

''Well, certainly,'' she said. ''I—''

''Give me the keys,'' Lang ordered.

Betty Dickenson dug into her purse and came up with a set of keys. ''It's the Toyota on the side of the building,'' the woman said. Her voice was filled with enthusiasm now.

She was helping the police. She didn't know how, but it had to be the most excitement she'd had in years. Lyons just hoped he wouldn't have her heart attack on his conscience before it was all over.

They started for the door. ''Wait a minute,'' the Able Team leader said suddenly. ''Cube will recognize us when we get close. Even in these coveralls.''

Dickenson jumped to her feet. ''Come with me,'' she said, trotting around the desk.

Lang and Lyons followed Betty Dickenson out the door. The woman led the way around the build-

ing to a row of parking spaces. She opened the
trunk of a Toyota and pulled out a square black
case. Flipping the latches, she opened the top.

Lyons looked in, and he cocked an eyebrow. "A
wig?"

Dickenson shook her head. "You men," she
said. "It's not a wig, it's a fall." She pulled the
hairpiece out and turned to Lyons. "It's my daughter's. You'll look like a hippy." She giggled as she
began to pull bobby pins from somewhere inside
the case.

Blancanales and Schwarz grinned as the Able
Team leader leaned over so the woman could pin
the blond fall into his hair.

"That takes care of him, Betty," Blancanales
said. "What about us?"

Dickenson didn't break stride. Reaching up to
her own hair, she jerked off her wig.

"You," she said, smiling and pointing to Blancanales. "It almost matches your own hair."

Blancanales, who had been prematurely gray for
years, laughed out loud. "Betty, baby," he said,
stooping over so she could reach his head, "do that
thing you do!" A moment later his hair was halfway down to his shoulders.

"That's all the hair," Dickenson said, turning
toward Schwarz. "But come with me." She trotted
to the driver's side of the vehicle, unlocked the door
and pulled out a brown leather driving cap and a

pair of thick black eyeglasses. "My husband's," she said, handing them to Gadgets.

Schwarz grinned as he donned the hat and glasses, then suddenly winced. "Good night," he said, looking over the top of the frames. "What's his prescription, 20/1000?"

"Something like that. But he's a good man."

"He'd better be," Blancanales said as he took the key chain from the woman and handed it to Lang.

"What do you mean?"

"I mean," Blancanales said as the other men got into the car, "that if he isn't, I'll be back to steal you away from him."

Betty Dickenson smiled broadly as the Toyota tore off down the service road toward the refueling line.

Lang guided the Toyota with one hand, ripping the Ranger cap off his head with the other. He looked over at Lyons who was seated next to him. "I'm going to take you right up to the pumps," he said, "which means the Cessna will be able to see me." He blew air through his clenched teeth, then went on. "Help me out of this vest, will you?"

The Able Team leader reached over to assist as the captain shrugged out of his tactical vest.

"The side arm and belt should be hidden below the window," Lang said. "But what do I do about these damn captain's bars?" He twisted his neck to look at his shoulder.

Blancanales and Schwarz, seated behind the SWAT man, moved as one. Reaching up, they each ripped a bar off the man's combat suit. An inch of material came away with the insignia in Schwarz's fist, leaving a hole and frayed white thread sticking up at Lang's shoulder.

"You don't know how long I've wanted to do that to somebody," Schwarz said.

Blancanales laughed. "Me too."

The Toyota cut diagonally across the apron in front of one service area, eliciting several shouts and one raised middle finger from the crew working there. Lang piloted the vehicle to the next station, where small private planes were being refueled. He pulled to a halt just as the Cessna taxied up.

Lyons had found a red cotton scarf on the front seat and rolled it quickly into a headband, tying it tightly around the hair falling past his shoulders to further distort his features. He glanced over the backseat. The cap and sunglasses altered Gadgets's face pretty well. But Pol just looked like Pol wearing a gray wig.

"Gadgets," the Able Team leader said. "You come with me. I'll take the pilot side. Walk casually."

"How about me?" Blancanales asked.

"Do something around the pumps," Lyons said. "And face the other way. You look like your mother."

"If your mother missed a few estrogen shots and liked other women," Schwarz put in.

"Thanks," Blancanales said as the three men got out of the Toyota. "Mother jokes. They're even beneath *you* two."

Two real flight-line attendants stood at the pumps. Lyons walked up to one and grabbed the clipboard from his hands.

"Hey," the man said. But before he could continue Blancanales had grabbed his arm and spun him around for a quick debriefing.

Lyons and Schwarz walked toward the Cessna together. Lyons kept his gaze on the clipboard, trying to keep his face as hidden as possible. The two men split as they neared the plane.

At the top of his field of vision, Lyons saw the door on the pilot's side begin opening. Good. Cube was getting out to stretch, which would make him more accessible. Six feet from the plane, the Able Team leader reached inside his coveralls and drew his knife. He kept the blade hidden beneath the clipboard.

Lyons didn't look up until he was within arm's length of the door. Then, letting the clipboard fall to the ground, he reached up to grab a handful of the pilot's hair with his left hand and pressed the blade against the man's throat with the other.

The man who had flown the Cessna froze. Lyons looked over the thick blade to see the horror in the eyes above it. "Don't move," he growled.

The pilot didn't.

There was only one problem.

The man who had flown the Cessna wasn't Cube.

Stony Man Farm, Virginia

AARON KURTZMAN pulled his fingers away from the keyboard as the intercom on the console next to the screen began to buzz. For two days, ever since Phoenix Force had left to baby-sit the President, and Striker and Able Team had begun hunting for Maestro, he'd had his cybernetics team following computer leads of the sort that you pursue when you have nothing better to go on. These searches hadn't just been busy work, but they had about the same probability of leading to anything of value.

Then things had started to break. Both Bolan and Lyons had suddenly come up with Intel he could feed into his magic machines that began to make things take shape. By tapping into America Online's files, Kurtzman had been able to trace the E-mail address to one Mary Click at an apartment in Virginia Beach, Virginia. Further electronic investigation had come up with the facts that Mary was a widow with no police record.

Her thirty-two-year-old son, however, who according to the Virginia tax rolls still lived with his mother, didn't fit that profile. He had a long string of arson arrests dating from the time he turned eighteen and first entered the adult criminal justice system. Although he hadn't bothered to check Kurtzman knew if he tapped into the sealed juvenile records of the State of Virginia he would find similar entries.

Pyromaniacs like Desmond Click didn't wait until they were of legal age to begin setting fires. Like most sexual offenders, they started young, with signs of their dysfunction usually beginning to exhibit itself around puberty.

Kurtzman reached for the buzzing phone. He also learned that Click had been caught up in one of his own fires. Since then, the man had been in a wheelchair. He stayed in his room most of the time and, according to the records of Virginia's Probation and Parole Board, he spent most of his time with a computer.

Kurtzman had passed on the information to Barbara Price. Stony Man's mission controller had immediately dispatched Leo Turrin and Yakov Katzenelenbogen to lead a team of blacksuits to Virginia Beach. Kurtzman glanced at his wristwatch. With any luck, they should be taking Click into custody in the next few minutes. That might even be what the call he was answering now was about.

The phone buzzed again, and the computer genius pressed the receiver to his ear. "Yeah, Barb?"

"Lyons on 44," Price said. "He needs to talk to us both."

Kurtzman heard the click as Price connected the line to his phone. "Yeah, Ironman?" he said.

"Barb still on?" Lyons asked.

"I'm here."

"Okay. Cube wasn't flying the Cessna. He hired Harley—Harley was one of the bouncers at the Alamo when we arrived—to create a diversion in case someone was onto him. He also had Harley charter another plane, which Cube has flown to Washington. That's D.C., not State."

"You got a lot out of this Harley in a short amount of time," Price said.

"I used some not-so-gentle persuasion," Lyons replied.

"So you need to know if Cube has landed in D.C. yet, right?" Kurtzman asked. "What's Harley's last name?"

"Just a second," Lyons said.

Kurtzman heard Lyons's muffled voice on the other end of the line. Then he heard someone scream.

"Belzer," Lyons said into the phone a moment later. "Harley Parsons Belzer. You need anything else?"

"No. Give me a second." His fingers flew across the keyboard and a second later the charter flight records of both D.C. airports appeared next to each other on the screen. "Sorry," he told the Able Team leader. "He's come and gone."

Lyons cursed.

A beeping sound came over the lines and Price said, "Hang on. That may be Leo or Katz. If it is,

I'll patch them in.'' Her end clicked for a moment but her voice returned a few seconds later. ''Everybody still there? Go ahead, Katz.''

The former Phoenix Force leader came on the line. ''Click's flown the coup,'' he said. ''All we found here is a dead woman we assume is Mary.''

''He killed his own mother?'' Price asked.

''Looks like it,'' Katz said. ''There's one bullet hole between her eyes and two more in her chest.''

''Any clue where he's gone?'' Price asked.

''Not so far. The blacksuits are still searching the place. Leo's gone to…just a second. Here he comes.''

A second later Turrin said, ''One of the neighbors just told me they heard the shots, then saw Click rolling down the hall to the elevator. He also said Click has a disability-equipped van, which means he's mobile.''

''Wait a minute,'' Price said. ''Hal just walked in.''

Kurtzman turned his head to look through the glass wall separating the Computer Room from the mission control center. He saw Brognola hurry to Price's console and take the receiver from her. Price said a few words, then the big Fed pressed the phone to his ear and spoke into the mouthpiece.

''Carl,'' Brognola said, ''have Charlie get you to Washington on the double.''

He turned to Price, ''Barb, contact Striker and get him back this way, too. We'll all meet at my office at Justice. Whatever's happening is going to happen fast. And it looks like its going to go down in D.C.''

Washington, D.C.

MCCARTER HAD SPENT close to two hours trying to decide what to do about Special Agent Richard William when the answer came to him. He could just confront the man with the evidence and watch his reaction. All he needed to know really was whether the man was the leak that the President suspected. The Phoenix Force leader wasn't a cop; he wasn't trying to make a case to take before a jury, and it didn't matter if the evidence got tainted because William hadn't been advised of his rights or other proper procedures had been ignored. McCarter would know if the Secret Service man was dirty by the way William responded to the accusations.

And if he *was* dirty, Stony Man Farm had its own way of prosecuting that wouldn't get thrown out of court for technical violations.

The phone on Eileen's desk suddenly rang, breaking the silence that had fallen on the reception area. The woman lifted the phone and said, ''Oval Office.'' McCarter watched her listen to whomever it was on the other end, then heard her say, ''All right. I've already told the President, and he's planning to work in his study while they're here. Send them up when they get here.'' She disconnected the line with a long red fingernail, then tapped another button. ''Mr. President,'' she said, ''the exterminators will be on their way soon. Shall I send anyone in to help you carry your things?''

William shot from his chair next to McCarter as Eileen hung up. ''What's this about exterminators?'' he demanded.

''Didn't I tell you?'' Eileen asked. ''I found a cockroach in here this morning.'' Her shoulders shuddered in revulsion.

''No, you *didn't* tell me,'' William said in an agitated voice.

Eileen shrugged. ''Well, it's hardly the first time they've come, if you'll remember. This is an old building, Agent William.'' She stood and smoothed the skirt over her thighs. ''In the meantime, the President needs one of you to help carry some files to his study.'' Without another word she picked up her purse and walked out into the hall.

William let out a puff of air in disgust. He looked at George, then nodded toward the door to the Oval Office.

McCarter, Encizo and Manning followed William and Howard out into the hallway. The Phoenix Force leader looked at William, and decided now was as good a time as any to speak to him. Stepping up to the man, he said, ''I need to see you for a few minutes. Privately.''

William frowned, then looked at Howard. ''Take

over. Grab a couple of uniforms and escort the President to the study.'' He glanced curiously at McCarter, then walked down the hall toward the Secret Service office.

McCarter followed him into the command post where two uniformed officers sat at desks facing each other. William hooked a thumb over his shoulder at the door he and McCarter had just come through. The uniforms understood. They got up and left without a word.

The two men took the seats the others had vacated. McCarter stared across the room at the agent. Depending on what he saw and heard in the next few minutes, he knew he might have to kill Richard William. And he wasn't looking forward to it.

McCarter opened his mouth to speak when the phone in front of William rang.

The Secret Service agent lifted the receiver and said, ''William.'' He glanced across the room to McCarter, then said, ''It's for you.''

McCarter lifted the phone on his desk as William hung up. ''Yes?'' the Phoenix Force leader said.

''David?'' Akira Tokaido's voice asked on the other end.

''That's me,'' McCarter answered. He could hear the babel that the young Japanese computer ace called music exploding faintly in the background.

''Aaron asked me to check further into Special Agent Richard William's financial status,'' Tokaido started.

"I'm aware of that," McCarter said. "Get to the bottom line."

"Okay," Tokaido said. "The bottom line is that his wife was the only child of a very wealthy widower. Her father died roughly three months ago, and she and William inherited a small fortune. It's all on the up-and-up. Looks like William is clean."

McCarter was surprised at the extent of the relief that suddenly swept over him. Until then, he hadn't realized just how much he wanted to find the man at the desk across from him innocent. "Okay," he said into the phone. "Thanks."

"So what did you need to talk to me about?" William asked as the Phoenix Force leader replaced the receiver on the cradle.

McCarter looked across the room. The head of the President's protection team was nervously tapping his fingers on the desktop, which the Phoenix Force leader now realized meant nothing more than the fact that William was reacting fairly normally to the pressure of the assignment combined with a death in the family.

"I need to ask you a question only an American can answer," McCarter said.

"What's that?"

"Who do you think is going to win the Super Bowl this year?"

CHAPTER FOURTEEN

Washington, D.C.

Desmond Click released the clamps holding his wheelchair in place behind the steering wheel of the van. Backing the chair away from the wheel, he turned and rolled forward again, much like a car leaving the driveway. He hit the brake in front of the sliding door on the side of the vehicle, and an index finger rose to one of the buttons of the control panel mounted behind the van's driver's side. The door in front of him slid open. A tap to another button lowered a platform like a drawbridge spanning a castle moat.

Click rolled through the opening onto the platform and reached back inside the vehicle for a third button. A moment later the hydraulic lift whined and moaned as the platform lowered him to ground level. He wheeled the chair off the steel platform onto the sparse grass behind the shack in one of Washington's countless ghettos. He stopped for a moment, staring at the back door of the dilapidated dwelling. The walls of the house had once been covered with tar shingles, but few remained over the gypsum-board facing. There were more shingles, or rather pieces of shingles, on the grass than on the house, Click thought, as he listened to a chorus of crickets sing in the early-evening darkness. He rolled himself toward the door.

Beneath the heavy sweater he wore against the evening chill, Click's heart clubbed his chest with excitement. It had been months since he'd been farther from his bedroom than the bathroom down the hall. Now, he had driven all the way to Washington. There was a time in his life when driving the short distance from Virginia Beach wouldn't have seemed like such an adventure. But over the past few years—ever since his accident—he had rarely left the house. One quickly lost social skills in isolation, and tonight he felt like a man on safari facing a charging lion. He was the Great White Hunter, and the exhilaration flooded his veins.

Click reached the back door of the shack and paused. No, he wasn't a Great White Hunter. He was black now. He had been a black man ever since the accident. And in a few moments he would be face-to-face with other black men who had been persecuted for the way they looked just like he had. He would meet Bernell Dixon again after so many years. The adrenaline rush was almost overpowering.

Taking a deep breath to calm himself, Click

pulled a scarred hand from under the blanket on his lap, rapped on the door and waited.

It took a few moments for a face to appear in the window at the top of the door. Click recognized it immediately. Dixon's features had aged, of course, since they had been friends at Cub Scout camp. The face around the eyes was even slightly pudgy as Zulu fast approached middle age. But the penetrating brown eyes were the same, and Click knew he could have picked out his friend on the street in the midst of the Million Man March if he'd had to.

The door opened and Bernell "Zulu" Dixon looked down at him. For a moment, surprise touched the brown eyes. Then Zulu said, "Come in, Maestro. It's good to finally meet you."

Click rolled through the doorway into a kitchen piled high with dirty dishes, fast-food wrappers and other trash. "We're in the living room," Dixon said, then turned his back on Click and led the way through a small bedroom as slovenly as the kitchen. Click saw Zulu's computer half hidden beneath a pile of dirty clothes.

Rap music drifted into the bedroom as Click wheeled into the front of the small house. Two other black men sat on threadbare furniture. Click's chest threatened to burst with excitement as he rolled to a stop in front of them. Finally he was among his own. Men like him. Men who were oppressed for what others saw on the outside rather than what they truly were in their souls. He couldn't have controlled the smile that stretched his mouth and cheeks if he had wanted to, so he didn't even try.

Bernell Dixon looked down at him and a thin smile crept over his face. "Sorry if I stared at the door. For some reason, I thought you'd be black."

Click chuckled in delight. "I am, Zulu," he said. He watched curiosity enter the brown eyes but didn't follow up on the statement. There would be time to explain later. Right now he couldn't wait to remind Zulu that they already knew each other. "I remember you, Bernell," he said.

Dixon's eyebrows lowered to the bridge of his nose.

"I'm Desmond Click," the man in the wheel-chair said.

The confusion on Dixon's face only intensified.

"Cub Scout camp," Click reminded him. "When we were eight years old." He shouldn't expect Zulu to remember without some help; he didn't look anything like he had in those days, of course.

The nod of recognition that came from Dixon was forced and Click felt his enthusiasm start to fade. The man didn't remember him, not even now that Click had refreshed his memory.

"This is Bobcat and Fisherman," Dixon said, not bothering to explain the nicknames. "Brothers, say hello to the Maestro."

The man called Bobcat stared at Click in fascination. Fisherman looked away.

Zulu rested a hand on Click's shoulder, then suddenly jerked it back as if he'd touched something too hot. "Excuse the brothers," he said, his voice embarrassed. "They didn't know...I mean, I didn't tell them...look, you told me over the Net you were in the chair, man. But we didn't know you'd been...that the rest of you had been...hurt."

The thrill in Click's chest instantly evaporated, replaced by a burning thousand-pound rock. He sat still in his chair as an uneasy silence filled the room. Dixon and the other two men weren't going to accept him any more than anyone else did. They weren't going to be his friends. He was still alone.

Click reached under the blanket and pulled out the thermal charge, holding it in the air like a child giving his parents a picture he'd drawn.

Dixon nodded, obviously grateful for any diversion from the mood that had fallen over the house. "Man, that's great," he said with forced eagerness as he took the charge from Click. "How much we owe you?"

Click forced back the tears threatening to pour from his eyes. "Nothing," he whispered, his voice sounding hollow and far away. "It's a...gift."

Dixon's piercing eyes met Click's for a moment, and in them the man in the wheelchair saw both compassion and pity. But Dixon could hold the gaze only a moment, and he turned away to look at the men across the room. "Okay, my brothers," he said, "as soon as the detonator gets here, we're on. Fisherman, did you—'' He was interrupted by a knock at the front door.

He glanced through the curtain covering the window next to the door, then looked in Click's general direction. ''I think it's the cowboy you told me about,'' he said. He drew a small .380 automatic pistol from the back pocket of his jeans.

''Maestro? Hey, anybody in there named Maestro?'' a Texas twang said through the door. ''Dammit, get me inside before the blacks eat me alive out here. Why'd we have to meet in the middle of the ghetto anyway?''

Dixon opened the door but stayed behind it out of sight. Cube fairly leaped into the living room and said, ''Damn, talk about jungle-bunny central. I—'' Suddenly he saw Fisherman and Bobcat, and the face beneath the rancher's hat turned purple.

Bernell Dixon closed the door behind Cube and the fat man whirled and found himself staring down the barrel of the .380. ''Oh, shit,'' he said. ''Hey listen, I didn't mean that stuff about—''

''It doesn't matter,'' Dixon said. He stuck the weapon back in his jeans. ''You bring the detonator?''

Cube nodded as sweat broke out beneath the brim of his rancher's hat.

''Where is it?'' Dixon asked.

Cube started to relax, realizing he wasn't going to be killed for his earlier choice of words. ''It's nearby,'' he said. ''Where's the money?''

Dixon nodded to Bobcat. The man stood, pulled a roll of bills from his jeans and handed it to Cube.

The fat Texan took the money and counted it. "I know that's what Maestro and I agreed on," he said. "But I've had unforseen expenses." He looked around the room suddenly, his eyes falling on Click. "*You're* Maestro?" he said.

Click nodded.

"Damn, I didn't know…" Not knowing how to finish the sentence, Cube let his words trail off into the air. He adjusted the belt around his immense waist, then turned back to Dixon. "Look, I had expenses," he said. "It's gonna cost you double."

Dixon's eyes flashed with anger. "That wasn't the deal."

"It is now. That is, if you still want it."

"Maybe we don't," Dixon said.

"Then maybe I ought to just get the hell out of here." Cube stuck his fat chin out belligerently, the jowls beneath it wobbling like a rowboat riding an ocean wave. His hand fell into the side pocket of his Western-cut sport coat, and the movement brought out new confidence. "I didn't know I was dealing with blacks anyway." He glanced at Click. "Or freaks."

Bobcat suddenly sprang, and now Click knew where he'd gotten the name. Before Cube could move, the revolver barrel was smashed against the back of his head. "Hey, wait a minute…" the fat man squealed.

Dixon reached forward, pulled Cube's hand from the pocket and removed an American derringer from the chubby fingers curled around it. "I think we'll pay you the same as we're paying the Maestro," he said, staring Cube in the eye. "And Maestro said what he brought us was a gift."

Cube's head bobbed up and down. "Yeah, sure," he said. "Whatever you say. The detonator's in the car. Just don't shoot me, brother."

"Call me brother again and you can count on it," Dixon said.

Fisherman rose from the couch and exited the front door. He returned a few moments later carrying a paper sack.

Dixon looked at him, and Fisherman nodded.

Dixon took two steps to the side of Cube, then nodded to Bobcat.

Bobcat pulled the trigger and Travis "Tex" Thompson's brains splattered past Dixon, slapping wetly against the wall.

Click reached under the blanket and curled his fingers around the grip of his father's Colt.

"We got work to do," Dixon said. "Let's go." He opened the front door and ushered the other two men through, started to exit himself, then turned back, remembering Click. "Hey, thanks again," he said. "You, uh, you can see yourself out, right?"

Click nodded.

The Free African Nation man closed the door behind him.

Click wheeled forward and stared at the fat body on the floor. Cube's death had come instantly. The fat Texan's face was almost peaceful. He had felt no pain.

Resting the Colt .45 on the blanket in his lap, Click stared at the closed front door. He sat quietly for a moment, a hollow numbness filling his soul. Then the pain that he had known so long, both physical and spiritual, returned to torture him.

And with the pain came the tears.

Washington, D.C.

DIXON PULLED the truck under the electronic arm at the guard post as it rose, then steered the vehicle down Pennsylvania Avenue to the front gate of the White House. He stopped again at the guard post in front of the gate and rolled down the window as a man in a Secret Service uniform approached the driver's side. The guard nodded as he looked first to the logo on the side of the truck, then down at the clipboard in his hands. "Yeah, Washington Street Pest Control," he said. "You're on the list. But you'll still have to get out while we search the vehicle. Sorry." He took a step back as four more uniformed men approached the truck.

Dixon, Bobcat and Fisherman, all dressed in khaki shirts with patches that read Washington Street Pest Control, climbed out of the truck.

"Please step over to the fence," one of the guards said as the other three began to search the vehicle.

Dixon watched the guards open the rear door of the truck as the fourth man ran his hands over the khaki shirt and pants. The man moved on to frisk the other two men. He saw a tall slender guard with blond hair climb into the back of the truck as the other two searched the cab. The blonde paused briefly at the tanks on the trio of sprayers, then went on.

A moment later, the guards signaled for the men to return to the truck. "You've got a problem," the man with the clipboard said.

"Sir?" Dixon said.

The guard tapped the windshield with his clipboard. "Your safety inspection sticker expired two days ago," he said. "Don't let the city cops catch you." He cleared his throat. "Proceed to the back of the building. Someone will meet you there." He handed a visitor's ID tag to each of the men, watched them climb back into the truck, then waved them through as the gate opened.

"Damn!" Bobcat said as they circled toward the back of the White House. "Safety inspection sticker, my ass! Bastard wanted to give me a heart attack."

Dixon's hands shook slightly as he pulled into an empty parking space by a service door. He'd had enough. He was glad he was doing what he was doing, but he was even gladder that he and his old lady would be skipping the country as soon as he finished rigging the bomb. It was all working out perfectly. Bobcat and Fisherman would flee the U.S., too, and the rest of Free African Nation would do nothing more than lay low while they tried to pick up how much the pigs knew.

No one else knew where Dixon and his woman were going. And no one knew they were taking every last penny of Free African Nation's financial resources with them, either.

Dixon, Bobcat and Fisherman stepped from the truck and began to unload their equipment as a contingent of Secret Service agents came out the service door. They were escorted into the building, then pointed through the metal detectors. All three made it through without tripping the alarm.

One of the guards even handed Dixon his steel tank and sprayer on the other side of the arches.

Dixon thought of his old lady again as they all rode up the elevator. He didn't plan to stay with her long after they reached Grand Cayman, and considering what she knew, he supposed that meant he'd have to kill her. Maybe take her out on a fishing trip and feed her to the sharks. The fact was, he'd probably have done something like that already if he hadn't needed her. She'd gotten a little too full of her own self-importance lately, and was fast becoming a royal pain in the ass.

The elevator came to a halt, and the Secret Service guards and pest control men stepped off. Dixon and his men went through another metal detector, then followed the uniforms down the hall.

A hard grin curled Dixon's lips as they neared the Oval Office. Then again, maybe he wouldn't have gotten rid of his old lady yet.

Sleeping with her was kind of a turn-on just because of who she was.

EILEEN PURSED her lips in front of the mirror as she ran the lipstick across them. She blotted her lips with a tissue and inspected her work. What she saw brought a smirk to her face. "You are so sexy. But then again, you always were."

The President's secretary stuck the lipstick in her purse and slid open the small compact of eye shadow. Removing the tiny brush in the hollow below the makeup, she began touching up her eyes as her mind drifted back over her past.

Eileen Oberlender had been born a Midwest small-town girl twenty-seven years ago last Thursday. Her parents and everyone else had assumed that like most of the other girls native to the village, she would marry a local boy and go to work at one of the grain elevators that were the area's biggest employers.

In a sense, she had gone to work at an elevator. But not in the conventional way.

Eileen dropped the brush back into the compact and dabbed a spot of blush on each cheek. She had learned early on that men liked her. She had noticed their stares as soon as she'd begun to sprout breasts, and it hadn't taken her long to recognize the power she possessed. A high-school affair with the rich owner of one of the elevators had insured a college education that her parents thought came from a scholastic scholarship. The memory still made Eileen laugh. The truth was, her grades were barely high enough to graduate high school. Georgetown University, her first choice of schools, had turned her down. So had George Washington—until she'd had a night to change the mind of the Director of Admissions.

The President's secretary smoothed the blush into her cheeks and used another tissue to wipe her hands. From the university, she had landed a good job at the Smithsonian after convincing the chief curator he couldn't live without her body. But the stupid bastard had wanted to leave his wife and kids for her, so it had been over to the Pentagon with a two-star general. That's where she met the President. He had been a senator then, but his office was still a step up. She helped him in many ways during his campaign for the Oval Office, and her reward was her current position.

And speaking of the Oval Office, Eileen thought, as she ran a brush several times through her long raven hair, it was time she got back. The exterminators would be arriving soon.

She was about to enter the office when she felt a hand on her arm. She turned to see the British guy, McCarter. He seemed to appear from nowhere. A moment of fear crept over her. That McCarter was heterosexual, she had no doubt. He probably even thought she was appealing. But he showed no signs of it like other men, and never let desire interfere with his job. He stayed in control.

Which meant Eileen couldn't control him, and that frightened her.

"Where are you going?" McCarter asked.

Eileen smiled sensuously at the man, more out of habit than the belief that it would work on the Englishman. "I've got a few things to do before the pest-control people get here," she said. "And of course I need to be here while they spray."

McCarter let her arm go. "The gate just radioed up. They're on their way."

"I'll hurry. It'll be thirty minutes to an hour before we can use the offices again."

The Briton frowned. "I thought it took longer than that."

"No, they've got some new chemicals that aren't as dangerous to people as the old ones," Eileen said. "I don't really understand it." She reached out, flicking some imaginary substance off McCarter's lapel, watching his reaction in her peripheral vision. She didn't get one, even when she let her fingers accidentally brush his face as she pulled her hand away.

McCarter just turned and walked down the hall.

As she'd known it would be, the reception area

was deserted. The Secret Service men, and whoever the hell McCarter's bunch were, had all gone to the President's study to guard him there. Taking a seat at her desk, Eileen lifted the phone. She had started to tap in the number when the hall door opened.

Several uniformed Secret Service officers and three black men in pest-control uniforms entered the reception area.

Eileen looked at the lead black man in khakis with dark brown eyes. They seemed to bore holes through hers. "How long will we have to stay out of the office after you spray?" she asked.

"An hour would be good," the man said. "But thirty minutes at least."

"No kidding?" the Secret Service uniformed supervisor Eileen knew only as Henry said. "My wife and I had our house done a few months ago. We had to rent a motel room for the night."

The pest control man shrugged his shoulders and grinned. "Progress, man," he said. "Chemicals have come a long way lately."

"I guess so," Henry said.

"Why don't you start in there," Eileen said, raising a long red fingernail at the door to the Oval Office. "I'll take you in." She turned to the Secret Service men as she stood. "You gentlemen make yourselves comfortable. We'll be right back."

"We really should go in with them," Henry said.

Eileen gave the man her sexiest smile and saw him blush. "Oh, relax, Henry," she said. "I remember these guys from when they were here before.''

Henry frowned. ''I don't.''

''Well,'' Eileen said, puckering her lips into a little pout, ''even a big strong guy like you can't work twenty-four hours a day, Henry. Maybe you had a day off.'' She watched Henry blush, then went on. ''Besides, we'll be right in there. You'll be able to see us through the door.'' She reached down to a knee with both hands and straightened her pantyhose, but her eyes never left the Secret Service man.

Henry's eyes, however, followed her hands. His face reddened. Then he shrugged and dropped into a seat against the wall. The other men followed his lead.

Eileen led the three men with the spray tanks into the Oval Office. Just inside the door, she stepped to the side, out of sight of the reception area.

The man with the deep brown eyes set down his spray tank, took her in his arms and pressed his lips against hers. His hand fondled a breast as the other two men began spraying the baseboards of the office.

Eileen pushed Bernell Dixon away from her. ''You goddamn fool,'' she whispered. ''Why take stupid chances at this stage of the game?''

Dixon glanced around him. ''It'd be fun to get it on in here,'' he whispered back. ''Real power trip.''

''Well, it's not going to happen,'' Eileen said.

"We've got too much to lose." She led him to the President's desk and stood between him and the door as he unscrewed the false top of the spray tank. Removing the thermal charge and detonator, he quickly fastened them under the desk inside the chair well with fast-acting glue, then twisted the tank back together.

Bobcat came over and made a show of spraying around the President's desk. Eileen stayed where she was. To the men watching from the reception area, it would look like she was paying careful attention to what Bobcat did. Her real purpose, however, was to continue blocking their view.

She didn't want Henry or the other men to see that nothing was coming out of Bobcat's spray hose.

Eileen watched the Free African Nation man set his tank inside the chair well beneath the bomb. When the President returned later that evening, he would think one of the pest controllers had simply forgotten it. And if one of the Secret Service men happened to notice that Bobcat no longer had a tank, he could claim an oversight and go back and get it. The diesel fuel inside wasn't really necessary. The thermal charge itself would be more than enough to turn the President into charcoal. It was simply there to send more fire across this floor of the building, wiping out some of the Secret Service men, if possible. Icing on the cake.

Or rather, fuel to the fire.

"All finished in here," Dixon called out loud enough for the men in the reception area to hear. Eileen led him back to her desk and sat down while he and the other two FAN men sprayed the area. When they finished, she said, "I've got a quick phone call to make. Then I'll leave." She waved the others toward the door.

"Okay, but don't stay too long, ma'am," Dixon said. "This new stuff won't hurt you, but it won't be pleasant." He followed the other men out the door.

Eileen lifted the phone as soon as they had gone. Her nose twitched as she pressed in the number for the airline. "Yes," she said as soon as the voice on the other end answered. "I'd like to confirm two reservations for Miami, with a connecting flight to Grand Cayman." She opened her purse, took out the tickets and read the numbers to the airline reservation clerk. "That's right. Mr. and Mrs. Bernell Dixon. Thank you."

Eileen replaced the phone and stuck the tickets back in her purse. She had an hour or so to kill before she met the President back here, and she guessed she would spend it in the cafeteria downstairs. She sat back for a moment, and let a frown come over her face. The one weak link in her plan was this timing. In reality, there was no new chemical spray that kept people away from treated areas for only thirty minutes, at least to her knowledge.

But she had been forced to come up with something to get the rest of her timing to work out.

The president's secretary stood, reminding herself to make some excuse to leave on time. She'd have to give herself a cushion of time so she could get far enough away before Zulu detonated the thermal charge and turned the leader of the free world into a presidential "crispy critter."

Eileen grabbed her purse and walked to the door. The one flaw in her story bothered her. But there was something else about her plan that bothered her even more. This would be the first time she ever killed anyone. She had no doubt she could do it, but she wasn't really looking forward to it. Yet it had to be done.

After all, she thought, as left the office and walked past the lusty eyes that followed her to the elevator. How else was she going to get Dixon's money and get rid of him after they reached the Cayman Islands?

DAVE MCCARTER PACED up and down the hallway outside the Oval Office reception area.

"Relax, buddy," Henry said as he walked by. "This is SOP. The President never lets anyone but George, Howard and William into the reception area when he's working late with Eileen." He winked at the Briton. "And they aren't allowed to even knock on the Oval Office door—regardless of what they might hear.'' He chuckled under his breath.

"That's not what's bothering me," McCarter said, stopping next to the uniformed man.

"Well, something is," Henry said. "What?"

"I don't know," McCarter answered. "I wish I did.''

"Come on. I'll buy you a cup of coffee." Henry turned and led the way down the hall toward the Secret Service command office.

The aging friend of Brognola's lifted a carafe from the coffeemaker, poured two foam cups full and handed one to McCarter. "It could be worse," he said. "If it weren't for those new chemicals they're using, we'd have to wait hours. This way, they'll be done and Eileen can go home early." He dropped into a chair behind one of the desks and grunted. "Huh. The miracles of modern science."

"I suppose," McCarter answered, his mind on other things. "I'd never heard of a chemical like this before tonight." He glanced at the phone on the desk where Henry sat. He didn't know how long the President would be working, but he might as well put the time to some use. Lifting the phone, he connected to Stony Man Farm.

"Striker and Able Team have arrived in town," Price told him. "They're just down the street from you at Hal's office. Their Maestro thing has led back here.''

"Wish them luck for me," McCarter said. "And

tell them all I'll switch missions with them anytime they say the word.'' He started to hang up, then said, ''Patch through to the Computer Room for a minute, will you Barb?''

A moment later Carmen Delahunt picked up the line. ''Hello, David,'' she said. ''What's my favorite Limey up to?''

''Watch yourself, you bloody Yank,'' the Briton said. ''And to answer your question, I'm sitting on my arse while the President... Never mind. You have a second?''

''Sure. Since the Maestro thing started narrowing down, I've gone back to my serial killings.''

''Okay. There's some new bug spray on the market. Evidently it kills roaches but doesn't affect humans. Or maybe the half-life is just shorter. In any case, they can spray and you can be back at work in half an hour. It's got my curiosity up, and I've got nothing better to do at the moment than bother you with it.''

''Huh,'' Delahunt said. ''I had my apartment treated a few weeks ago. Wonder why they didn't use it— I had to stay over with my sister. But hang on, I'll check the Net and see what I can find.''

McCarter sipped his coffee as he waited. Two minutes later, Delahunt came back on. ''You've got me,'' she said. ''I couldn't find a thing. And no one else around here has ever heard of it, either.''

The Phoenix Force leader felt the same indefinable apprehension he'd experienced so many times since this mission began to creep back over him. "Okay, Carmen," he said. "Thanks." He hung up and seated himself on the corner of the desk.

"What was that all about?" Henry asked.

"Oh, nothing really," McCarter said. "Just had someone try to find out more about the new chemical spray."

"You got bugs at home?" Henry asked. "I can tell you got ants in your pants here. I swear, you're more fidgety than William tonight."

McCarter shrugged. "I just didn't know such a substance existed."

"Well, don't feel all alone. No one else did before that guy from the pest-control service told us about it."

The Phoenix Force leader's head swiveled toward Henry. "When?" he asked.

Henry shrugged. "When they came in to spray," he said. "Eileen asked how long we'd have to stay out and the guy said—"

"Wait a minute," McCarter cut in. "*Eileen* asked him about it?"

"Yeah."

"But I saw Eileen in the hall. Before those men even came into the building. She told me about it *then*."

Henry's lower lip dropped slightly. He leaned back in his chair. "If she already knew about it, then why did she ask again?"

McCarter stood and lifted the phone again. "I

don't know," he said, "but I suspect so that you and the others would hear it." He dialed the number to Stony Man Farm.

"Barb," the Phoenix Force leader said, his heart racing, "get Striker and Able Team over here at the White House on the double." He paused, then added, "I said earlier I'd trade missions with them. Scratch that. We've been on the same one all along and just didn't know it."

CHAPTER FIFTEEN

"Okay," Carl Lyons said impatiently. "We need a plan? I've got a plan. Kick in the door to the Oval Office and go get the bitch." The Able Team leader's eyes flashed with righteous outrage. "It's no secret that I don't like the guy. But he *is* the President of the United States. And he's about to get blown into little bitty pieces."

Hal Brognola shook his head. "It's not that simple, Ironman," he said. He looked at the men seated and standing around the Secret Service command post, down the hall from the Oval Office. He, Bolan and Able Team had arrived to join Phoenix Force and the President's personal protection team only minutes earlier. "Eileen Oberlender isn't in this alone. We need to find out who the men from the pest-control company were. My guess is Eileen will lead us to them."

"And what if the bomb goes off before that?" Lyons demanded.

Brognola's teeth clamped down on the unlit cigar. "While she's still in there with him?" he said.

"That doesn't make sense." He bit harder on the soggy cigar, at the same time issuing a silent prayer that he was right.

The Able Team leader grudgingly nodded. "Okay. And that means you need someone to follow her." His eyes fell on Schwarz, then Blancanales. "She hasn't seen me or my men. We'll take the job."

Brognola nodded. He turned to the uniformed Secret Service man who sat at the desk across from him. He had known Henry for over twenty years, and always liked the man. But Henry had screwed up royally by letting the pest-control men slip into the Oval Office and plant the thermal charge. Henry had grown too old for the tasks required of him. Sad, but true. "How many years have you got with the Service now, Henry?" he asked.

The gray-haired man swallowed hard. "My thirty's up in two months, Hal," he said. "Unless I get shit-canned over this."

Brognola smiled. The Secret Service could find a place to put him out to pasture for that length of time. For now, the Stony Man director needed some way to let the man save a little face. Or at least get him out of the way. "We need a scout, and it won't look out of place for you to be outside in the hall, old friend," he said. "Why don't you go down and watch the door? Hurry back and tell us when Eileen leaves."

Henry nodded his head. He looked depressed as

he walked out the door, but he also looked relieved to get out of there.

"I'd hate to be in his shoes," Blancanales said as soon as he left.

"If you'd been in his shoes the bomb wouldn't have been planted," Brognola said.

Lyons, Blancanales and Schwarz stood. "We'll pick her up downstairs in the employees parking lot," Lyons said. "Radio when she leaves, will you, Hal?"

Brognola nodded, then turned his attention to McCarter. "Eileen should be used to seeing you around too, David. Go keep Henry company and make sure he doesn't screw this one up, too."

McCarter gave him a quick salute and left.

Brognola watched the man leave, then turned to Bolan. "What are your ideas on the detonator, Striker? Timer or remote?"

"Remote," the Executioner said without hesitation. "This Eileen knows the charge is already in place. She's in there with the President, trying to act normal. I'm not sure even an ice queen like she seems to be could pull it off knowing what's ticking across the room. No, they'll be using remote. Which means they'll have to be close by. And they'll also have to be able to see her leave. Unless she's planning to contact them by phone."

"She might go straight to the site where they're detonating," Hawkins said.

Brognola turned to face Phoenix Force's youngest member and shook his head. "Unnecessary risk," he said. "She can call them if they aren't watching. No, I don't think she'll meet up with them until later."

Bolan stood. "Just in case, I'll go down with Able Team. They can follow the woman. I'll either go with them or break off if I see something that leads me toward her accomplices."

Brognola nodded as the big guy left the room. He turned to Gary Manning. "I guess I don't have to tell you what *your* job is," he told the Canadian explosives expert.

"I guess not," Manning said. "But I've got to tell you, Hal, we're cutting it thin. There's going to be a time period during which I can diffuse the bomb. I don't know how long it will be. It might be no longer than the time it takes Eileen to get down to her car and use a car phone."

"Then you'll have to work fast," Brognola said. "I've got faith in you."

"You better, 'cause I won't be the only one to enter the stratosphere if I'm not successful."

"Okay," Brognola said. "Raphael, T.J., Calvin. As soon as we get the word that Eileen's left, I want you to get the President and his family out of here. I mean out of here. We've already got his chopper waiting. I don't even want them on the grounds." He turned to James and Hawkins. "In fact," he said, "you two go get the First Lady and the children now. Take them to the helicopter."

The two Phoenix Force commandos hurried out of the room.

The door suddenly opened, and Henry and McCarter raced in. "Eileen just got in the elevator," McCarter said.

Brognola nodded as the men of Phoenix Force rushed out of the room toward the Oval Office.

Words made famous by Sir Arthur Conan Doyle suddenly ran across Hal Brognola's mind. "Yes," he said quietly under his breath, "the game is afoot." The Stony Man Farm director started out the hall as he lifted the walkie-talkie from his belt carrier.

He just hoped that everything turned out as well here as it always did for Sherlock Holmes.

SEATED IN a five-year-old Nissan from the Justice Department, Able Team watched Eileen Oberlender exit the White House. Schwarz and Blancanales ducked below the windows. Lyons, seated in the driver's seat, did too. But he stayed high enough to watch through the steering wheel.

"What's she doing?" Schwarz asked.

"Getting into a brand-new Mercedes," Lyons answered.

"The President's secretary gets paid that much?" Gadgets asked. "I might apply for the job. I've got a feeling it's about to be open."

Lyons started the engine and pulled out of the parking spot, staying a good twenty yards behind the Mercedes. He strained to see the reactions of the woman behind the wheel. He couldn't be sure, but she didn't appear to be paying attention to them. Just to be safe, however, he let a late-model Buick leaving the lot fall in between them. In the rearview mirror, he saw a pair of headlights come on and then another undercover Justice car pulled in behind the men of Able Team—Bolan.

Lyons lifted the walkie-talkie from the seat next to him. "Able One, Striker. That you?"

"That's me."

The four-car convoy passed through the gates and out onto Pennsylvania Avenue, turned right and left the closed area of the street. Two blocks later, the Mercedes stopped at a red light. The other cars halted in line behind.

The Buick turned right as soon as the Mercedes had crossed the intersection, and Lyons dropped back farther in the light traffic. Roughly two miles later they entered a run-down area of the city. A half-block after that, Lyons saw the Mercedes's lights suddenly die, then flick on again.

"Was I imagining things, or was that a signal?" Schwarz asked from the passenger's seat.

Blancanales's voice came from the back. "You weren't imagining anything. But who can be sure what it was?"

Lyons slowed, his eyes searching both sides of the street for anyone suspicious. He saw only empty cars parked parallel to the curb.

The Able Team leader drove on. As much as the cop in him wanted to find out what the flashing headlights meant, Able Team's assignment was to tail Eileen, and they couldn't do both.

Blancanales spoke from the backseat again. "I don't know if it was a signal or not..." he repeated.

Lyons glanced up at the rearview mirror and saw that Blancanales had turned to face the rear.

"...but Striker thinks it is," Blancanales finished. "At least he's pulling over."

BOLAN FOLLOWED Able Team down the street, stopped at the stoplight and waited. The more he thought about it, the more he believed that while Eileen Oberlender wouldn't go directly to the men she was in league with, she would have to signal them somehow when she left. They had to be relatively close to detonate the bomb by remote control, especially in an area that had as much electronic interference as this part of Washington. And while traffic wasn't heavy this time of night, they would still run the risk of missing her if they relied on visual surveillance alone.

The Mercedes pulled away as the light turned green and the Buick Lyons had used as a shield turned off. Bolan followed the Able Team car past seedy bars, pawn shops and a few other businesses that lined the street. All but the drinking establishments were closed but they were doing business big time—the parking spaces along the street were all filled.

No, the Executioner thought. Eileen would contact her associates somehow. If she didn't have a phone in her car, she'd stop at a pay phone or—

Ahead, the Mercedes's lights suddenly flashed off and on. Bolan frowned. Had it been an accident or a signal? He watched the Able Team car continue after Eileen's vehicle, and followed.

He had just passed a neon sign announcing Mitzi's Cocktails when the head popped up in the Ford directly to his side.

Bolan's warrior instinct went on red alert. He drove on, watching the Ford in his rearview mirror, then pulled over into a fire lane next to a hydrant. Swiveling in his seat, he looked back down the block.

The Ford pulled out of the parking space and made a U-turn.

It headed back toward the White House.

MCCARTER LED THE CHARGE down the hall and into the reception area.

George, Howard and William jumped to their feet. "You can't come in here," William said. "The President—"

"We won't be long," McCarter said, not breaking stride. He lowered his shoulder as he neared the Oval Office and practically drove the door off the hinges.

The President sat on a couch against the wall in his shirtsleeves and slacks. His suit jacket and tie lay haphazardly on the floor in front of him. He looked up from a highball glass in his hand, and said, "What's going—?"

"There's no time to explain, Mr. President," McCarter said, reaching down and hauling the man to his feet. "We've got to get you out of here."

"Tell me what's going on!" he demanded.

McCarter stared the man in the eyes. "There's a bomb in here," he said. "Is that good enough?"

The President looked shocked.

George, Howard and William entered the office with their guns drawn. "Don't move," William yelled, aiming his SIG-Sauer at McCarter. "I want to know what's going on."

"There's a thermal charge planted in here." Hal Brognola's voice behind them caused the Secret Service men to turn on their heels. "Mr. Brognola?" William said.

"Get the President down to the chopper," Brognola told the men. "His family should already be waiting."

George, Howard and William hurried the President out of the room.

McCarter, Encizo and Manning broke up the room into thirds and began searching for the bomb. The search didn't take long.

"Bingo," Encizo said.

McCarter looked across the office to see him

standing behind the President's desk. Manning joined him, dropping to his knees and pulling a flashlight from his pocket.

The Phoenix Force leader joined the other two men behind the desk. "How complicated is it?" he asked the explosives expert.

"Not bad," Manning said. He lay on his side beneath the desk and beamed the flashlight overhead. "But it'll take a little time."

McCarter took a deep breath. "Let's hope we have it."

LYONS FOLLOWED the Mercedes past the crumbling shacks and watched it turn down an alley. The car looked out of place, and he wondered if Eileen planned to stay long wherever she was going. His guess was that about fifteen seconds after she stopped the car it would be stripped to the frame. In this neighborhood that might happen even if she slowed too much.

The Able Team leader killed his headlights as he neared the mouth of the alley. He wondered briefly if the path the woman took was designed to see if she was being followed. Maybe she had even spotted them and was trying to lose the tail.

If that was the case, she had chosen a good method. Lyons couldn't be sure if she was stopping behind one of the houses or if she'd exit the other end of the alley and drive on.

The Nissan halted under the broken streetlight at

the edge of the alley. Lyons stared in the direction the woman had turned. He could see no taillights. She, too, had doused her beams. Had she parked, or had she turned her lights off and gone on to throw them off? There was no way to be sure. But he couldn't just barrel down the alley after her, even with the Nissan in darkness, without getting spotted.

The Able Team leader floored the accelerator and circled the block. He looked up and down the street but saw no sign of the Mercedes. That didn't necessarily mean she had parked behind one of the houses. There had been plenty of time for her to escape while he was circling.

Blancanales answered the unspoken question in Lyons's mind. "Might as well give it a shot," he said from the back seat. "If she made it out, we'll never find her again anyway."

Lyons pulled the Nissan over to the curb and the three men got out, quietly shutting the doors behind them. Their white faces drew a few curious looks from the porches lining the street, but the voices that belonged to the faces stayed silent.

Entering the alley, the Able Team leader drew his .357 Magnum Colt Python and led the way over the broken glass, rotting garbage and other trash that carpeted the dirt. He spotted the Mercedes behind a house in the middle of the block and drew a breath of relief. Stopping next to a fence, he turned to his teammates. "Go to the front," he said. "Wait until you hear me kick in the back door."

The two men nodded and cut between two houses.

Lyons hurried to a splintering garage detached from the house and used it for cover. He eyed the shack where Eileen had parked—a long jump down from the elegance of the White House she had just left. It had one, maybe two bedrooms tops. Lights shone though the back door and the side window he could see.

The Able Team leader wasted no time. Sprinting to the back, he raised a foot and sent it crashing into the door. The glass in the top half shattered with the blow, raining on him as he rushed inside.

At the front of the structure, Lyons heard a similar crash as either Blancanales or Schwarz kicked their door.

The kitchen Lyons found himself in was empty. He raced into what looked like a combination bedroom-computer room and heard voices screaming in the front.

"Freeze!" Blancanales shouted.

"Drop it!" Schwarz ordered.

When Lyons reached the living area, he saw Eileen Oberlender standing in shock in front of the two Able Team men. A pair of black men flanked her, also looking toward the door where the invaders stood. They looked shocked as well, but the surprise on their faces quickly faded.

''You bitch,'' one of the men screamed, turning to Eileen. ''You brought these mothers here!''

In one lightning-fast movement, the man drew a revolver from under his shirt and shot Eileen in the side of the head.

Lyons, Schwarz and Blancanales opened fire a microsecond later with Lyons pumping out .357 Magnum rounds as fast as his finger could pull the trigger. The man who had killed the President's secretary fell to the floor. A heartbeat later, the other man fell on top of him.

The Able Team leader stepped forward and picked up the men's guns. It was only then that he noticed the dead man on the floor. A familiar short-brimmed rancher's hat, now soaked in blood and brains, lay on its side next to him.

What looked to be a small dining room was situated just off the living area. A cheap tapestry hung over half of the wide doorway, restricting the view. The Able Team leader kept the .357 in front of him as he hurried to check it out.

Lyons threw the tapestry back and stepped into the room. More blood and brains covered part of the ceiling and one of the walls. A wheelchair sat next to that wall, occupied by a man who had been burned badly sometime in the past. The top half of his head was blown away.

The Able Team leader stared at the monster that could only have been Desmond Click. The Maestro.

An old Colt Single Action .45 rested on top of a blanket covering Click's legs.

THE EXECUTIONER knew there could be only one reason the man in the Ford was driving back toward the White House. He was too far away to use the remote control. But as soon as he got close enough, that was exactly what he'd do.

Bolan didn't know exactly where the edge of the range stood. He only knew he couldn't let the man reach it.

The Executioner cut the wheel and stood on the accelerator. His tires squealed in agony as the Nissan reversed directions as the Ford had done. He straightened the wheel and saw the car two blocks ahead.

The Executioner's jaw set firmly as he leaned forward. He stared at the Ford ahead as the gap began to close. All he could do was ram the other vehicle and force it to a halt. He'd just have to hope the car wasn't yet close enough to detonate the bomb when he did. Or else hope the man inside didn't have the remote in his hand when it all went down.

His face almost against the windshield, Bolan tried to will more speed into the Nissan. He passed two more intersections and came to another streetlight. He watched the Ford pass through on amber, and saw the light turn red. He couldn't afford to stop, or even slow down, and his foot didn't rise from the accelerator.

A Jeep Wrangler approaching from the intersecting street honked as Bolan shot through the red light. The Wrangler's front bumper struck the Nissan's rear fender, causing Bolan's vehicle to fishtail down the block. The Executioner fought the wheel, straightened the Nissan and raced on.

He was still a block behind the Ford, and guessed them to be a half-mile or less from the White House, which meant the Ford was well within range for any but the least sophisticated remote-control detonators. Still, they were far enough away that the Executioner wasn't likely to see or hear the explosion. Had the man set off the bomb yet? There was no way of knowing. But Bolan would proceed as if he hadn't.

They had gone another block when a Mustang pulled out from the curb. The Ford was forced to slow behind it.

Bolan tightened his seat belt with one hand. He let up on the accelerator slightly and braced himself for the impact. A second later he rammed the rear of the slow-moving Ford, still running close to sixty miles an hour.

Rubber squealed and steel screeched as the bumpers of the two cars locked. The mass of steel turned sideways and spun down the middle of the street like motorized conjoined twins, barely missing the Mustang.

It seemed to take hours for the two cars to halt. In reality, it was a matter of seconds. When they had finally careened off the parked cars on one side of the street, crossed over and done the same on the other, they finally stopped.

The Executioner staggered from the wrecked Nisson to the Ford, drawing the Desert Eagle as he went. He stopped at the driver's-side window and looked inside to see the driver, dead behind the wheel. The man still wore the khaki shirt of the pest-control company but the letters were now all but unreadable beneath his blood. What looked like bottomless brown eyes stared sightlessly into space.

Bolan wrenched open the door, and Bernell Dixon fell out onto the concrete.

The remote-control device was still clutched in his lifeless fingers, his thumb on the button.

McCARTER WATCHED as Gary Manning carefully worked the screwdriver into the apparatus beneath the President's desk. Encizo had dropped to the floor next to him, squeezing into the chair well to serve as flashlight bearer.

The Phoenix Force leader heard footsteps outside in the reception area and looked up as Brognola entered the room. "How's it going?" the Stony Man director asked.

"Taking longer than we thought," McCarter

said. "Gary found a bunch of trip wires he didn't see at first."

"Booby-trapped?"

McCarter nodded. He watched Brognola drop to one knee. "How much longer, Gary?" he asked.

The big Canadian dropped his arms for a rest. "No way to tell for sure," he said. "Depends on whether I find any more surprises." He paused and took a deep breath, his big chest heaving. "I was going to just take it off and work on top of the desk where I'd have more room and light," he said. "But they thought of that. Whoever set this thing up glued one of the trip wires into the desk. I can't take it off without moving the wire. So if I don't diffuse it before it's moved…boom."

More footsteps sounded outside, then George, Howard and William entered the Oval Office. They were followed by Calvin James and T. J. Hawkins.

"The President and his family just took off," James said. "They've decided to take a few days at Camp David."

"Good," McCarter said.

"You guys should get out of here," Brognola suggested, looking at William. "There's no reason for you to stay. For all we know this thing could go off any second."

William shook his head. "It's our responsibility to stay," he said. "It's our fault it's here in the first place."

"Everybody makes mistakes," Brognola said.

"We can't," William countered. "We can't afford to."

"Still, there's no reason to risk your lives. It's not accomplishing anything."

William shook his head. "You stay, we stay." The Secret Service men came behind the desk and joined the Phoenix Force commandos.

A moment later, they all heard a tearing sound beneath the desk. Then Manning scooted out of the chair well holding the thermal charge and detonator. Thick dried strings of glue hung from the trip wire he had mentioned.

"So," the big Canadian said with a straight face, "does this mean I can have tomorrow off to go hunting?"

A sudden screech sounded outside the window. It was followed by the sounds of crunching metal. The noises went on for several seconds as all heads in the Oval Office turned toward them.

"What was that?" James wondered aloud.

McCarter walked to window and peered out into the night. "Can't see really well," the Phoenix Force leader said, "but it looks like one hell of a wreck down the street."

In the badlands, there is only survival....

JAMES AXLER

DEATH LANDS

Crucible of Time

A connection to his past awaits Ryan Cawdor as the group takes a mat-trans jump to the remnants of California. Brother Joshua Wolfe is the leader of the Children of the Rock—a cult that has left a trail of barbarism and hate across the ravaged California countryside. Far from welcoming the group with open arms, the cult forces them into a deadly battle-ritual—which is only their first taste of combat....

Available in January 1999 at your favorite retail outlet. Or order your copy now by sending your name, address, zip or postal code, along with a check or money order (please do not send cash) for $5.50 for each book ordered ($6.50 in Canada), plus 75¢ postage and handling ($1.00 in Canada), payable to Gold Eagle Books, to:

In the U.S.	In Canada
Gold Eagle Books	Gold Eagle Books
3010 Walden Ave.	P.O. Box 636
P.O. Box 9077	Fort Erie, Ontario
Buffalo, NY 14269-9077	L2A 5X3

Please specify book title with order.
Canadian residents add applicable federal and provincial taxes.

GDL44

TAKE 'EM FREE

2 action-packed novels plus a mystery bonus

NO RISK

NO OBLIGATION TO BUY

SPECIAL LIMITED-TIME OFFER

Mail to: Gold Eagle Reader Service
3010 Walden Ave.
P.O. Box 1394
Buffalo, NY 14240-1394

YEAH! Rush me 2 FREE Gold Eagle novels and my FREE mystery bonus. Then send me 4 brand-new novels every other month as they come off the presses. Bill me at the low price of just $16.80* for each shipment. There is NO extra charge for postage and handling! There is no minimum number of books I must buy. I can always cancel at any time simply by returning a shipment at your cost or by returning any shipping statement marked "cancel." Even if I never buy another book from Gold Eagle, the 2 free books and mystery bonus are mine to keep forever.

164 AEN CH7Q

Name	(PLEASE PRINT)
Address	Apt. No.
City	State	Zip

Signature (if under 18, parent or guardian must sign)

* Terms and prices subject to change without notice. Sales tax applicable in N.Y. This offer is limited to one order per household and not valid to present subscribers. Offer not available in Canada.

GE-98

Desperate times call for desperate
measures. Don't miss out on the
action in these titles!

#61910	FLASHBACK	$5.50 U.S.	☐
		$6.50 CAN.	☐
#61911	ASIAN STORM	$5.50 U.S.	☐
		$6.50 CAN.	☐
#61912	BLOOD STAR	$5.50 U.S.	☐
		$6.50 CAN.	☐
#61913	EYE OF THE RUBY	$5.50 U.S.	☐
		$6.50 CAN.	☐
#61914	VIRTUAL PERIL	$5.50 U.S.	☐
		$6.50 CAN.	☐

(limited quantities available on certain titles)

TOTAL AMOUNT	$
POSTAGE & HANDLING	$
($1.00 for one book, 50¢ for each additional)	
APPLICABLE TAXES*	$
TOTAL PAYABLE	$
(check or money order—please do not send cash)	

To order, complete this form and send it, along with a check or money order for
the total above, payable to Gold Eagle Books, to: **In the U.S.:** 3010 Walden Avenue,
P.O. Box 9077, Buffalo, NY 14269-9077; **In Canada:** P.O. Box 636, Fort Erie, Ontario,
L2A 5X3.

Name: _____

Address: _____ City: _____

State/Prov.: _____ Zip/Postal Code: _____

*New York residents remit applicable sales taxes.
Canadian residents remit applicable GST and provincial taxes.

GOLD
EAGLE

GSMBACK1